# LIES I CAN'T UNSEE

Jane Fitcher

GS Publishing

This book is a work of fiction. Names, characters, places, and incidents are the product of the author's imagination or are used fictitiously. Any resemblance to actual events, locales, or persons, living or dead, is purely coincidental.



First edition 2025



Library of Congress Cataloging – in — Publication Data has been applied for.

ISBN (Print) : 978-1-963404-00-5

ISBN (eBook) : 978-1-963404-01-2

# Contents

***

To all that there is, and to all that there was.
For everything seen, unseen, and endured.
To the noise of two children echoing
while I read and write,
to the yes from a man,
and the weight of his approval.
To the mother who picks up where I pause,
to a father who went,
sisters who love far and wide,
in-laws who lend and stay,
friends whose smiles remain the same,
and neighbors who remind me I belong.
To all that feels far, and to all that is near—
may you always know that words remember
what hearts cannot always say.

•••••

*A single lie can grow and consume all that is good in this world, and all that is good in me.*

# 1

# Something about the Suit

"Where are you going all dressed up like that?" I ask my husband as he comes out of our bedroom, his footsteps echoing down the narrow hallway. He looks sharp. The suit hugs him like it was tailored with precision. The fabric catches the light, bold and expensive. Like something out of a Tom Ford campaign. He's got that I'm-about-to-impress-someone vibe. And judging by how good he looks, plus that scent I haven't caught in months, I doubt any woman would dare to refuse. Or maybe a man, for that matter.

I catch myself staring, racking my brain to remember if we had plans tonight that I somehow forgot.

The only thing is... I don't remember him ever asking.

"Just meeting up with Owen for a beer at Ambrosius," he replies. His tone is neutral, but his eyes don't meet mine.

Surprised, I arch a brow. "In a tuxedo?" I try to smile, but it slips away as a chill creeps into my chest, wrapping around my lungs.

He nods, adjusting his tie, still not meeting my eyes. "I have a business dinner afterward."

"A business dinner? On a Sunday...?"

The question escapes before I can stop it. My tone is calm, but inside, doubt thickens.

"Does this business associate of yours know it's the Lord's day?" I offer it with a smile, meant to be light, maybe even playful. But it comes out with more edge than ease.

It doesn't land. Not even close.

His lips twitch, not in amusement. A flicker of irritation crosses his face.

"Not everyone follows such traditions," he says, clipped, like he's brushing off a piece of lint. He adds, "Not even you."

I almost drop the coffee mug in my hand. I hold it tight, worried the spill would bother him more than what I'm trying to say.

Owen. Wait—wasn't he still in Peru this week?

The thought slams into my chest. Loud. Clear. But the words stay stuck, somewhere between my heart and my throat.

I want to ask. I want to press him.

But I also know how this goes.

Two more questions, and he'll act like I'm picking a fight. Like I'm the problem. And just like that, the conversation shifts, and the truth slips away.

A month ago, during our couples' date night, Owen and his wife had mentioned they would be celebrating their tenth anniversary in Peru. Will he really be having a drink with Owen, or is something more going on?

His hands fidget in his pockets, and he keeps avoiding my eyes as he grabs the car keys.

"Well. Have fun then."

The words are flat, my jaw locked tight as I fight to keep the confusion from surfacing.

Ignoring him as he leaves, I turn toward our bedroom. The pulse in my ears drowns out everything else as I try to make sense of what just came to light.

Should I listen to my heart, or let it go? The heart is deceitful...but what if this beat is a buried truth, whispering a reality I'm too scared to believe?

"Are you okay?" he calls out, his voice cutting through my thoughts. I flinch, steadying myself.

"Yes. I'm fine," I say, steadying my tone.

"Did you hear what I said?"

I blink, reeling my mind back. "Sorry...what?"

"I said no coffee in the bedroom. You might spill it on the carpet," he says. Like he's correcting a child.

As I tighten my grip on the mug, coffee spills over the rim and scalds my skin. I don't flinch. My thoughts are moving too fast to feel it.

Can I ignore the truth when it's staring me in the face? The words, 'God help me!' trembles on my tongue like a warning bell I'm too afraid to ring.

*What if I spill coffee on the carpet? Do you have a problem with that?*

The comeback flares inside me, sharp and tempting. But I swallow it. Picking a fight now won't help. Defiance only gives him something to control.

The dull rhythm of my usual Sunday, laundry, leftovers, and low expectations—suddenly feels electric, with a hum of something I can't quite trust.

Something's shifted. And I feel it in my bones.

As my husband keeps talking, his words start to blur. Just noise floating around the edges of my mind. I'm still stuck on the lie, trying to make sense of it while pretending it doesn't bother me.

"I'll text you when I join you for dinner tonight," he says.

"Huh? Dinner?...Okay." I nod, too quickly, my voice lighter than it should be.

But my thoughts are miles away. A knot pulls tight in my stomach. His words carry something underneath. I can feel it, sharp and buried, like a splinter under skin.

I had hoped my brain would let this go, but instead, it convenes a full-body town hall.

"You have to investigate this kind of stuff," it announces with authority. My heart chimes in like a loyal co-conspirator: "Oh yeah, let's not brush this off. It *could* be something, you know?"

In that moment, my entire body joins the cause. My back aches in agreement. My shoulders whisper tension. Even my stomach sends a nervous memo: "There's nothing wrong with being a little curious."

Curiosity, though, is a tricky thing. It starts small, a soft itch of uncertainty. Harmless. But it shapeshifts into something bigger, sneakier. Like a fox in the shadows, it tempts you to poke around, to question everything you thought you understood about your relationship.

At first, it's just mild curiosity, a quiet wondering born from nothing you can name, a feeling that won't sit still. But left unchecked, it spreads like wildfire, searing through trust and scorching every word and gesture with suspicion.

Am I ready to ignite a fire in my marriage?

Or open the door to a truth I can't unsee and a mess I can't undo.

I step into our bedroom, coffee in hand, trying to keep myself steady in more ways than one. I set the mug down on the small espresso side table, but as I turn, my foot catches the edge of our oversized four-poster bed.

The stumble happens fast. My hip clips the mattress, momentum pulling me forward. I flop onto the silk sheets, arms flailing, and slide right off the edge, landing on the carpet with a dull thud.

Perfect. Just what I needed.

My husband's voice floats in from the hallway.

"Everything okay in there?"

"Yes, yes!" I reply a little too quickly, my tone exaggerated, an awkward attempt at cheerfulness. "Just tripped over my own feet."

A pause, and a question, "Did you spill the coffee on the carpet?"

I raise my voice slightly, aiming for casual. "No...I

set it on the side table before the grand tumble." I try to laugh, but it comes out thin.

My husband's footsteps thud down the hallway. Steady. Deliberate. Coming closer. It stops. They start again, followed by the slam of a door. I let out a breath I didn't know I was holding.

Still sprawled on the carpet where I fell, the tension in my chest burns, my breaths fast and uneven. The clock on my bedside table glows in harsh green: **4:30 PM**. Mocking me with its cold silence.

Scenarios spin through my head, each more unsettling than the last. Should I follow him? Or would that only confirm what I don't want to admit?

Should I go?

No. I should stay.

Maybe it's nothing.

But what if it's everything?

In one motion, I spring off the carpet and make a beeline for the front door. I grab my running coat, shove on a hat, and jam my feet into my shoes.

But as my hand closes around the doorknob, my stomach drops.

He has the car. Of course he does. Our only vehicle: a brand-new, glossy Range Rover hybrid. I freeze, hand still on the knob.

It bugs me though. Why do we have a car like that? Maybe because it's a statement. A reflection of his taste. He needs to have the best. The most. He's the kind of man who curates appearances, even as everything underneath slowly falls apart.

What would I know, anyway? I'm only a writer. I don't need a car to do my job. Just a quiet space, a reliable laptop, and a steady internet connection. Or at least, that's what I've always told myself.

Now, standing here with my heart thudding and my husband's truth dangling out of reach, I wish I had my car. Turns out, chasing down suspicion requires wheels.

Sure, I could call a rideshare. But what if something goes sideways? Chaos. Confrontation. The worst-case scenario is that the driver remembers me. Me, of all people. As a potential suspect.

Okay...maybe I'm overthinking it. But can you blame a woman's intuition?

With no other options, I resort to the oldest form of transportation: my own two feet. He mentioned meeting Owen at a bar a few miles away, so I slip on the sunglasses I grabbed earlier. More disguise than necessity, and head out.

As a writer, I've learned the best cure for a mental block is to lace up my shoes and hit the pavement. The rhythm of each step clears the fog. Sparks new ideas. Sometimes it's an escape. Other times, a revelation. Either way, it moves me forward. But today, my mind isn't on my story. It's on his.

Tough luck, the rain has impeccable timing.

It starts as I break into a run. First, light pinpricks on my skin. Then harder. More insistent. It falls in step with the weight pressing down on my chest.

And, a question, *why is my husband lying to me?*

My pace slows—not from the slick sidewalk, but from everything churning inside me. The rain drowns my thoughts, mirroring the confusion in my head. Each drop feels like a question I don't want to ask, and an answer I'm not ready to face.

As I near the bar, my breath comes in short, shallow bursts. My heart hasn't stopped pounding since the moment he walked out the door. This can't be good. A sense of foreboding prickles through every nerve ending.

This could go one of two ways: Either I retreat into the familiar role of the dutiful housewife, willfully blind to whatever secrets my husband is hiding. Or I uncover the truth and watch the life I know crumble around me.

I stop a short distance from the bar and restaurant, my body slick with rain and adrenaline. A knot of fear twists in my stomach. I can't let him see me. Not yet.

If he catches me here, if he thinks I'm watching, he'll say it. "Are you spying on me?" That one accusation could destroy everything I'm trying to uncover.

The windows are floor-to-ceiling—sleek, cold, glass walls that watch like silent witnesses. They stretch across the building like mirrors, reflecting what shouldn't be seen. One glance in my direction, and he'd spot me. It would be over. The truth, still out of reach. The investigation, pointless.

I can't risk it.

With my pulse thudding in my ears, I circle to the

back entrance, each step quiet but urgent. My soaked coat clings to me as I duck into the shadows.

Please, don't let anyone recognize me. Not now.

Being a bit of a recluse has its perks. Plenty of people have read my books, yet almost no one knows my face. It's a strange kind of anonymity, and in this moment, a gift.

When a secret keeper finds something worth uncovering, she doesn't hesitate; she digs. She pushes past every warning, every wall. But this time, the secret isn't about a stranger. It's my husband. And the truth feels like a loaded weapon aimed at everything I thought I knew.

Five years ago, he made trust non-negotiable. "We need to trust each other," he said, voice firm. "I can't be in a relationship without it." I agreed. I believed him. I still do or I want to. But right now, something in me has changed. It's no longer about trust. It's about truth. And the truth doesn't always wait for permission.

And here I am with my pulse drums against my ribs, wild and erratic. Each step drags like molasses. Or denial pretending to be courage. I tell myself I'm just checking. Just confirming.

*God, please—let me be wrong. Let this be nothing.*

There's no turning back now.

I close my eyes and try to breathe. It comes out shaky. I search for rhythm, something to hold onto. My breath snags, caught between fear and recognition. Something inside me winds tighter. The door stands before me. Whatever lies behind it, denial is no longer an option.

The door is locked. Ha, what did I expect?

Still, I wait. Hoping someone comes through the service entrance. The one the staff use to take out the trash. The one I shouldn't be standing near, but am.

Five minutes pass. Nothing. Another five. Still no one.

I lean into the brick, the chill and grit pressing through my coat like it wants to settle into my skin. Try to look casual. Try not to think too much. Someone has to come out eventually. They always do.

But time stretches. Five minutes turn into seven. Maybe more. The silence feels heavier now. Like the building itself is holding its breath.

And I start to wonder, what if no one comes out? What if this door stays shut, like the truth I'm trying to pry open?

Frustration rises, hot and tight in my chest. And then, doubt. Creeping in like a slow leak.

What am I doing here? Everyone knows the rule: never go digging into your husband's secrets unless you're prepared to choke on the dirt. It never ends well. More pain. More mess. More proof you should've left the lights off.

Maybe I should let it go. Keep the peace. Don't poke the bear. But then again...what kind of wife ignores the feeling that something's off? Still, nothing good ever comes from digging up dirt on your husband, does it?

Where did I ever hear that? One of those dog-eared paperbacks I used to burn through late at night, the kind with secrets and affairs and warnings masked as clichés.

But no. A lie is still a lie, no matter how it's dressed. And he's lying. I know it. The only question now is: what am I willing to do about it? Will someone step in and take action on my behalf? Will fate intervene?

As I turn away in resignation, the door opens.

Hallelujah! Which means the saga of spying on my husband commences.

A balding, middle-aged man pushes through the door, juggling three overstuffed garbage bags. Opportunity.

"May I hold the door for you, sir?" I ask, layering my voice with polite concern.

He grunts a quick thanks, stepping past me to heave the bags into one of the large bins outside.

I keep the door propped open with my foot, eyes already scanning the dim interior beyond the threshold, narrow hallway, the hum of fluorescent lights, and muffled clatter from the kitchen up ahead.

Then, as he turns back, he squints at me. "Are you one of the new waitresses they hired recently?"

My mouth goes dry. For a half-second, I freeze.

His question catches me off guard. For a beat, I say nothing. Mind blank, my cover is already starting to slip.

But in that flicker of silence, I imagine it. Me, as

the new waitress, a job I'd always wanted to try.

Despite the question I'm afraid to answer, he doesn't press. He gives a polite nod, like he's too tired to care, and disappears down the hallway. He turns back once, eyes narrowing with a flicker of confusion at the sight of my drenched ponytail and running clothes. I hope he doesn't say anything. Not to anyone.

I stand there, still holding the door open, watching him go. The moment lingers, too long to be casual, too loaded to ignore.

A whirlwind of emotion rushes through me. I let the door close softly behind me, peel off my sunglasses, and shove them onto the top of my head. Then I breathe. Slow and deep, and start walking.

The hallway is dim, fluorescent lights flickering overhead, casting the walls in a tired yellow. My footsteps echo softly on the linoleum. Each one is steadier than the last.

The smells hit first—grease, fryer oil, beer that's been mopped up but never really gone. It clings to the walls, to the floor, to the people who pass through here.

Head down, loose hair clinging to my neck, I move slowly. Every second feels too loud. Any second now, someone might stop me. Ask why I'm here. Ask who I am. I inch forward, mind racing, heart on the verge of retreat.

*God,* I plead silently, *please don't let me discover something about my husband I can't unsee.*

The bar is right beyond the kitchen, and the noise

slams into me like a wall. Laughter. Cheers. A TV blaring over it all.

It dawned on me, it's football Sunday. Of course it is.

Suddenly, the room roars to life. Someone jumps up on the bar counter and drops to one knee. The crowd hushes in a ripple of curiosity.

He's holding a ring.

A woman stands before him in a red dress—tight, radiant, the kind of red that demands attention. She's the type who turns heads just by breathing. Her blonde waves tumble down her back like something straight out of a commercial.

Then I hear it.

That voice.

That *familiar* voice.

"Will you marry me?"

My stomach drops.

My head spins.

No.

It can't be.

But the tuxedo. The slicked-back blond hair. The posture.

It's him.

My husband.

He's kneeling in front of that woman, holding out the diamond like the recycled promise he gave me five years ago.

She says yes. The crowd erupts.

And I freeze. Shocked.

I want to tell myself I'm wrong. That's someone else. That...I'm confused. But I know that suit. I know that face.

*Oh Lord, help me.*

The weight of it all, the betrayal, the spectacle. The lie crashes into me, and I can't move. Can't breathe.

I'm watching my marriage dissolve in the middle of a bar, like it's just another Sunday show.

Is this even possible?

The world tilts. It blurs.

The cheers dissolve into a muffled hum, like I'm underwater. I can't breathe. Shock rolls through me in jagged waves, sharp and endless.

This can't be real. It has to be some cruel, cosmic joke. Some twisted narrative the universe dreamt up to see how much I can take.

My thoughts scatter, darting in every direction. Is there some old tale, buried in history or myth, about a married man proposing to his next bride while still tethered to the first?

Maybe.

Probably.

Writers make that stuff up all the time. We spin heartbreak and betrayal into page-turners and call it art.

But this? This isn't fiction. This is my life. And maybe this kind of betrayal only happens to naive, reclusive writers who spend too much time in their heads and never see the plot twist coming.

*Oh God, have mercy!*

As I'm spiraling, lost in thought, a tap on my shoulder jolts me back. A tall man in a white chef's uniform stands in front of me, concern etched into his face.

"Are you alright?" he asks.

I must look like a disaster—drenched, pale, shaking. Like I wandered in from a storm, I created myself.

"Yes, I'm fine," I manage.

"Huh? You look like you're about to faint," he says, eyes scanning me.

"I'm okay," I repeat, the lie flimsy on my lips. "Do you have a bathroom here?"

Of course they do. What kind of question is that?

He points behind me. "Yes, that way, miss."

"I think I'm going to throw up," I blurt. My stomach churns, liquid and loose. I reach for something. Anything. But there's nothing. He steps forward and steadies me, hands firm on my arms.

"I got you," he says. "This way."

He guides me through the blur of bodies and noise, steady as I stumble beside him. My eyes drift, for a moment, back to the bar. To *him*. My husband. Beaming. Holding and kissing another woman. Son of a gun.

The memory of his proposal, the way he looked at me, once—slices through my thoughts

"Try to hold it," the man pleads.

We make it to the bathroom. He holds the door like a gentleman. But before I reach the toilet, I throw up—right on his shoes.

He doesn't flinch. He helps me to the toilet, holds my head over the bowl as my body continues to convulse. I heave until there's nothing left but bile and shaking.

I want to apologize, but he's gone, disappearing without a word. Of course. Who would stay?

But then, he returns.

A mug of warm water in one hand, a paper towel in the other.

"I think you could use this," he says.

I lean back against the cold tile and accept both with shaking hands. I sip it. Breathe. It helps.

He watches me with a gaze that lingers a little too long. Curious. Kind. Maybe even...familiar.

I wipe my mouth. Then, self-conscious, I glance at his shoes, still smeared with my vomit.

God, I'm so sorry," I mumble, grabbing a clean patch of paper towel. I'm already on my knees, wiping, like an apology might live in the motion.

He leans down and gently takes my hands, stilling them.

"Don't worry about it. No harm done," he assures.

I look up, riveted by his gaze.

His eyes. Silver-grey. Piercing. Unsettling in their stillness.

I've seen them before.

*I wrote them.*

"You have breathtaking eyes," I whisper, stunned.

He doesn't react to the compliment. Instead, he

shifts the subject. “Do you know those people who just got engaged?”

“Engaged?” I echo, blank.

And then it all floods in. Like the a vacuum seal breaking. The bar. The ring. The red dress. *My husband.*

“I’m sorry. I have to go,” I say, voice tight, legs already moving.

He calls after me. Once, maybe twice. But I don’t look back. I tear through the same door I came from and run.

Run like I can outrun what I saw.

What I now know.

# 2
# Run

Rain pours steadily as I run. My coat holds most of it back, but passing cars spit cold water at the sidewalk, like the city taking cheap shots. My heart pounds, matching the rhythm of my feet hitting the pavement.

A horn blares. "Hey, watch it!" someone yells.

I flinch but keep going. Numb to the chaos, locked inside my own.

The sky mirrors what I feel. Heavy. Dark. Furious. Thunder rumbles like it knows. Lightning splits the clouds, each flash a raw reminder of the pain clawing at my chest.

My shoes are soaked, squishing with every step, and even under my hat, wet strands of hair cling to my face. There's no escaping it. I can't outrun what he did. His lies are etched now, burned into me.

This marriage—our marriage—is in shambles, and here I am, running nowhere, trying to shake the ache like it's something that can be left behind in a puddle.

I want to scream. Not just in my head, but out loud. I want the whole world to hear it, to see the storm I'm carrying inside.

"How could you do this to me?" I scream, the words tearing out of me with more force than I intended.

The downpour doesn't let up. If anything, it joins in. Each drop a note in the sad, the background noise of me losing it.

I don't even know where I am anymore. The streets blur, the lights smear, and my path home feels as lost as I do.

Does it matter? Will going home fix this? Will anything?

No one's after me. So why am I running? Why am I doing this to myself?

Maybe it's not about escape. Maybe it's what happens when everything you believed in breaks, and there's nothing left to stand on.

I gave him everything. My trust, my love, my future, and now all I have left is a soaked hat, aching feet, and a pain that feels like it's chewing through my chest.

God, this hurts.

This sucks.

Heartbreakingly sucks.

Despite the burning in my legs, I keep going. My breath hitches. Shallow, uneven. Then everything in me gives out. I drop hard, knees smacking the wet pavement. I stay there, folded into myself, soaked and shaking. Crying like I've lost more than I can hold.

But even in the wreckage, something in me refuses to quit.

Somehow, I get up. Shaky, dripping, but upright. The street blurs around me, all grey and water. And I can't run anymore. So I walk. Slow. Numb. One foot, then the other.

My muscles scream—enough. My chest burns from sobbing. But the tears keep falling, heavier than the rain.

Tears I thought were long gone rise from some hidden vault deep inside. A place I didn't know still held anything. How can one heart hold this much grief?

I walk. Cry. And breathe. All at once.

Somehow, it fits. Each step feels like dragging my heart across broken glass. My mind, still reeling from what I saw—his face, her laughter, the casual cruelty of it all.

Is this karma for ignoring every red flag? For choosing silence when I should've spoken? Or is this just life showing me its sharp edges, daring me to bleed?

What now?

There's nothing to grab onto except this hollow, pulsing ache in my chest. But maybe that's something. Maybe the pain means I'm still here. Still thinking. Still trying.

How can someone you love hurt you like this? Like they're hurling bricks at your chest. Each one heavier, more deliberate. Like they know exactly where to hit.

I keep walking, trying to find my way home. Without warning, the street ahead looks familiar. This is my block. The one I've walked and jogged a thousand times. The trees, the sidewalk, the curve near the corner store. I know them all. But it feels...different now. Like the place stayed the same, but I didn't. Something in me cracked, and nothing around me fits quite right anymore.

This street used to be my anchor. It always felt solid. Unchanging. It'll still be here long after I'm gone, just like this moment will linger long after tonight ends.

The rain comes harder now. Sharp and merciless. I squint through it. The world has gone flat and colorless. The red door I once adored. Mrs. Delgado's ivy, brittle and brown, still twisting along the fence like it's clinging to memory. The soft gold glow from porch lights, they're all bleeding into gray.

My legs are shaking, like rubber bands pulled too tight, trembling from the strain. I don't know if it's from exhaustion, or heartbreak, or the weight of the storm pressing down on me.

Nestled beneath the towering oak's outstretched limbs sits an old wooden bench, weathered and worn. It looks oddly out of place here, wedged between prim townhouses, iron fences, and parallel-parked cars—but in this moment, it's the only thing that feels solid. Anchored. Still.

I make my way over and sink into the seat, all the energy draining out of me.

The bench is damp and cold, and my yoga pants cling to my skin, soaking up the chill. I just sit there, trying to breathe, trying to slow the thunder in my chest. Rain taps through the leaves above me, and I stare at the pavement, watching droplets shatter like tiny truths hitting the ground.

Minutes pass. Maybe hours. I lose track.

A woman in a bright green parka approaches and eases herself onto the bench beside me. Her breath is visible in the cold air. She glances over and offers a kind, cautious smile.

"Are you okay, miss?" she asks. Curious.

Miss.

People always assume. They see my face and think "young," "lost," maybe even "naïve." I hate that. Can't they see the ring on my finger? It's not for decoration. It's a promise. A vow I kept. A title I wear—Mrs, not some wandering girl. I don't do betrayal. I don't run around breaking hearts.

But apparently, some people do. People you trust. People you love.

The tears threaten again, rising like a wave I can't hold back.

I glance at her. There's something familiar about her face, but I can't quite place it. She watches me with concern, then says, "Do you want me to call the police?"

Her voice is laced with a thick accent. That's it. She's one of the vendors at the Saturday flea market. I see her every week, just never up close like this.

"Police?" I echo, blinking, confused. I must look more wrecked than I thought.

She's already pulling out her phone, tapping the screen.

"Please don't," I say, rising from the bench as panic creeps in. "I'm fine. Really."

She doesn't argue. Just gives me a skeptical look and mutters under her breath, "Crazy people these days..."

I wish I were crazy.

At least then I'd have an excuse. Some diagnosis, some detachment, something that explains the noise in my head and the break in my heart.

But I'm not. I'm just awake. Hurting. And trying way too hard to make sense of a world that no longer makes sense

So I walk. Again.

Before I even realize it, I'm standing in front of our house. I climb the granite steps to the porch, my palms slick from the rain still clinging to my skin. The stone-brick townhouse glistens under the soft drizzle, catching just enough light to look almost elegant, like it's trying to impress someone.

Funny. It used to impress me, too.

But now, it feels cartoonish. Overdone. Like something from a show about people pretending to be happy. Five bedrooms. For two people. My husband always bragged about it. The space, the finishes, the resale value. But what's the point of a dream home if the dream inside is broken?

I let out a short, humorless laugh. It's just a house. Nothing more. Nothing special. Not anymore.

As I reach the door, the weight of what's happened presses down on me. I left in such a daze. No phone, no keys. Just instinct and questions I still can't answer.

I stare at the keypad, trying to will the code into my memory. My brain, fogged with rain and grief, draws a blank. I curse under my breath and crouch down, flipping back the doormat with trembling fingers.

There it is. The spare key, tucked in its usual spot. Some tiny miracle, still where I left it.

A small mercy. One thing, at least, hasn't changed.

As I step through the door, a blast of cold air hits my skin. I shudder, clothes damp and clinging, the scent of wet wool riding the draft. The thermostat's low, too cold for me, just how he likes it.

The house feels hollow, echoing the emptiness in my chest. I walk through the hallway, past all the carefully chosen pieces we once collected together. They used to tell a story. Now they just look like things. Faded. Lifeless.

I sink into the couch, soaked clothes pressing into the cushions, and I almost laugh. He'd hate this. The mess. The moisture. He always reacts. But I can't sit here too long.

I push myself up, limbs heavy, and head to the bedroom. The silence follows me like a shadow. I peel off my wet clothes and step into the bathroom, needing to feel something other than this swirling confusion.

I turn the faucet on and wait for the scalding heat to settle. When I finally step in, the water hits me hard—tiny needles of fire pelting my skin. It stings, but strangely, it helps. It's real. It cuts through the numbness.

Tears fall freely now, mixing with the water, washing over me without mercy. My chest tightens, like a hammer just struck something deep inside.

I sink to the shower floor, hugging my knees. The hot water streams down, muffling everything. My sobs, my thoughts, the weight of it all.

I don't know how long. Minutes. Hours. At some point, the truth returns: I can't stay in the shower forever.

I turn off the faucet and step out into a cloud of steam. The mirror is fogged over, but as I wipe it clean, a version of myself stares back. Flushed skin, puffy eyes, and damp hair clinging to my cheeks.

I look like someone who's been hit by a truck.

Over and over.

Emotionally wrecked, physically drained.

And still trying to understand why.

The images won't leave me.

Him. Her. That bar.

The scene replays on an endless loop. My outburst echoes in my ears, louder than the rain ever was. Regret curls in my stomach like smoke, thick and suffocating.

Now I get it. Why do they say ignorance is bliss? Because knowing... hurts.

Truth doesn't just open your eyes. It guts you. Once it's out, there's no unknowing, no unseeing. It shatters everything. Your image of them, of the world, even of yourself.

And yet...what would secrecy have done for me? Prolonged the ache. Stretched it out into something quieter, but deeper. The truth has a way of surfacing, whether you're ready or not.

He's always had that charm. Maybe a little too much. He's obsessively neat—maybe even borderline OCD. But I let it slide. He's my husband.

I know he's attractive. And women stare. I noticed. Of course I did. But I never let myself worry. Why should I? He was married to me. We made a promise. Till death do us part.

And yes, I laughed at his dry jokes—even when they didn't land—just to keep things light. I cared. Deeply. And I think... he did too.

Once.

His eyes are like sapphires. That stupid-perfect skin. The way his blond hair always fell just right without trying. He looked at me once like I was everything. Like the world began and ended in my smile.

But now? Now I wonder if he ever truly loved me at all...Or if he was just really good at pretending.

Is our marriage even real anymore? What are his intentions now? To leave me?

Or worse...To erase me?

The thought comes out of nowhere, dark and cold. It slides in like a knife. What if he wants me gone?

To be free. To be with her.

I shake my head, trying to push it away—but it lingers. These thoughts are driving me to the edge. And I don't know what's real anymore.

My phone rings, sharp and sudden. I don't need to look—I know it's him. Five missed calls.

"You scumbag. Lying... son of a gun," I hiss through clenched teeth, shouting it loud enough for the walls to echo. Let the neighbors hear. Let the world hear. At this point, who even cares?

Then—Buzz.

A new message pops up on the screen.

Oscar: How many times have I told you not to hide a key under the rug? We'll talk about this when I get home.

Oscar: Anyway, Owen and his wife invited me to an after-party for the football game. So, don't wait up.

I stare at the screen, numb. That's it? No apology. No guilt. Not even a flicker that he knows I know. Still playing the role. Still texting like everything's normal.

My fingers tighten around the phone. Does he think I'd respond with my usual, "Have fun"?

Not anymore. I'm not the clueless wife I used to be.

He probably saw me on the door camera—the one he insisted we install "for safety." Maybe he saw me soaked, shaking, fumbling for the key. But he has no idea what I've seen. What I know.

Rage simmers beneath my skin. How long has this been going on? How many carefully constructed lies has he fed me?

My fingers twitch. I want to hurl the phone, hear it crack against the wall. But I don't. Not yet.

Because before anything else, I need the truth. The full truth.

When did it start? Who is she?

Would knowing even help?

Was any of this real?

The questions spiral in my mind like broken glass in a storm—cutting, sharp, endless.

I sit, paralyzed. Staring at the phone like it might confess something on its own.

I don't know what I'll do next.

Confront him?

Leave?

Forgive?

But this much is certain: My life split in two the moment I found out.

And nothing will ever be the same again.

# 3

# The person you see is not the real me.

People often say I'm easygoing, compliant, agreeable, and always pleasant. I don't argue. I don't make waves. I just...go along.

My family, especially my husband, once called me a pushover. They said it like a joke, tossed out with a laugh, but it stung more than I cared to admit.

"That's ridiculous!" I protested, the words flying out instinctively the moment he said it. But later, in the quiet, a small voice inside me whispered: Is it, though?

Maybe there's some truth in what they say.

I forgive them for the remark, of course. I always do. They don't know me—not the parts I keep tucked away. And I never want to make a fuss.

But deep down, it bothers me. Is that who I've become? Is that the image I've been projecting all this time?

One thing's certain: I avoid conflict at all costs. Not because I don't feel things deeply, but because I don't want to prolong tension. Especially with people I love. It's a pattern I've lived in for as long as I can remember, sacrificing my feelings for the sake of peace.

Since childhood, I've been the quiet one. The good one. The girl who never caused trouble, never raised her voice. I wore that role like a badge of honor. Now... I'm not so sure.

But what am I, really? Who am I when no one's watching? And does that even matter?

What defines me—who I've been, or who I'm meant to become?

These questions swirl around my mind like loose threads I can't quite tie together. I want to say it doesn't bother me. That I'm above it all.

But the truth?

It does bother me. Not loudly. Not all the time. But enough to make me wonder—If they're wrong about me...why have I spent so long acting like they're right?

I tell myself I've learned to pick my battles. That some things aren't worth the fight. And maybe that's true. But sometimes, I wonder if I've been choosing silence out of wisdom...or out of fear.

These days, I keep my distance. I see my family and all their handpicked guests mostly during the holidays. Thanksgiving. Christmas. Twice a year, I put on a brave face and step into their world.

It's loud. Chaotic. Full of opinions I don't agree with and questions I don't want to answer. But I smile. I serve. I make conversation like it's my job. And leave.

Because when there are so many people around, it's easier to hide in plain sight. I can disappear into the crowd. Endure the performance. Then go home and fold back into the version of myself no one ever really asks about.

Growing up, my sisters and I dreaded our father's yearly Christmas ultimatum: Spend a full week at his house or risk being cut out of the will.

It was never said in so many words, but we all knew what was at stake. So year after year, we packed our bags, showed up, smiled, and counted down the days.

But one Thursday night, during our weekly dinner, I finally found the courage to speak.

"Dad," I began, "would it be okay if I only stayed for one night every year? Just Christmas Eve?"

He didn't answer right away. He looked at me over the rim of his glass, eyebrows raised. Then he smirked.

"You're not worried about your inheritance?" he teased, as if daring me to flinch.

I smiled. "It's okay, Dad. I don't need it."

We went back and forth a little—his stubbornness, my resolve.

But eventually, he gave me a pass. "One night. Don't make me regret it. And you're still required to come to Thanksgiving."

I didn't make him regret it. And so, every year since, I make it a point to show up; Thanksgiving and Christmas Eve.

My dad and I still made a point to have dinner together every Thursday. No bail, but if it's an emergency at his work, he would call and make it up to me next time.

Late that same evening, as we sat across from each other in our usual booth at an old diner, he looked up from his plate and asked, "Tell me, kid...why aren't you worried about your inheritance?"

He always calls me kid or kiddo, like I'm still five. I asked him once to stop, but you can't tell my dad what to do. He built a multi-million-dollar empire by being immovable.

"I'm kind of okay," I said, keeping it vague.

"What does that mean?" he pressed.

My dad always got answers. One way or another. That's how he ran his company, and that's how he ran our family.

"I work, you know."

He raised an eyebrow. "What kind of work?"

Dad never minded that my sisters didn't have jobs. He encouraged us after college, but never pushed. When two of them dropped out, he threatened to cut them out of the will, and because of that, they went back and finished their degrees.

"Are you a spy?" he asked, only half joking.

"I wish," I said.

"You wish what?"

"That I were a spy."

"Okay, kiddo, you're stalling," he said, leaning forward. "What kind of work do you do?"

I hesitated. "You have to promise not to tell anyone. Not even Mom."

He held up his hand. "Scout's honor."

"I write," I blurted out.

He laughed. "You're joking."

I grinned. "Nope."

"Okay, so you write. What's the big deal? Writers are broke, kiddo."

"Not always."

"Have I read anything you've written?"

"Yes."

He squinted at me. "Which one?"

"That one." I pointed to the book sitting beside his plate, the one he'd been reading when I arrived. Dancing With the Gods, the third installment in my fantasy series.

"This?" He lifted the book. "Nah. You're toying with me."

"I'm not. I'll send you the next one once you finish reading that one."

"It hasn't come out yet."

"I know," I said, leaning back. "But I already finished writing it."

He blinked, stunned. "Noooo..."

"It's true."

His brows pulled together. "Shut up. You're J.G. Bowler?"

"In the flesh."

He stared at me, jaw slack. "I don't believe you."

I met his gaze, steady and silent.

"No way, kid," he said, shaking his head. "How could you not tell me?"

"You never asked. And...I didn't think you'd be

interested."

"Me? Not interested? My kid's a bestselling author? Are you kidding me? You're not serious, are you?"

"Yes, Dad. I make things up for a living. Legally."

He looked down at the book like it had turned into scripture.

He chuckled, still processing. "So, nobody knew?"

I nodded. "Nobody. Well... you, my editor, my publisher, and Arabella."

He went quiet for a moment. "Where's Arabella these days?"

"Last postcard was from Nepal."

He nodded slowly, narrowed his eyes, and asked. "Does your husband know?"

"Nope."

A slow, knowing smile spread across his face. He looked at me like he was seeing me for the first time.

As we said goodbye, he ruffled my hair like always and pulled me into a rare, tight hug.

"I didn't know you had it in you... kid," he said, his voice thick with pride.

And for once, I didn't mind being called kid at all.

I used to be close to my sisters, back when we were kids. Before everything got complicated. Before they found out about my Thursdays with Dad. Or used it as an excuse to stop liking me.

That changed things. Maybe not all at once, but enough to make the distance grow. Enough to turn warmth into suspicion.

Mom is a completely different story. She's rarely home, always off somewhere—traveling, cruising, indulging her vices with Dad's money. Dad doesn't seem to mind. Or maybe he's too numb to care.

"She's happy when she's away," he says. That's it. No judgment. No bitterness. Only resignation.

On weekends, he retreats to his lakeside cottage. Sometimes he's joined by his brothers, old friends, or their wives. He always sends a group text to us kids, inviting anyone who wants to come. Mom never does. And I never do either. Well... when Dad insists, I go. Otherwise, I make excuses, always have.

The truth is, I avoid conflict like it's my job. It's second nature by now. When I sense tension, I don't push back—I disappear. I plan my exits before others finish their sentences.

My sisters aren't like that. They confront. Loudly.

When I'm around them, they never stop confronting me about everything. About Dad. About Mom. About why I don't answer their calls. Why do I always slip away before the drama starts?

Alexi is the loudest, always accusing, always assuming the worst. Marie just echoes her, nodding along like she's too tired to form her own opinions.

They don't ask how I'm doing. They ask why I always have Thursday dinners with Dad, why I get a pass to skip a week at Christmas, and everything else.

I told them not to worry. That nothing is going on.

But that's not what they want. They say I'm too

close. That I'm swaying him. Working an angle.

And no matter how many times I say I've got nothing to hide, it never lands. They've already decided—I must want more. I must be hiding something.

And maybe I am. Just not what they think.

My husband, however, is a different tale altogether. He's perfectly content with me being sequestered in the basement. I told him I needed the space for painting, but the truth is, I don't paint. I like the idea of it. Sometimes I create a mess with brushes and color palettes, enough to make it look convincing. Chaos, it turns out, is a great deterrent.

The day he came downstairs and saw the disaster I'd staged, he didn't ask questions. He took one long look and said, "It's all yours." He's never come down since.

And I'm fine with that. Down there, in the basement, I find a kind of therapy, not in painting, but in writing. It's the one place my imagination is allowed to roam free, unobserved.

Before we married, Oscar was clear about his preferences and pet peeves. He couldn't stand messes. Growing up in a military household, order wasn't expected—it was the law.

If I spilled a drop of coffee on the counter, he wiped it up before it dried. So I learned to be careful, especially in our kitchen: the pristine white one, gleaming like a showroom. The whitest part of our house.

The bathrooms were another sacred zone. They

had to be spotless—or he'd sulk. Or worse, seethe in silence. He never yelled. He disapproved. And somehow, that was worse. His disappointment was the punishment.

In the basement, I have my bathroom. I tucked a small bed into the corner—nothing fancy, enough for when I need to reset during the day.

It's the only space in the house that feels like mine. Not because I was given it, but because I claimed it.

Either way, it's mine. My space. My rhythm. My rules.

Oscar hired Maria, a young woman from Guatemala, to clean the house once a week. She doesn't speak English, and every time she sees me, she blushes, bows her head, and murmurs, "Lo siento, señora," before walking away.

I've never quite understood her blushes. Maybe she's just shy. Or maybe she senses something I can't admit out loud.We bought the house five years ago. Oscar said it was perfect for the two of us. Endless white walls. High ceilings and quiet corners.

Who was I to say it was too big? Too cold? When he asked if I liked it, I remember answering, "Hmm...not too shabby." And that was that.

We never really talked about having kids. I wanted them. Someday. He always said he wasn't ready. And I didn't push. I told myself the timing wasn't right, that the conversation would come later, when things were more settled. But now...I often wonder when we'll revisit it. Or if we ever will.

The thought creeps in during quiet moments. When I see a stroller on the sidewalk, or a child's laugh filters in from the street. But I push it aside. Every time. It's easier not to ask. Not to hear the answer I already suspect is coming.

Our intimate moments have changed. Slowly, then all at once. What used to be spontaneous and passionate has become a carefully scheduled event.

Now, before anything physical happens, he consults his calendar. It feels less like a shared connection and more like a business transaction.

In the early years of our marriage, those scheduled sessions were at least regular. Predictable, yes. But still satisfying. But over time, they've grown fewer and farther between. And during those long, dry spells, I lose myself in writing. It's convenient when my publisher is breathing down my neck... but it also reminds me how far we've drifted.

It's been six months. Half a year since he's even attempted to pencil me in.

I've tried initiating. Once, I bought a negligee—something soft, hopeful, maybe even a little bold. It had lace, a hint of mystery, and enough risk to make me feel like I hadn't entirely disappeared.

But my attempt at seduction landed with all the passion of a cold casserole. He grew tense. Defensive. Like I'd crossed some invisible boundary neither of us had agreed to, but I was expected to honor.

And somehow, I still walked away feeling like

I had done something wrong. Like wanting to be touched, something so basic, so natural in a marriage—was an inconvenience.

Maybe... my sexy days were over. Maybe I'd quietly crossed that line without knowing it, slipping from desirable to dutiful. From lover to roommate. And he never said a word. Not when the shift happened. Not even when the spark fizzled out and got replaced with shared calendars and polite nods across the kitchen.

He always promises we'll make time. That he'll "schedule something soon." But the thought of being slotted between meetings or chores...it makes me feel small. Insignificant. Unwanted.

So I retreat. Emotionally. Physically. I avoid the conversation altogether. Because every time I try to reach for him, I'm reminded of how far he's already gone.

I've had the feeling something wasn't right for a while now. Couldn't quite put my finger on it, but I chose to ignore it.

Well...not anymore.

I can't unsee what I've seen. And one thing about me? I don't tolerate cheating. Even if I wanted to turn a blind eye...I couldn't.

"An after-party for the football game, my arse," I mutter under my breath.

But here's the thing, now I'm the one ignoring his calls. And that feels like a shift. Like the first stone in an avalanche.

Normally, I'd text back something cheerful,

"Okay!" or even call and say, "Have fun, and be safe." I played my part well.

Supportive. Sweet. Predictably trusting.

I bet he's enjoying his time with his fiancée right now. Should I call and congratulate him on the engagement?

Yeah. Right.

Maybe he's been sabotaging our marriage from the start. And I? I was the perfect mark—naive, non-confrontational, never one to pry.

He knew exactly what I wouldn't do. That's how he got away with it. His sly charm, his carefully timed lies, and that quiet confidence that always left me second-guessing myself instead of him.

But now the truth is unraveling, thread by thread. And I'm starting to see it for what it is.

Maybe I wasn't blind. Maybe I didn't want to see.

But now the cracks in our relationship, so neatly disguised by his manipulative hands—are finally starting to show. And I can't help but feel like a fool for not noticing sooner.

I slip into our perfectly arranged bedroom, the soft glow of lamplight filtering through sheer curtains. The silence feels staged—like everything else in this house.

I sit at the edge of the bed, my mind racing: thoughts, timelines, backup plans.

The clock reads past nine. I have three hours. Oscar is obsessively punctual—always home before midnight, like some twisted version of Cinderella. Only if he's late, nothing turn into a pumpkin. Something far more dangerous shows up instead.

I need to be gone before then.

I'm not ready for a confrontation. He has a gift for flipping the script—gaslighting me until I'm the one apologizing. I'm not ready for that battle. Not yet.

I scan the closet and pull out my largest suitcase. I pack quietly, carefully—only what he won't notice is missing. With every folded item, I feel something stirring inside me.

Power.

Freedom.

One blouse at a time.

Down in the basement, I erase every trace of myself. Desk cleared. Files gone.

As for my "paintings"? I laugh softly. What paintings? Just staged chaos for a man who never looked too closely.

I double-check everything. Then check again. No evidence. No mistakes. I hope.

But where will I go? That question still lingers. Dad's place is out of the question. Right now, I need distance. Room to think. Room to breathe.

I call a limo company, not a ride-share. Oscar tracks everything—apps, cards, locations. He's thorough like that. So instead, I give the limo driver my neighbor's address. Not mine.

Quietly, I ease open the back door, wincing at the faint creak. I can't risk being caught on the front-door camera, dragging a suitcase like a neon sign. I crouch behind a bush and wait, heart pounding, breath thin. Five minutes. Then ten.

Finally, headlights sweep the street. A sleek black sedan pulls up in front of my neighbor's house.

I spring to my feet and wave. The driver sees me and opens the door.

"Thank you," I whisper, slipping inside like a fugitive.

He buckles in, checks his mirrors.

And that's when it happens.

A Range Rover glides up the street and parks just ahead. Oscar. Fifteen minutes early.

My heart slams into my ribs.

I lean forward, my voice low and urgent. "Do you mind waiting a few minutes?"

The driver nods.

I watch as Oscar walks inside, unaware. He hasn't seen me. I hope not.

My fingers tighten around the seat. This is it. My last window.

I take a breath that weighs a thousand pounds.

"Let's go," I say.

The car pulls away—quiet, smooth, deliberate.

And I don't look back.

# 4

# Dinner is a chore.

Dinner with my husband was always precise, neat, quick, and timed like a military drill.

"You're late. What are you doing downstairs?" he'd say, glancing at his smartwatch like it was my superior officer.

The message was always the same: Chop, chop. You're wasting my time. It felt like he had somewhere more important to be. Always.

After dinner, the routine clicked forward: rinse his plate, change clothes, call his mother or brother, then lights out. No detours. No surprises.

If I ever missed dinner, I paid for it the next day, with a full lecture on commitment, discipline, and how skipping meals was the first step toward moral decay.

He treated our dinner conversations like museum displays—carefully chosen, sterile, untouchable. Nothing messy. Nothing emotional. And nothing that might spark joy or discomfort. Anything that stirred the water, even a little, was off-limits.

"You know, Brenna's pregnant again. Her third," I said once, trying to open a door. Brenna had become a friend. Her husband and Oscar went way back.

But his response was as curt as ever. "I don't want to talk about children tonight." His voice had that edge—calm, clipped, final. Like a door clicking shut.

"Please, eat your dinner," he added without looking at me, as if the word children had left a bad taste in his mouth. As if I'd said something obscene.

He never brought up the subject himself, sidestepping it like a cat on hot coals. His discomfort was thick, like a fog that settled between us and refused to lift. A whirlwind of thoughts would spin through my head as I weighed whether to push the topic or let it drop.

Oscar hated messes. A single dish left in the sink would make him twitch. The same thing happened when he saw my clothes on the bedroom floor. It wasn't anger, exactly—just this constant hum of disapproval. Tension. Control. Always pressing in.

"What's all this mess?" he'd ask.

"My clothes," I'd reply.

"And what are they doing on the floor?"

"Well, you don't like them on the bed, so I put them on the floor so I can fold them," I'd answer, sarcasm barely disguised.

His nostrils would flare, face flushed with irritation. Sometimes he'd walk away. Other times, he'd rattle off a list of things wrong with me. But that night, he didn't. He turned around and said, "I need it to be gone when I return, or you'll never see them again."

Moments like that always made me retreat, do what he wanted and keep the peace. But the air would thicken. Heavy. Unspoken judgment clinging to every gesture, every sigh. It was exhausting, living under that microscope. The constant pressure to be perfect according to his impossible standards.

So I learned to stay quiet. I didn't push back when he criticized me—not at home, not at family gatherings, not in front of friends. I'd just nod and smile, hoping it would blow over.

But sometimes, it didn't. Sometimes the anger lingered—infecting the next morning, trailing me to work, making it hard to focus. And even though I hated how much control he had over me, giving in was easier than another battle.

He expected obedience—his version of what a "good wife" should be. And maybe, for a while, I convinced myself that was normal. That all wives were experts at pretending. Pretending to be okay. Pretending to agree. Pretending obedience was love.

But is it me? Am I the only one wearing this mask?

Sometimes I wonder if it's all just a necessary façade—to keep him from nagging, correcting, controlling. Shouldn't it be the other way around? Isn't it the wife who's supposed to nag the husband? Isn't that the joke?

I don't know. I struggle with communication. Maybe that's the problem.

Whenever I tried to convey something to him, it inevitably escalated into a fight that required prolonged conversation. But deep inside, I constantly tried to control my emotions and words. I didn't like to fight or make a fuss over things. It took time. The tension built up gradually, and it didn't help me when I had to finish a book.

Our deal breaker came over the basement. I flipped and confronted him when he tried to get Maria to clean the entire space.

"No. You've got the whole roof to yourself. The basement is mine. There's nothing down there, and I need it for my sanity." I may have overreacted, but I needed to clarify my point and carve out a space to immerse myself in my little world.

So, he compromised on the basement arrangement. Whenever he wanted to be with me, he insisted I shower before joining him in bed. He had his quirks. The thought of a messy space beneath his meticulously maintained house unnerved him.

His family, who live in Ohio, have an annual reunion called "The Grand Chambers." His mother, Brenda, personally arranges and organizes the event in detail. Everything has to be flawless, from the smallest part of the event to the flowers and decorations. Everyone would feel her wrath if she found something that wasn't up to her standard.

Brenda is not fond of change. She's a meticulous woman who always finds fault in everything.

In the first three years of my marriage, I attended the family reunion the way she expected. But over the last two years, that changed. I started showing up only on the day of the event instead of arriving a week early, like she preferred—and she hated that. Oscar didn't like it either, but I stood my ground. I told him plainly: either I go for one day, or I don't go at all. So he compromised. But every time I arrived, I was met with a non-welcome party—cold stares, tight smiles, and the kind of silence that says more than words ever could.

The reunion is set to happen in the next two weeks. And I hate to say I can't make it this time. Well, my husband could bring his new fiancée. That would certainly stir the pot. I bet his mom would have a fit. And do I care? Huh, why should I?

My phone won't stop ringing. Only nineteen percent battery left—and I should charge it—but in my rush to get out, I left my charger behind. I didn't think it through. So I wait. Wait for it to die. And when he calls for the umpteenth time, it finally dies.

I ask the limo driver if he can keep driving until I figure out where I'm going. He's understanding and agrees. I promise him extra for the trouble, and he nods. His name is Leo. He hands me his business card, which I stash in my backpack without looking.

We drive in silence for a while until Leo glances at me and asks, "You got a destination in mind yet?"

I shake my head.

He mentions needing to stop for gas, so we pull into a station. Once we're back on the road, he speaks again, his voice warm—almost paternal. "Now, tell me straight...you runnin' away from your husband?"

My eyes widen.

"Don't worry," he says, lifting a hand. "Ain't my

business. But I been doin' this almost twenty years. I know that look when someone's tryin' to disappear."

He pauses.

After a moment, he says, "I just need to know where to drop you. My wife's already blowin' up my phone, tryin' to figure out if I'll be home before breakfast."

"I don't know where to go," I admit.

"What if I drop you at a hotel?" he offers.

I nod, then hesitate. "Do you know a place where I can pay in cash?"

Leo nods, eyes on the road. "Don't worry, I got you. Been in this line of work too long not to know the perfect spot. Though...she probably gon' hate me even more for helpin' you out," he says with a chuckle.

At the mention of she, I finally exhale. The tension in my chest loosens. As we reach the edge of the city, a small bed and breakfast comes into view. It's not fancy, but it has a quiet charm. Leo pulls up and cuts the engine.

"You'll be safe here. I know the owner. Be good, now. Tell her I sent you."

He hands me my suitcase, and I give him cash for the ride.

"Now hold up—this too much," he says, trying to pass some of it back.

But I shake my head. "I might need to call you again. Please, keep it."

He studies me for a second, and nods. "Alright then." He pulls out his phone. "Lemme call my wife before she sends a search party. Told her I'd be home before breakfast."

The clock reads past one in the morning as I approach the entrance and attempt to open the locked door. After knocking three times, I waited patiently for a response. When there is none, I knock again on the beautifully crafted wooden door. The only sound in the chilly night air is the chirping of crickets. With no other options, I persevere; I have nowhere else to go. Thankfully, the door finally opens.

A sophisticated woman in her mid-fifties greets me with a smile and introduces herself.

"Good morning! Please come inside," she welcomes me. "I'm Angela, the manager."

Dragging my luggage behind me, I enter the inn.

"I was hoping you might have a room available?" I ask.

Angela nods, "Yes, that's correct. Let's get you settled."

"Leo brought me here," I admit to Angela.

"I figured as much," she replies, with a smile on her face.

"I'm sorry for showing up so late," I say.

"Don't worry about it, dear," she replies, opening a drawer and pulling out a large black notebook that looks like a ledger. "How long are you planning to stay?"

I'm unsure, so I ask her to keep extending it as needed. I promise to pay in cash for my stay and hand her the ten-day total. She asks no more questions but informs me of the breakfast hours and offers to provide lunch and dinner upon request.

It's crucial for me to always have cash on hand, whether in my backpack or pockets. Sometimes, I stash it in my books or anywhere, just in case I need money. I hate to use my credit card. After all, everything I have is tied to my husband. I don't want him to find me yet, and I don't want anyone to know where I am. I need to clear my head and figure out what to do with what I have just witnessed today. I still can't process what my husband did.

Where does that leave me? Does he think I will not find out? If he's so keen on hiding his secret, why not do it elsewhere?

Is that even legal? To propose to someone else while still married?

Even if you're legally separated, that doesn't mean you get a green light to remarry.

It's insane. Either he's lost his mind, or he's got a plan.

A way to push me out of the picture.

I bet he's spiraling right now, losing it because he can't get a hold of me.

Well, good. That would serve him right.

As Angela hands me the key to my room, she mentions the breathtaking view, particularly at sunset. But before heading to my room, I asked Angela if I could use the phone.

I need to call my dad to let him know where I am. But, before dialing his number, I press *67 to ensure the number in the inn remains unknown.

"Hello!" answers my dad on another line.

"Hi, Dad," I greet.

"Where are you?" he asks me right away. "Oscar has been calling, asking where you have been," he tells me, panicking. "Are you alright?" he asks. His voice is full of concern.

"Yes, Dad, I'm fine!" I answer.

"What happened?" he asks.

"I can't tell you on the phone. I'm just calling you so you know I'm fine," I tell him.

"What happened to your phone?"

"I forgot to bring the charger," I say, trying to sound casual. "Listen, Dad, I have to go."

I tell him I love him. Then hang up before he can talk me into giving him my address.

I can't let anyone know where I am—not yet.

I need space.

I need time to figure out my next move.

# 5

# How I Met Oscar

Oscar was intimidating—in looks, in manners, in the bullet points of his résumé. I still don't know how I ended up talking to him that night. My first impression? He was out of my league, and fully aware of it.

Every year, my dad threw a Christmas party for his company. He insisted, without fail, that the entire Green family attend. No matter what. They treated it like a social summit. Plus, they could bring a plus-one of their choosing.

I dreaded it. Every single year.

Social gatherings, any kind of party, were never easy for me. The anxiety always came in waves: the twisting in my stomach, the damp palms, the way my chest tightened with every unfamiliar voice.

I preferred the edges. Corners. Hallways. Bathrooms with the door locked and the fan running.

If someone wanted to find me, they'd have to look behind the scenes. I was never on the dance floor—unless Dad insisted, dragging me out for a forced spin under the lights, smiling like it was all normal.

If it were up to me, I'd be one of the people passing hors d'oeuvres. Blending in, staying busy, staying invisible. But that would've driven my father up the wall.

My sisters were different. Parties lit them up. They seemed to follow some unspoken code. How to glide from one conversation to the next. When to laugh. How to make everyone feel seen. It looked effortless. Natural.

They were magnetic. I, on the other hand, found the whole thing exhausting. Like trying to speak a language I was never taught.

My mother used to say I was like a fly on the wall. Easy to miss, easier to ignore. She said it with a sigh, like it explained everything. I once overheard her tell a friend, "Oh, that poor, poor girl," as if I were a burden she hadn't quite figured out how to carry.

I was raised by a nanny. My mother only made appearances on holidays: Thanksgiving, Christmas, and Dad's annual party. She floated in. Elegant and distant, like a guest in her own home. Then she'd vanish again, back to whatever life she lived outside of us.

But one thing became clear as I got older—when she was around, she always made time for my sisters. Marie and Alexi got the warm smiles, the lingering hugs, the whispered jokes meant just for them. With me, it was silence. Or small talk, if necessary.

I tried to act like it didn't matter. Played it cool. Distant. But inside, it hollowed me out.

The difference in how she treated us wasn't

something we talked about. But it was there, sharp and constant—a quiet wound that never scabbed over.

I used to ask myself, What's wrong with me? Not out loud, of course. Just enough for it to echo.

I remember the night I first saw Oscar. It was at one of my father's over-the-top Christmas parties—high ceilings, crystal chandeliers, laughter that never quite reached the eyes.

I was doing what I always did: trying not to be noticed. Hovering near the edge of the room, a glass of something untouched in my hand, pretending to be part of the décor.

That's when I saw them—Marie and Alexi, front and center in a cluster of women, giggling and leaning in just a little too close. And at the center of it all, him.

Tall. Composed. Blond hair perfectly styled, suit tailored within an inch of its life. He had that ease about him. The kind that draws attention without trying.

I wasn't especially interested. But I watched anyway. Maybe because they couldn't stop watching him. I slipped over to the bar, hoping for something cold to steady my nerves. I stood at the far end, away from the crowd, pretending not to watch the scene unfolding across the room.

Then I felt him. A presence beside me. Quiet. Intentional.

I turned, and there he was. The man they couldn't stop looking at.

Up close, he was even more composed. Effortlessly elegant. I opened my mouth to say something, anything, but nothing came out.

He smiled, extended a hand, and asked me to dance.

Before I could respond, Alexi materialized at my side like she'd been waiting for the moment. "She's one of us," she said, all teeth and charm.

I smiled stiffly. One of us. The phrase stuck in my mind like a splinter.

What did that even mean?

For a second, I pictured us in some secret society. Not the glamorous kind. More like a gathering of wolves in silk dresses, sniffing out weakness. Or vampires, introducing their next victim.

Alexi's brows arched, then drew together—displeasure flickering across her face like a shadow she didn't bother to hide. Marie didn't say a word, just looked at me like I'd wandered into the wrong room wearing the wrong dress.

Here we go again, I thought.

I grabbed my drink, swallowed the tightness in my throat, and offered a smile that didn't quite reach my eyes. "It was a pleasure meeting you, Oscar."

Then I turned and walked away. Calm on the outside, brittle on the inside. I could feel their eyes on my back, sharp and assessing.

I didn't need to look back to know the truth.

I wasn't invited into their circle. I never had been.

But Oscar didn't seem to get the message. Or maybe he did, and ignored it. He stayed close, too close, a persistent presence trailing just behind me wherever I went.

"Dance with me," he said, his voice low and melodic, like a challenge wrapped in charm.

"I don't dance," I replied, keeping my tone flat. "And I don't think it's wise for you to be following me around."

Marie, never far from a good eavesdrop, drifted by just in time to hear. "You're quite the threat, little sister," she murmured with a sly smile before disappearing into the crowd, pleased with herself.

Eventually, I ended up dancing with him, only because my dad insisted. "Give the man a chance, will you?" he said, nudging me toward the floor like it was a harmless favor.

"Dad, he's got women hovering around him like flies. Look at Alexi—she's about to murder me with her eyes."

He shrugged. "He seems fine. And you've always had an active imagination."

So, I agreed. One dance. That was it.

Before the music started, I looked up at Oscar and said, "You may lose a toe. I'm a terrible dancer."

He chuckled. "I'll take my chances."

And sure enough, I stepped on him twice, maybe three times. But honestly, how could I not? Alexi's stare was locked on me the whole time, like she was willing me to trip just so she could say I told you so.

When the song ended, Oscar asked for my number. I said no.

To my surprise, Oscar later told me that Alexi had given him my number. The next day, he called and asked me out to dinner. Again, I said no. "It's not a good idea," I repeated.

"I've heard that phrase since last night," he replied, sounding amused.

I had plenty of reasons not to date him. He felt like trouble—the kind of man who stirred up silent wars in rooms full of women. And he'd caught Alexi's attention, which made him strictly off-limits. I'd spent most of my life avoiding conflict with her. She already wasn't thrilled with me. I didn't need to give her another reason.

Then came the text.

Alexi admitted she'd given him my number. Said it was fine if I wanted to go out with him.

It stopped me cold. Alexi wasn't exactly known for her humility. This was her version of an apology. Indirect, calculated, but still unexpected.

Even with her blessing, I didn't feel any pull toward Oscar. Just a quiet wariness. A man like that? He had trouble written all over him, in perfectly embossed, monogrammed letters.

Despite his persistent calls and texts, I chose not to engage. I let his calls go to voicemail, left his messages unopened. When they finally stopped, I felt...r elieved. Like a weight I hadn't realized I was carrying had slipped off my shoulders.

Two years later, I saw Oscar again, at another one of my father's Christmas parties. I had skipped the previous year's event, blaming it on a last-minute trip I planned with Arabella, and for once, my dad didn't push back. In the time since, Oscar had faded to the background.

Seeing him again jolted something loose. Especially because he was standing next to Alexi. I assumed the obvious. They looked comfortable. Familiar. The kind of ease that didn't come from just being acquaintances.

But when Oscar asked me to dinner, I looked at him and said, "Aren't you and Alexi a couple?"

He shook his head. "We're just friends," he said, like that settled everything. Then he looked at me, like he was pleading with me to say yes. Like none of the time or distance had changed a thing.

Alexi confirmed they were just friends, her tone light, dismissive. So I agreed, telling myself it was nothing more than a casual meal.

But our first date wasn't forgettable.

He was charming, attentive in a way that caught me off guard. He made me feel...seen. Like I was the only person in the room.

One dinner became two. Three. He told me how he felt—plain and direct. He wanted something real.

I liked the attention. More than I wanted to admit. So I told him exactly what I was looking for: marriage, kids, faithfulness. No games. No half-truths. No disappearing acts.

He agreed.

We kissed on our fifth date, and soon after, he

proposed. When I told my dad, he asked, "As long as you're happy, go ahead."

I replied, "Yes, I'm happy."

We got married a year later.

On the day of the wedding, Alexi didn't show. She texted that she had the flu—said everything was spinning and she couldn't keep anything down. It was from a night out clubbing, she admitted, almost proudly. I told her to rest and feel better. I believed her.

After the wedding, life felt...normal. Or close enough. The marriage worked. No major fights. No glaring red flags. We went out often. He seemed content, as long as I was home when he walked through the door.

He supported my hobbies. Within reason. As long as they didn't interrupt his schedule.

Asking about his day or what he had planned seemed to grate on him. In the end, I stopped asking.

For reasons I still can't quite explain, I never told him about my writing job. I wanted to. I kept waiting for the right moment. But the moment never came.

Maybe I was just making excuses. Or maybe I already knew. It wouldn't have made a difference.

Looking back, I wonder if I was just avoiding confrontation. Probably. I've always been good at that. But knowing what I know now? No. I wouldn't have agreed to a date. Not for a second.

What he did was unforgivable. Betrayal has a way of hollowing you out. You give your trust fully, freely, only to have it broken by the one person meant to protect it.

I believed he was faithful. At least for the first two years. But then the doubts came—quiet at first, then constant. I clung to the man I thought I married, convincing myself I had no reason to worry.

Now I catch myself replaying old conversations, searching for something I missed. A glance. A hesitation. Anything that would've warned me. But people don't always leave clues. Sometimes all you're left with is the ache of not knowing for sure.

Still, I know I played a part. I didn't press. I didn't challenge. I let things slide for the sake of peace.

I trusted him.

He broke that trust.

And I won't let that happen again.

# 6

# The Day After

Oscar and I had a bedtime routine that ran with quiet precision. At exactly 9 PM, the lights went off and we went to bed. No exceptions. He was firm about getting enough rest. Sleep, to him, was non-negotiable. Peaceful nights, predictable mornings. That was the goal. I agreed to the routine for two reasons: one, to keep my writing life hidden; and two, because early mornings gave me a clean slate. Space to think, to create, before the rest of the world woke up.

I've been lying in bed for what feels like hours, staring at the blank white ceiling. Time stretches, slow and indistinct. My stomach growls, but I don't move. A dull ache settles in my chest. This isn't the life I pictured—not even close. I used to imagine waking up to sunlight, the quiet hum of the coffee maker, and words spilling out before the day began.

Now those mornings feel like someone else's dream.

The room is cold. Still. I sit up slowly, fingers brushing the rose-colored bedspread—soft, comforting, almost tender. For a moment, I let myself sink into it, wishing my life felt more like this. Warm. Familiar.

Safe.

But it doesn't.

I sigh and place my feet on the floor, grounding myself in the only truth I know: I have to get up. I have to keep going.

As I swing my legs over the side of the bed, a sudden wave of dizziness hits me. I steady myself with the bedpost, waiting for the room to settle. Food has lost its appeal lately. I can't remember the last real meal I ate. My stomach is either in knots or silent, like it's given up asking.

Running used to help. It cleared my head, kept me grounded. But for days now, the thought of tying my shoes has felt impossible. Except for yesterday. Yesterday I ran—hard, fast, like I was trying to outrun something I couldn't name.

Today, though, even the memory of that run feels heavy. Like it belonged to someone else.

I drag myself into the bathroom and splash cold water on my face, hoping it'll shock me awake. The woman in the mirror looks hollow. Dark circles. Tangled hair. Skin a shade too pale.

I let out a long sigh and step back into the room. My eyes fall on my dead phone. Holding it feels like holding everything that's broken in my life.

I need a new charger. But that feels like the least of my problems.

I think about my husband more than I'd like to admit. I can almost hear him now: *"Quit throwing tantrums and come home."* He's probably pacing the house, checking his phone, maybe even debating whether to call the police.

And the last thing I want is to explain myself—to anyone. Not to them. Not to him.

But then I pause. *Is* he still my husband?

Technically, maybe. But after what I found out yesterday, I can't see him the same way.

What we had. Whatever it was—is broken. And once it shatters, you can't put the pieces back together.

Is the universe steering me into a new phase of my life?

Is that why I had to face the painful truth of my husband's betrayal?

Like something—life, fate, God—is pushing me to move. To let go of what's safe. To finally face the truths I've been avoiding, even if it hurts so much.

Now the weight of it all is settling in. I think about how many times I stayed quiet when I should've spoken up. How often I buried my feelings just to keep the peace.

If I could rewind, I would. But time doesn't bend like that. It teaches on its own schedule—never when we're ready. And still, I can't bring myself to face Oscar.

How long can I hide behind the lie that there's still time? Asking someone else to marry him, while still married to me. That's not how I pictured married life. Not even close.

But how do I unsee what I saw yesterday? The

memory clings. It won't loosen its grip, no matter how hard I try to scrub it off my mind. There are things in life you wish you could unlearn. Realities you never asked for. But you don't always get to choose what people throw at you.

In a perfect world, what I saw would've been a scene on TV. Something to shake your head at before flipping the channel.

Not real.

Not mine.

But here it is, looping in my mind like a song stuck on repeat.

I slip into black yoga pants and a loose T-shirt, tying my hair into a messy bun. A small thought creeps in—*Maybe Oscar cheats because he wants someone more polished.* But no. I won't let myself believe his betrayal has anything to do with my clothes.

I leave the room and head to the front desk, nerves tightening as I approach.

"Hi, um...do you happen to have a spare phone charger I could borrow?" I ask, forcing a lightness into my voice I don't feel.

Angela smiles, warm and familiar. Something about it reminds me of my grandmother.

"Yes, some guests leave theirs behind all the time and never come back for them," she says. "I can give you a spare if you'd like."

Guilt flickers in my chest. "Thank you, Angela."

She tilts her head.

"Do you need anything else? Maybe something to

eat?"

I hesitate. My stomach growls, a gentle reminder that I haven't eaten since that chaotic run to the restaurant. But the thought of food turns my stomach. Maybe it's the stress. Maybe it's everything.

"I think I'm good for now," I say, trying to sound casual. "Thanks for offering, though."

Angela nods, her smile as warm as ever. "Of course, dear. Just let me know if you need anything, alright?"

I nod, grateful for her kindness.

As I walk away, a flicker of regret hits me. Maybe I should've said yes. Heading back to my room, the same problem keeps circling in my mind. Smartphones track everything. Their built-in GPS can betray your location with a single ping. If I want to stay hidden, my only option is to either keep it off, or not use it at all.

Which, honestly, feels like cutting myself off from the world. Isolating. Suffocating. But what's worse? Disappearing or being found?

Will Oscar grow suspicious? Will he search harder? Or just write me off as insignificant?

I pace the room, trying to think. I need answers, real answers. Why did he propose to someone else? Who the heck is that woman? Was it planned all along? Or spontaneous betrayal?

I can't stay completely disconnected. I need to reach my father. The thought of him worrying makes my chest tighten. A prepaid phone would solve it, but even that feels like too much right now.

Maybe I can risk turning my phone back on. With the location disabled. I just need to be fast enough to disable that feature.

I plug the charger in and brace myself. Within seconds, my screen lights up like a Christmas tree. Notifications pile in—texts, missed calls, voicemails. I dive into settings, scroll to privacy, and shut off location services. Just to be sure, I disable tracking too.

Then I just stand there, staring at the glow of the screen. Trying to decide what to read first. And what I'm not ready to see.

I can't risk Oscar tracking me down. I never want to be found. Well, at the moment. But deep down, I know that "never" is a word I can't use when it comes to Oscar. He's relentless and persistent, always wanting to control things or those around him.

My eyes scan through the notifications, some from my dad, who always checks on me.

Dad: "Call me soon, kiddo."

Marie: Where in the world are you?

And then there are the ones that make my chest tighten—Oscar. My finger hovers over the screen. I'm not sure I'm ready for his voice, even if it's only in text. But curiosity wins.

Oscar: Where are you?

Oscar: What is this?

Oscar: Why is your phone off?

Oscar: Call me at once... or else?

*Or else what?* my mind snaps. I scoff. After what I saw yesterday, how can he still act like life is normal? I scroll through the rest of his messages, each one more frantic than the last. The missed calls are endless. A hundred or more. I don't know where to start with him—and I'm not ready to try.

But I do need to call my dad.

"Hello?" he says.

"Dad," I reply, my voice sounding slow and low.

"What's going on, kiddo? Where are you?" he asks, sensing the tension in my voice.

I hesitate. I'm not ready to share the truth with him. Now is not the time. But I have to say something.

"Oscar is here," he reveals, his tone tense.

"What? In the cottage?" I ask, surprised.

"He's looking for you. He didn't believe you weren't here, so he came early this morning to see for himself. Now he's telling everyone you're missing."

"How can I be missing? It's not even 24 hours..."

"Then why are you hiding from him?" Dad asks.

"I'm not. I just need some time to gather my thoughts," I reply, trying to sound calm.

"Alexi, your mom, and Marie are all here too," my dad adds.

"What? Why? Is he calling all of New York? I'm actually surprised his mom isn't here," I mock.

"Oscar called everyone. I bet he's calling his mom in Ohio, too. They're all worried about you. It's not like you to just disappear without a word," he tells me.

"Are they near you?" I ask, feeling uneasy.

"I'm by the docks, fishing. They're inside the cottage having breakfast," my dad replies.

I let out a deep sigh, feeling overwhelmed by the situation. "Okay, thanks for letting me know, but I'm not coming anytime soon," I say, letting him hear the frustration in my voice.

"Whatever it is, I'm sure it can be resolved through some negotiation," my dad advises, his tone that of a businessman.

"Not this time, Dad..." I reply.

"There's no problem that can't be solved by sitting down with a drink. After all, you're both adults who can talk it out," he continues.

"Dad, don't!" I tell him firmly.

"I'm just saying that—" he starts, but I cut him off.

"Dad, you need to hear the whole story before convincing me to talk to Oscar!" I remind him.

After a long silence, I change the subject. "I owe you, though," I say playfully.

"What for?" he asks, curious.

"I lost a bet," I say with a laugh.

"Ha! What about?" he asks, amused.

"Mom finally came to the cottage, huh?!" I reply, and we both laugh.

In the midst of laughter and reminiscing, we playfully speculated long ago about what it would take for Mom to finally agree to a trip to the cottage. I can still hear my own voice teasing my dad, saying it was a lost cause.

He laughs. "I thought I would never see the day. I almost believed you. But hey, she did show up." I can picture my dad's smile, but then his voice turns somber.

"Is there something wrong, Dad?" I ask, genuinely concerned.

There's a brief silence. Then he replies, "Nah, nothing I can't handle."

"Aren't you supposed to be in your office?" I ask. "Isn't today Monday?"

"Well...everyone's here. They even arrived before I started my coffee. So, I just called the office to let them know I'm working from home," he explains. Then, trying to sound upbeat, he asks, "So, what do I get for winning the bet?"

"I don't know. What would you like?" I respond.

"I want the first copy of every book you publish—before anyone else," he says with mock seriousness. "Signed, of course, with a note that reads, *'To my ever-loving, adorable dad—you're the best, and the very first to read this book.'* That kind of stuff."

I laugh, picturing the grin on his face as he teases me. "Oh, come on, Dad—every volume? That's a little ambitious, don't you think?

He laughs and says, "Well, kiddo, that's what I

want. And remember, you lost." He laughs at the end.

"I'll see what I can do, Dad, but I can't promise," I answer.

"Nope. You lost the bet. And I demand it," he chuckles.

Before we hang up, I hear my mom's voice and ask, "Is that Lila you're talking to?"

He lies and says, "Nah...it's my business partner, Boyd."

# 7

# The Jack Stone

When I'm in doubt, I usually let things flow. I trust the universe to nudge me in the right direction. It's like writing a story, I never know exactly where it's going, but somehow, one sentence leads to the next until something whole takes shape. Or maybe it's more like a game of signs. The universe drops clues, and I piece them together like a cosmic jigsaw puzzle. Even if the final image isn't what I imagined, it often turns out to be a masterpiece I didn't know I needed.

But when I try to force things, when I push too hard—it's like trying to shove a square peg into a round hole. It doesn't fit, and I just end up feeling like the blockhead holding the hammer. So usually, I surrender. I laugh along with the universe's twisted sense of humor and let it steer the ship.

I'm not one to rock the boat, but something about this situation tells me that going with the flow won't cut it. So, taking the initiative is the right thing to do.

Well, why not?

This isn't the universe trying to send me signals. This is the multiverse grabbing me by the shoulders and shaking, "Tip the damn boat."

So here I am, standing on a nondescript street in mid-Manhattan, trying to track down the man the internet promised would help: Jack Stone Agency. Four and a half stars. Dozens of glowing reviews. Honestly, it was a no-brainer. Well, he was also the first result that popped up. And let's face it, *Jack Stone*? That name has a certain...credibility. Like a guy who wears sunglasses indoors and gets things done.

This is my first foray into hiring a private investigator. I tried calling to schedule an appointment, but no one answered. The voicemail was full, so leaving a message wasn't even an option. Showing up in person wasn't my first choice, more like my last resort.

According to the website, his office is on the second floor—room 209. I take the stairs instead of the elevator, telling myself it's for the extra steps, maybe even a little exercise. A few minutes later, I'm standing in front of the door I came here to find.

The tag on the door reads *Jack Stone, Investigator*, but it's locked. I knock for five solid minutes. No answer.

With no other option, I slide down to the floor and wait, my back against the wall. I don't know how long I'll be here, but for now, waiting feels better than walking away.

I pull a book from my backpack, hoping to pass the time, but the words don't stick. My mind is too noisy.

The hallway is dim and quiet, lit by a single flickering bulb overhead. The concrete wall at my back is cold, grounding. An hour crawls by without a sound, and unease begins to settle in.

I tell myself to give it five more minutes. Maybe ten. I should come back next time. But just as I brace to stand, the sound of footsteps breaks the silence—slow, deliberate, growing louder with each echo.

My heartbeat quickens as I start to rise, but the footsteps stop, and then I see him.

A man stands before me, tall enough to make me hesitate. I freeze halfway standing, caught between getting up and bolting.

His eyes lock onto mine, and I can't move.

He's wearing faded blue jeans and a tattered brown coat that hangs loose over his broad shoulders. But it's not the coat, or the height, or even his sudden appearance that stops me.

It's his eyes.

Silver-grey. Mesmerizing. Like molten metal—fluid, unreadable. There's mystery there. Stillness. And something I can't quite name.

Whatever I was about to say vanishes on my tongue.

*Have I met this man before?* The question drifts through my mind, uninvited. There's something about him, something vaguely familiar. But no matter how hard I try, I can't place where or when. Still, the sense lingers, like a word on the tip of my tongue.

I stand fully now, brushing off the moment and

pushing through the nerves.

"Hi, I'm Lilanie Green Cham...err—" I stumble mid-syllable and stop myself. No. I don't want to be known by that name. Not here. Not now. "You can call me Lila," I say instead, forcing a smile. "Everyone does. But Lilanie works too... whatever suits your fancy."

The words tumble out faster than I mean them to, a babbling attempt to smooth over the awkwardness.

That fell flat.

No smile.

No chuckle.

His face doesn't move at all. Hands tucked casually into his back pockets, he just stands there, watching me.

Those sharp grey eyes bore into mine—steady, unreadable. Is he trying to read my thoughts? Is this part of the job?

I fight the urge to look away. I won't let his stare rattle me.

Summoning what little confidence I have left, I break the silence.

"You're Jack Stone, the investigator...right?" My voice wavers slightly, just enough to betray the nerves I've been trying to hide.

His first words land with a thud. Firm and dismissive. "We're not taking on new clients."

Without waiting for a response, he strides past me, pulls a key from his pocket, and unlocks the door to his office. Just as I move to follow, he steps into the doorway and stops, his body a literal and figurative barrier.

*Ooh la la... would you look at that?*

My brain chimes in before I can stop it. Apparently, this man owns a gym membership—and actually uses it. Broad shoulders, defined arms, the kind of physique that practically writes itself into a leading role.

I let my eyes linger a beat too long. Artistic appreciation, purely professional, of course.

His brow lifts ever so slightly.

Yep. Caught.

Trying to regain control of the conversation, I ask, "What do you mean?" My tone light but coaxing, angling to keep the door open. "You came highly recommended," I add, hoping that flattery might shift something in his stance.

He doesn't budge.

"Who gave you my information?" he asks, voice calm but alert.

His gray eyes flicker—not quite suspicion, more curiosity. And I find myself caught in them again. There's something still and deep about the way he looks at people, like a quiet lake that dares you to step in.

I forget what I was going to say.

Then he clears his throat. "Ahem."

The sound jolts me back. Busted, again.

*What was the question?* My mind blanks for a beat, then catches up.

"Oh—right. The internet," I say, trying not to

sound as embarrassed as I feel. "You've got a 4.5-star rating and a lot of good reviews."

I hesitate, then let the words come, quieter now. "I need someone to investigate my husband. I've been scrolling for hours, and...you seemed like the best lead."

I let just enough desperation edge into my voice. A little exaggeration never hurt.

Mr. Stone's face shifts. Subtle but telling. A crinkle of the nose, furrowed brow, and a long, tired sigh. Not quite a no, but definitely not a yes.

"My agency doesn't handle marital investigations," he says, voice flat. "You should try room 303. They specialize in that."

He moves like he's about to close the door.

My heart kicks.

"But I want you," I say. Softer than I mean to, but still out loud.

Too loud for comfort. Not loud enough to take back.

But I can't give up that easily.

"Please, Mr. Stone. I need your help." I reach out instinctively, but he takes a slight step back. I stop myself and let my hand drop. "I don't want someone else," I say, softer now. "You seem...capable. Experienced. Can I come in and talk? Just like I'm your next client?"

I fold my hands in front of me, almost prayerful, aware of how ridiculous I probably look—but hoping it works anyway.

Then, of course, my stomach betrays me. A loud,

unmistakable grumble cuts through the silence.

He shoots me a look. Part exasperation, part disbelief.

Maybe it's my obvious desperation. Maybe it's the sad sound of hunger. But he steps aside with a sigh. Not a welcoming gesture, exactly—more like reluctant tolerance.

Still, I take the opening.

And step inside.

The office is compact yet cozy, with a coffee machine and a tray of pastries in one corner. Filing cabinets line one wall, while another desk, neat and organized, contrasts sharply with Mr. Stone's cluttered workspace.

"Mind if I help myself to some coffee?" I ask, inviting myself without waiting for a real answer. The nausea's creeping in, and I need something warm to anchor me.

He gestures wordlessly—go ahead.

I walk over, then stop. The machine stares back at me, all smooth lines and chrome. Sleek. Complicated. The kind of appliance I've never met in my life.

I'm used to the old-school kind: scoop four tablespoons into a filter, fill the tank, flip a switch, and wait for that comforting burble that says, *almost there.*

But this?

*Ha.*

Mr. Stone must catch the hesitation on my face, because without a word, he steps over and takes charge.

He stands beside me, so close. And he smells so good. He's not imposing—and starts the process with practiced ease. A small capsule, like a futuristic vitamin, clicks into his hand. He taps a hidden panel, and the top of the machine lifts open.

He drops the pod in, sets a paper cup beneath the spout, and closes the lid.

A low mechanical hum starts up. Then, finally, the familiar sound of coffee dripping.

Something about it feels...normal. And right now, normal feels like a gift.

"Wow, that's pretty cool," I say, genuinely impressed. "I'm definitely getting one of these."

He gives me a look—somewhere between amused and baffled—like I've just emerged from a pre-internet century.

I spot a tray of pastries nearby, grab one without hesitation, unwrap it, and take a bite. I'm so hungry, I devour it in seconds.

"What?" I say, catching his glance. "It looked like it was asking me to eat it."

He almost smiles.

*Almost.*

He heads to his desk without a word. I follow, matching his pace. He sits in his swivel chair, and I take the seat across from him.

Now, at last, we look like investigator and client.

And for the first time today, I feel the tiniest flicker of relief.

"So, as I told you...we're not accepting new

clients," Jack Stone says, eyes on the scattered folders in front of him, hands sorting through them like this conversation is just background noise.

My hand trembles slightly as I take a sip of coffee. I set the cup carefully on the table, steadying it like it matters.

I inhale deeply. Then I speak.

"Please, Mr. Stone," I say, my voice catching. "I'm at my wits' end. My husband asked someone to marry him—while still married to me."

His hands pause, just for a second.

"I just found out yesterday," I continue, forcing the words out. "It's insane. Cheating is one thing. But proposing to someone else? That's another level of insanity."

As I speak, tears start to gather—threatening to betray the storm inside me. But I blink them back, refusing to show weakness in front of this man.

Mr. Stone looks up at me again. For a beat, his gaze softens.

"I understand," he says. "But our agency doesn't handle this kind of case. You need to find another investigator."

"I just need to know the truth," I reply, my voice breaking slightly. "I haven't been home since I found out. He's probably already reported me missing."

The words spill out faster than I can catch them, tangled in panic and disbelief.

"Who does that?" I mutter, mostly to myself, but loud enough for him to hear.

He studies me for a moment. "Well...?" he says, quietly drawn in.

"Who proposes to someone when they're already married?" I ask, shaking my head, dazed. "What kind of person does that?"

And then it hits me, how freely I've been talking. Spilling my story to a stranger without second-guessing myself. Without hesitation.

Jack Stone just looks at me, like he's deciding whether my question even deserves an answer. His gaze doesn't waver—sharp, unblinking, calculating.

It's unsettling. And oddly comforting.

Maybe this is why he's got four stars and a trail of glowing reviews. He listens. He pays attention. Even when he says nothing.

His eyes catch the light for a moment—silver-grey, piercing. It's easy to get pulled in. Too easy.

And yet... there's something else.

A flicker of recognition. I can't place it, but I *swear* I've seen him before.

I try to remember. When. Where. But the memory stays just out of reach.

Oh my! Holy moly.

"Wait a minute," I blurt, hands flying to my mouth. The pieces click all at once. "Were you... the man...err...the chef?"

The words barely land before the memories do—me, disoriented, throwing up in front of strangers... on his shoes.

My face burns. Suddenly, his piercing stare makes

perfect, horrible sense.

Of course he remembers. That's what the smirk on his face is about.

Mortified, I want to disappear. Or rewind time. Or both.

"I'm—I'm so sorry," I stammer, voice trembling. "About your shoes. The restaurant. And... everything."

My hands fly up to cover my face, and I start to shake—just slightly, but enough.

I don't dare look at him. Not yet.

I shoot to my feet, ready to abandon the plan entirely and make a run for it. Suddenly, room 303 sounds like paradise.

I need to get out of here.

Clutching my bag like it's a life raft, I avoid his eyes. "Sorry again...for what happened," I mumble. "I meant to come back and clean it up, but I... forgot. Until now."

My thoughts are scrambled, tripping over each other.

"Maybe room 303 isn't such a bad idea after all," I mutter, mostly to myself. "Thank you for the suggestion."

I force a sheepish smile. "Have a good day, Mr. Jack Stone."

And because apparently one apology wasn't enough, I add, "And sorry again. For yesterday."

I turn, praying the door is closer than it suddenly feels.

But then I stop, pausing just long enough to grab

my abandoned coffee. My hands tremble. *Oh God, this is mortifying.*

"That took you a while, huh?" he says behind me. "To recognize me."

His voice carries a spark now—warmth, even. I freeze.

"I...please forgive me," I stammer, turning halfway toward him. "I'm a scatterbrain sometimes. It's... a curse I'm working on—"

"Sit down," he says, cutting me off. His tone is softer this time. Unexpectedly so. "I might consider your case."

I blink. Did I hear him right?

The room softens—warmer now, less sharp. Despite the humiliation, despite everything, I feel it: a pull toward this man I barely know. Somewhere in the back of my mind, a tiny voice whispers, *Hallelujah.*

I ease back into the chair. "So... not just a chef, eh? Investigator by day, apron by night?"

"Primarily the latter," he says with a shrug. "I only cook on Fridays. Yesterday was... special. Super Bowl Sunday."

I raise an eyebrow. "Your restaurant?"

He doesn't answer. Just watches me with that unreadable stare that makes me want to fidget and freeze at the same time. A clean dodge. He's not ready to talk about it, and I'm not sure why I want him to.

So I shift gears.

"What made you change your mind?"

His mouth twitches. "Didn't you want me to?"

Then, as if quoting my earlier plea: "Internet says I'm the best out there."

He delivers the line deadpan, but something dances behind his words—teasing, maybe.

I say nothing. Just sit there, half-hypnotized, hoping he doesn't stop talking. His demeanor shifts, and he continues, "I'll see what I can do, but I can't make any promises. Investigations can be complicated and time-consuming."

He leans back, eyes narrowing slightly. "Do you have a copy of your husband's driver's license? Social Security number?"

My stomach knots.

Oscar always handled that stuff—meticulous, obsessive, the kind of man who had color-coded folders for taxes and utilities.

I shake my head, hesitant. "Honestly...I'm not sure."

He doesn't react, just keeps pressing, methodical. "Ever get an email from him with a tax form? Anything official?"

That lights a spark. I pull out my phone, hands slightly shaky, scrolling fast through years of cluttered emails.

"Wait—yes. I think so. Give me a second."

Pulling out my phone and navigating to my emails. I search, keywords flying—"W-2," "Oscar," "TurboTax." And then there it is: an email from two years ago, subject line: *1099 Copy – for our records.*

I jot down the numbers on a small notepad from

the desk. My handwriting's a mess, but the digits are legible.

"Thank you," I say sincerely. "I appreciate your help with this."

He nods, tucks the note away. No smile, but not cold either.

As I stand up to leave, Mr. Stone follows suit, escorting me to the door. Before I go, I ask, "Can I have the rush service? I promise I'll pay and give you a big tip."

Jack Stone's expression sends a chill down my spine, so I quickly add, "Take whatever time you need. Have a good day!"

"I'll be in touch once I have any updates or information for you," he says, his silver eyes boring into me as he holds the door open.

"Thank you again, Mr. Stone," I say gratefully before stepping out into the hallway.

# 8
# Threat

My phone buzzes violently in my hand, an ambush of missed calls, texts, and push notifications lighting up the screen like a warning flare.

I squint through the chaos, pulse quickening with each alert. Oscar. Again and again. As if he doesn't know that I know.

The audacity.

Putting him in the dark is the only revenge I can afford right now, but it doesn't settle me. It rattles. I'm still raw from yesterday, still trying to process what it means when your husband proposes to someone else while still married to you.

I sink into the armchair in my room at the Bed and Breakfast. It swallows me up, cushions soft against my spine, but there's no comfort in it.

My fingers tremble as I scroll through the backlog, trying to decide what deserves a reply. I've been ignoring everything. But Mr. Stone's voice—cool, clipped—echoes in my head. His stare, the quiet intensity of it, still lingers. Like he saw too much. Like he knew more than I did.

Then a new message flashes across the top of the

screen—Oscar, again, followed by another name.

Alexi.

Ugh!

Whatever peace I'd carved out for myself dissolves. One name claws at my guilt. The other? At my curiosity.

> Alexi: Where the hell are you? What kind of wife just disappears like that...with no word, no warning? Not even a trace. Don't be selfish. Go home, you ungrateful b****. You're unbelievable. Not even the decency to leave a trace?

I sigh and reread the message, the words seeping under my skin like cold water.

Leave it to Alexi to say something like that. Sharp. Loud. Entirely missing the point.

I mutter it aloud, more to the silence than to anyone listening. She doesn't know. That much is clear. She's reacting to the surface—to the vanishing act. Not to the reason behind it.

Still, the sting lingers.

Permission. Selfish. Ungrateful. All the classics.

She's always been that way, cutting through nuance like it's tissue paper. Call it honesty. Call it concern. But I know better.

Do I tell her? Do I unravel the whole mess right here, lay it bare in blue bubbles and long-winded voice notes? Or do I let her sit with her version of the story, the one where I'm the problem?

I don't know.

Maybe silence is safer.

Maybe silence is survival.

My fingertips hover over the screen, ready to reply. Just a few taps. One sentence, maybe two. But something holds me back.

Not fear. Not exactly.

It's that quiet tug in my gut—the one that shows up when someone's trying to pull strings.

Alexi's always known how to manipulate the conversation. How to steer it just enough to make you question your judgment. She doesn't smile and nudge. She shouts. She corners you with volume and blame until you forget who started it. And somehow, you're the one saying sorry for bleeding.

I know her tells. And this message? Classic Alexi.

No wonder she and Oscar get along so well. Two artists of control, fluent in guilt and gaslight. I wouldn't be surprised if he asked her to reach out. In fact, I'd bet on it.

His own texts are bad enough—thinly veiled threats dressed as concern. Now he's sending reinforcements.

> Oscar: Why are you doing this? If you're not coming home, I'm calling the police.

Does he really think that'll scare me?

I stare at the message, blinking slowly. The words look like concern, but I know better. Oscar doesn't plead, he pressures. He doesn't worry, he warns. This isn't love. It's leverage. Call the police, then. I think. Then, tell them your wife left after finding out you're not just unfaithful, but unoriginal.

I won't be intimidated. Not anymore. And yet, my thumb hovers over the reply button.

The truth, that I know about her, about the proposal—sits on the edge of my tongue, but I can't bring myself to type it.

Not yet.

The second I show my hand, he'll twist the narrative. He's good at that. Too good. I need time. Space. A plan I don't have.

So I settle for something safer, something vague.

Even if I look like I'm holding it together, the truth is—I'm not ready.

Not ready to see his face shift from confusion to denial to that smug kind of anger he wears like cologne. Not ready to let him spin this into my betrayal. Not ready for the explosion that will follow.

That's why I haven't told anyone. Not even Alexi, whose version of concern feels more like a leash. Letting someone in might mean losing the only quiet power I still have—if I even have any at all.

I don't have a strategy, just instincts, adrenaline, and a knot in my stomach that tightens with every new message. But one thing I do know: I won't be bullied. So I type slowly,

Me: Don't call the police. I need time to think.

Oscar: WHERE ARE YOU? Why are you doing this?

Oscar: What's going on? Are you hiding from me?

Taking a deep breath, I type back a message.

Me: I need to take a little break. Don't worry. I'll be back soon before you know it.

I hit send, hoping the message would carry enough calm to keep him from spiraling—just enough reassurance to stall the chaos. The last thing I need is Oscar dragging the police into this, turning my quiet escape into a spectacle. But Oscar can't be silenced. Not when he feels control slipping. Not when someone tells him no.

Oscar: Whatever this childish act of yours, come home. Otherwise, I'm going to call the police and report you missing. I'm alerting the bank of all your credit cards.

"Yeah, right. Go ahead, buddy. As if the police force will bend to your will," I mutter, tossing my phone onto the bed with more force than necessary.

But the smugness fades almost instantly. Oscar has friends, powerful ones. A close buddy in the NYPD, the kind who could make a few calls and turn my disappearance into a manhunt if it suited his narrative. I exhale sharply. Oh well, what can I do? I'm not going back. Not yet.

Maybe not ever?

It's like being trapped between a rock and a duplicitous place.

Confrontation is the last thing on my mind. Not until I have a plan. Not until I know what to say and how to say it, with proof in hand to keep him from spinning the truth like he always does. He thrives on control—needing to know my every move, tracking my steps like I'm something to manage, not someone to love.

But nothing could've prepared me for this. For him asking someone else to be his wife while I still wear that title. The betrayal slices through me again, sharp and fresh. It's not even the cheating that stings the most—it's the gall. The complete erasure of me. My life, my vows, discarded like an expired lease.

"You'd think after a certain point, the heart would simply be numb to such treachery," I murmur to the empty room, rolling my eyes at the bitter irony. But mine still breaks. Over and over.

My phone buzzes again—Oscar. I stare at the screen, the name glowing like a warning, and let it ring until it dies into silence. I can't bear to hear his voice right now. Not when the echoes of his betrayal are still bleeding beneath the surface of my skin.

Threats about money? Please. That's the oldest trick in his book, and I've memorized every page.

The buzzing won't stop. I power off the phone entirely and toss it back onto the bed like it burns. What I need is air. Something quiet. Something away from my phone.

I grab my jacket and slip into the hallway, my steps slow, careful. The inn is still, hushed, like it's holding its breath.

As I pass the front desk, Angela glances up. She lifts a hand, still mid-call, her headset slightly askew. With a kind, curious look, she motions for me to wait.

And I wonder, does she know?

Has she guessed?

Is the storm inside me really that visible?

I hesitate, my feet sinking into the plush carpet as I weigh whether to approach. Angela's back is turned, but I can feel the tension in her posture, hear it in the low urgency of her voice as she speaks into the phone.

Finally, I move toward her, unsure if I want to be seen or just...acknowledged.

She ends the call with a click, then turns to me with a smile that feels too knowing.

"Hello, dear," she says, her voice warm—gently disarming.

My shoulders drop a fraction.

"Are you doing alright?"

I try to sound casual. "Um, yeah, I guess so."

What I want to say is: Considering I've just confirmed my husband's moral compass is permanently jammed on 'deceit,' I'd say I'm doing spectacularly well.

But those words never make it past my lips. They rattle around my skull and lodge somewhere between defiance and despair.

Angela's smile fades. Her expression sobers as she leans in, voice barely above a whisper.

"I thought you should know," she says. "Two police officers were here earlier today. Asking about you. They showed me your picture... said you're listed as missing."

The carpet shifts under me. Or maybe it's just the knot tightening in my stomach.

My mind scrambles to process her words. Two officers. A photo. Missing.

This isn't just about lies anymore. It's an escalation. A trap tightening.

Didn't I text him not to call the police? The thought screams through my skull, sharp and useless.

I force my voice to stay even. "Did you tell them I was here?"

Angela shakes her head. "They asked for the guest list, but... you paid in cash. So I didn't have a name to give."

Relief brushes past me, too brief to hold onto.

"But," she continues, lowering her voice, "they were convinced you were here. Said your iPhone pinged the Inn as the last known location. I didn't know what to say."

My stomach turns. Of course. The phone. My phone. The one I turned off but never left behind.

Man... I thought I'd turned that locator feature off fast enough. Did it already ping my location before I shut it down?

I frown, the realization settling like a stone in my gut. Technology—the great betrayer.

"Did you tell them anything else?" I ask Angela, trying to gauge the situation.

"No, I didn't," she replies—her voice firm. "I didn't want to get involved, so I told them I couldn't be sure since many people come and go. But they seemed pretty determined that you were here."

I sigh, appreciating Angela's discretion but feeling the pressure of the situation closing in on me. "Thank you for not giving them any more information," I say. "I'm dealing with some personal issues and need to stay under the radar right now."

Angela nods, her expression understanding. "Don't worry, you're safe here. My bed and breakfast seem to be the best solace there is. If they return, I'll do my best to keep them off your trail."

As I think about it, I can't help but feel like Oscar might have called the police even before our recent text exchange. It just seems too coincidental that they showed up so quickly otherwise. Knowing he's probably already done that makes me feel even more urgent and anxious.

"Thanks for letting me know, Angela," I say, trying

to sound as calm as possible. "I appreciate it."

She nods, her eyes full of concern. "If there's anything I can do to help, just let me know, alright?"

I give her a weak smile. "Thank you, Angela. I'll keep that in mind."

I have to put my stroll on hold for now. It seems likely that Oscar's men are lurking outside, waiting for the perfect chance to coax me back or snatch me away. I'm not going to fall for that.

On my way back to my room, Angela intercepts me and hands over a flyer with a warm smile. The flyer advertises a luxurious getaway destination.

"Take this with you," she instructs. "If you ever need a getaway or a safe place away from everyone, use the number I wrote there. Let them know I recommended it," Angela explains.

I glance at the colorful flyer, which displays a tranquil island retreat promising relaxation and a break from the daily grind.

"Thank you," I say, appreciating her thoughtfulness. This looks like just what I need."

Angela smiles warmly. "Sometimes, a little escape can do wonders for clearing your head and figuring things out. I hope it brings you peace and clarity."

Her words linger longer than I expect, like warmth I didn't know I needed. I nod, murmuring thanks, and head back to my room, the flyer still clutched in my hand.

Maybe distance is what I need.

Not answers.

Not confrontation.

Just space.

I slide the flyer into my backpack, careful not to fold it. It feels like a lifeline, or at least the idea of one. And right now, that's enough.

His betrayal presses in again as I sit on the edge of the bed. The idea of a quiet island, of vanishing for a while, it doesn't just sound appealing. It sounds necessary.

I turn my phone back on, my thumb hesitating over the settings. I double-check the location feature—off. Or at least, I think it is. Can you ever really be sure with these things?

Then the screen lights up.

A message.

One name.

Dad.

Dad: See you on Saturday, kiddo. Big day!

With that message lingering in my mind, I know a good night's rest is now out of the question.

# 9

# Proof

Saturday comes like a sentence. I feel like a prisoner being pulled from her cell—not by force, exactly, but something quieter. Heavier. An invisible obligation that drags rather than shoves.

The day's social expectations press down on me before I even get out of bed. I used to love Saturdays. Used to linger through the market, savoring the scent of herbs, warm bread, and overripe fruit bursting with color.

Now, even that feels distant. Erased.

Today, there's no market. No familiar rhythm.

Just a new, unspoken assignment: find the perfect dress.

My mother, in her infinite flair for control, issued a dress code for her three children for her birthday celebration—silver, thin-strapped, backless, and floor-length. No blazers, she added, as if preemptively swatting down my only form of rebellion.

Apparently, freezing to death in style is the goal. Never mind that spring feels more like winter's unfinished business.

Two hours of shopping and not a silver dress

in sight. What I *did* find was a black version of her specs—close enough to pass inspection, far enough to still feel like mine.

It's not ideal. But it's better than showing up in jeans and a loose shirt, which—let's be honest—was always Plan A.

For as long as I can remember, my mother has dreaded turning sixty. According to her, who really celebrates getting older, especially when sixty comes with its own brand of finality?

Retirement. Relevance fading. A mirror that doesn't lie.

Well...not in my eyes.

But in hers, it's all downhill from here.

I used to love birthdays, back when my mom still came to celebrate them. Well, *came* might be generous. Dad forced her to show up for every family birthday. After my seventh, I can't remember the last time she actually came on her own. It became routine—her forgetting. Or maybe just not caring enough to come.

And honestly, I don't even blame her anymore. Why celebrate the birth of a child you barely know?

So when the invitation to her 60th birthday arrived, I couldn't help but feel it—resentment, sharp and immediate. Skipping it would've been the perfect gift... to myself. But of course, that's not an option.

Family expectations. Social niceties. The unspoken rule: smile, show up, keep the peace. Pretend history never happened.

But deep down, I wish there were a different rule.

One that said: if a mother can skip her child's birthday, then the child gets a pass on hers. Seems fair enough.

A trade-off for the forgotten milestones. The empty chairs. The birthdays I learned not to expect her for.

Right?

I'll have to face them all again—Alexi, Marie, and the same old crowd I've known since childhood. The ones who never missed a party. The ones I started skipping as soon as I was old enough to say no.

The plastic smiles. The rehearsed laughter. The endless game of pretending everything's fine.

And of course, my mother—it's her birthday, after all. She'll be holding court, surrounded by her polished circle of wealthy socialites, each one silently competing for the title of *Most Extravagant Life.*

Ah, First World problems. So shiny, so loud—so utterly unbearable.

And, oh God—Oscar.

I'll have to smile when I see him. Pretend the betrayal didn't splinter something vital inside me. Like my heart didn't crack open the moment I stopped pretending not to know.

I dread the fact that I'll have to face the man himself. Oscar has kept sending police officers to the inn. But Angela, bless her heart, keeps denying that no Lilanie Green Chambers is occupying the inn.

"Let me see your guest list, ma'am," the officer with a beard longer than his hair, as Angela described, asks.

"It's confidential."

Then, they produced a piece of paper that permitted them to search her computer. Angela obliged. And when they couldn't find any Lilanie Green Chambers on the guest list, they moved on. I thanked Angela profusely for protecting me.

Meanwhile, I'm messaging my dad.

Me: Can I skip the party?

Dad: No

Me: I want to skip the party.

Dad: No, kiddo. No excuses.

Me: I actually have one, Dad. Hear me ou
t...

Dad: Okay. Make it a better one.

Me: I don't want to see Oscar.

Dad: You have been hiding from him since Saturday. What's going on?

Me: :-(

Dad: What is that supposed to mean?

Me: I am not ready to see him.

Dad: That's not an excuse to skip your mom's birthday.

Me: Yeah, it is. Because Oscar's going to be there.

Dad: What really is the problem?

Me: Everything, Dad. Everything!

Dad: You skipped Thursday, too. You could have told me during our regular session together.

Me: You called our time together a session?

Dad: Why not?

Me: The word "session" feels like therapy. Like psychiatrist use it for their patients. Or somewhere where rehab is happening.

Dad: What would you call it?

Me: I don't know. Our time together?

Dad: You can't run from everything, kiddo.

Me: I'm not running....

Dad: Then, what are you doing?

Me: Hiding.

Dad: (smarty pants) See you tonight!

Me: I couldn't get away with that one, huh?

Dad: Well, nice try.

Seeing Oscar at the party tonight throws off everything. He'll expect an explanation. I still don't have one—at least not with proof. Jack Stone won't return my calls, and now his voicemail is full.

Full. Who even lets that happen?

I suppose when you've got a four-and-a-half-star rating online, your phone number gets popular. Still, ignoring desperate calls from a client? That feels personal. Or at least unprofessional.

Maybe if I show up at his office, he'll finally answer. Or maybe I'll just become another unread notification.

Just then, a call from an unknown number flashes across my screen.

"Hello?" I answer, cautious.

"Hey, it's Jack Stone," he says on the other end. Voice quick, a little breathless, like he's already moving. "Headed into the city now. Less than three hours out. I've got everything—you're gonna want to see this. It's all there.

Relief pulses through me.

His voice is confident. Direct. Rushed. *Where is he even coming from?*

But then the weight returns. In less than three hours, I'll be at my mother's party. And Oscar will be there.

I can't exactly conduct business with the subject of the investigation hovering near the shrimp cocktail.

"Hello? You there?" Jack Stone asks.

"Yes," I say, trying to walk the tightrope without slipping.

"Do you want to see the file tonight?"

"Yes." Too fast. Too eager.

He doesn't miss it.

"Where will you be?"

"At my mom's party."

There's a pause on the line. Then—

"Where is that?" he presses, voice low and pointed.

I hesitate. "Well...you see, my husb—sorry. Oscar—will be there." A pause. "Don't you think it might raise a few eyebrows if I'm seen whispering to some silver-eyed guy no one recognizes?"

"Who's that?"

"You," I say, a little amused despite myself.

"It's just grey," he replies. Flat. Factual. Not a flicker of humor.

A beat of silence stretches between us.

"Enjoy your party then," he says, clipped and efficient. "I'll meet you tomorrow."

"Nope. It's not happening. I need to see you. I need to know—now."

The words burst out before I can stop them. Too loud. Too fast. Too much.

My mind's racing, desperate to uncover the truth before I come face-to-face with Oscar again.

"Hello?" I say, my voice small now.

Silence.

*Did I scare him off? Did he hang up?*

Then—his voice, calm and steady: "I'm still here."

I exhale, shoulders dropping slightly. "You see...I didn't mean to raise my voice. I just—panic, sometimes. Lately, it happens before I even realize it."

A pause.

"And I'm sorry about that."

Another pause. "What do you want to do, then?"

"I'll figure something out," I whisper, more to myself than to him. "I can be late to the party."

"Send me the address," Mr. Stone says.

Then hangs up.

No goodbye. No see you soon. Just silence.

*What did I expect?* Considering I threw up on his shoes the first time we met, we didn't exactly start on the right foot.

In frustration, I sent him another message—told him to meet me at Central Park instead. No response. Of course. Classic investigator move: minimal communication, maximum mystery.

But as long as he shows up, and gives me answers before I see Oscar—that's all that matters.

My heart feels like it's trapped in a jar, fluttering hard against the glass. Waiting does this to me. It stretches time, sharpens edges. My fuse shortens with every silent minute.

Still, I keep reminding myself: once Jack Stone tells me what he knows, things will come into focus. And maybe then, I'll finally know what to do about my husband.

It's not every day you find yourself in a situation like this. There's no roadmap. No script. Just instincts I'm not sure I trust anymore.

All I can do now is hope—That whatever Mr. Stone's about to show me will bring some kind of clarity to the wreckage of my life.

However, I'm sending a text to my Dad.

Me: Hi Dad, I'll be thirty minutes late for the party.

Dad: Not good. Your mom will not be happy with you.

Me: Ha, she's been unhappy with me since I was born.

Me: I will try my best, Dad.

Dad: No excuses. Come when you can. But not more than an hour late.

Dad: But we need to talk.

Me: I will tell you everything, Dad. I prom ise...

Standing in the middle of Central Park, I wait for Mr. Stone to arrive—heart pounding, nerves fraying. I force myself to appear composed, still, unbothered. Inside, I'm anything but.

Earlier, I made arrangements. I called Leo, hired him as my driver for the night, paid him in advance. It wasn't about luxury. It was about control.

I need a clean exit when I leave the party. No questions. No lingering family glances. No interruptions. Just a quiet escape from a night I already dread.

"Hey..." a voice from behind calls my attention.

My pulse quickens at the sound of Mr. Stone's voice. I turn, and there he is. His steel-grey eyes lock onto mine, and for a second, something flickers in them. Just enough to make my breath catch.

I can't look away. His tall frame, the quiet strength in his shoulders—it all pulls me in like gravity.

I let out a shaky breath, eyes dropping to the manila folder in his hand. The edges are worn, creased. Like it's been held too tightly. Or kept too long.

My stomach twists. Whatever's in that folder, it feels like my future is folded inside it.

"Let's find a spot where we can sit down and talk this through," he suggests, nodding toward a nearby bench. As we walk over, his eyes stay fixed on me, sharp and probing, sending a chill through my skin as if he can see right into my thoughts. Now that he seems to know the story of my life, I feel exposed. Yet, I refuse to succumb to vulnerability—I still have something to fight for.

"What's with the gown?" he inquires, his tone curious yet with a hint of a smile. I look down at my black dress, feeling slightly self-conscious about how it clings to my figure.

"It's required for this event," I say, keeping my tone light. I glance around the park, noticing how everyone else is dressed in comfortable, casual clothes. My hands smooth down the fabric of my dress, as if that might somehow make me blend in. But I hold my head high, determined not to let this investigator see even a flicker of my unease.

"Aren't you cold?" he asks, catching my slight shiver.

"I left my coat in Leo's car," I confess.

Mr. Stone slips off his coat and drapes it over my shoulders. "Here, take mine," he says softly.

"Thanks, but I'm fine," I reply, trying to sound resolute.

He firmly presses it onto me. "You need it. Don't resist."

I give in, pulling the coat tighter around me, feeling the warmth seep into my skin. "Thanks," I murmur.

"You look fetching," he says, a small smile tugging at his lips.

I lift an eyebrow, meeting his gaze. "Fetching, huh?" I echo, a mix of doubt and something else fluttering in my chest. Despite myself, my heart skips a beat at his words. We sit down on the bench.

He hesitates, then speaks, his tone careful. "Are you sure you want to look at it now?" His voice is low, almost a whisper. "Knowing this before seeing your husband tonight...it might not be the best idea."

"That's exactly why I need to see it before I see Oscar," I say firmly, my voice trembling slightly. "Why? What's in there?" I ask, my hands shaking, a cold shiver running down my spine.

He looks at me, his expression unreadable. "I found everything I could on your husband."

As soon as he says that, I reach for the folder, but he pulls it back just before my fingers can grasp it. Mr. Stone leans in, a mischievous glint in his eyes, his smile sly and teasing.

"Guess what? I think you should wait until after the party to see the rest," he murmurs, his voice low and playful. With a deliberate flourish, he slips a single envelope from the folder and holds it out to me.

My heart pounds in my chest.

"What?" I breathe out, curiosity flaring in my eyes. "How many are there?" I ask, my voice barely more than a whisper.

He doesn't answer, his expression set on keeping the rest a secret for now.

"For now, here...open this," he says, standing up and gesturing for me to take the envelope.

My hands tremble as I hold the envelope, anticipation and dread tightening my grip. Am I ready to see what's inside?

Mr. Stone notices my hesitation, his eyes softening.

"Want me to open it for you?" he asks gently.

"No, I've got it," I say, but my hands are shaking even more. I instinctively bring them to my mouth, teeth pressing against my knuckles as if trying to steady myself. My stomach twists, threatening to rebel.

Mr. Stone places his hand over mine, his touch warm and steady.

"Please...don't tell me you're going to throw up again," he says, a hint of teasing in his tone.

A shaky laugh escapes me, surprising us both. I can't believe his little puns work. I take a deep breath, slide my finger under the flap, and open the envelope. The moment I see the contents, my mind reels, unable to process the shock and disbelief flooding in.

The girl he proposed to was named Antonilla. Seriously? Antonilla? It rhymes with Bougainvilla. All I can think is: perfect name for a character who meets a tragic end in my next book.

She is twenty-two years old and has been studying English at New York University since last year. Their affair started three months after she came to America. They met at a coffee shop near his workplace, exchanged numbers, and that was that. In the third week of November, Oscar and she went to her home country, Colombia.

Huh!? That son of a gun. That's when I wondered why he was suddenly traveling to South America during Thanksgiving week. I had a big fight with him about that. "Why Thanksgiving? I only come out on two holidays. Why pick this holiday?" I asked him.

"Not everything revolves around your special holidays, Lila. You can't have me every Thanksgiving or Christmas. I have other plans," he replied. I didn't press any further; I just became the quietest person in the room. He kept ranting, but I made my exit. I didn't argue with him again before he left.

When he came back, everything had changed. Our dinners together seemed bland. There were no conversations; sometimes, he would just ask, "How was your day?" He only spoke in short sentences, like when he asked why I was late for dinner if I didn't show up on time.

I couldn't believe our relationship still existed. How did we survive?

Or better yet, how did I survive?

# 10
# Showdown

I arrive at Rockefeller Plaza an hour and fifteen minutes late, my mind still reeling.

Oscar, my husband—is a fraud.

A cheat.

A shameless womanizer.

And the worst mistake of my entire life.

The words keep repeating, looping through the back of my mind like static I can't shut off.

As I step out of the car, Leo leans over from the driver's seat, his eyes steady but warm.

"I'll be close by," he says softly. "If you need anythin', you call me. I'm right here. You hear me?"

I nod. He says it like a fact, not a favor, like showing up is just what he does.

The elevator drags on. Each floor is marked by a slow, mocking chime. The air feels too thin, the walls too close—metal pressing in like a vise. My hands start to tremble. I shake them out, but it only makes it worse. The panic won't be reasoned with. Heat rises behind my eyes. A tear slips free. I wipe it away, quick. Hoping no one notices I'm coming apart.

The doors slide open with a soft ping, and I step

out, legs weak and unsteady beneath me.

I stride as if I fit in perfectly, concealing the fact that I'm aching inside.

Anger. Betrayal. Confusion.

Whirling so fast I can't see straight. Just trying to move without coming undone.

Then I see my father. The look in his eyes, worried, searching—nearly shatters me. A lump rises in my throat.

Beside him stands Boyd Flemming, one of his old friends. A familiar stranger. Steady. And somehow... his presence is just enough.

Enough to keep the tears from falling.

"Finally," my father says, gesturing with a gentle wave for me to come closer for a hug.

"Dad..." My voice catches in my throat as I embrace him, my mind screaming at me not to break down, not to make a scene. I force the biggest fake smile I can muster, trying to hide any sign of the storm inside. Please, tears, not now. Not here.

"Perfect timing, sweetheart. Your mother is just about to give her toast," my father says, a forced cheerfulness in his tone.

He notices the tremor in my body and leans in close, asking softly, "Are you okay?"

The gentle coaxing in his voice makes me want to bawl my eyes out.

I nod, swallowing hard.

He whispers, "Just hold it together, okay? Whatever it is, we'll get through it."

His reassurance is met with a tight squeeze, and a small wave of calm washes over me.

I turn to Mr. Flemming, forcing a smile, trying to mask the turmoil swirling inside. His warm grin always has a way of pulling me back to my carefree childhood days—so welcoming, comforting, and reassuring.

As we step into the grand ballroom, Alexi's voice slices through the air, echoing off the marble like a warning shot. "Well, well, look who finally decided to show up... my *dear* younger sister!" Her tone is sharp, arrogant, dripping with sarcasm. The knot in my stomach tightens.

The marble floors gleam under the crystal chandeliers, casting a golden glow across the room. Elegant couples twirl on the dance floor while others mingle in small groups, their laughter filling the air.

Some guests turn to stare as we enter, and I force a polite smile—nodding, as if everything is fine.

A string quartet hums softly in the background. It should feel elegant. Enchanting. But I can't focus on any of it.

Then I see Oscar.

His eyes are already on me.

I look away, but my gaze keeps drifting back, drawn by instinct, dread, some twisted magnetism. And he's making his way toward me.

My chest tightens, and I can't seem to catch a full breath. I take a step back without meaning to— then my body betrays me, refusing to move.

Don't run.

Don’t flinch.

Don’t let him see it.

But the panic is there, coiled tight beneath my skin.

As he gets closer, my heart pounds faster, and my thoughts scatter like leaves in the wind. Words slip through my mind, impossible to grasp. A surge of frustration rises within me, and I turn to my dad, whispering, "I can't face Oscar right now," my voice tight with restrained anger.

"Why?" he asks, his eyes searching mine for answers.

"It's complicated," I murmur, my gaze darting away. "I'll tell you later."

Unaware of, my dad guides me towards Mom, signaling the party organizer to begin the toast. I can feel Oscar's eyes on me, but I refuse to meet them, afraid of what might show in my gaze.

With a well-practiced enthusiasm, I exclaim, "Happy Birthday, Mom!" But my voice feels hollow, as if someone else's words are being spoken.

My mind is consumed with my troubles, but tonight is all about her, and I don't want to steal her thunder by drawing attention to myself. As soon as I say the words, my mother's sharp voice cuts through the air like broken glass.

“You’re late ... and you’re wearing the wrong dress. I told you silver,” she scolds, her finger pointed like a weapon. Every word drips with disappointment.

I start to apologize, trying to explain why I was

held up, but thank God, the event organizer's voice cuts through the tension.

"The toast will begin shortly."

She straightens, smoothing her expression with practiced grace. The spotlight calls, and she never misses a cue.

"Ladies and gentlemen, please welcome the birthday honoree to the stage."

Her gaze shifts to my father, subtle but sharp. A silent signal: *Come to me.*

He releases my hand and leans in.

"We'll talk," he whispers.

Just two words, but they carry more than comfort. They carry understanding.

The ballroom hushes as my parents make their way to the stage.

They walk hand in hand. Poised. Polished. Perfect. The couple everyone believes they are.

But I know better.

As the crowd rises, applauding with cheerful admiration, I remain still—on the outside looking in. Like a stranger pressed against the glass of someone else's life. A picture-perfect facade. Cracking, quietly.

I sense him before I see him—Oscar, too close. I turn, and there it is: his gaze, sharp as a blade, locking onto mine.

"We need to talk. Now." He grabs my arm.

"Let go of me," I snap, my voice low but shaking.

"What is this nonsense you're pulling?" he hisses, voice sharp and quiet—designed to cut without drawing attention.

My head throbs. My heart pounds as rage, grief, and panic crash into each other like a storm I can't outrun.

There's no more running. No more pretending. This is the moment I have to face him—and everything he shattered.

Marie's voice slices through the fog, low and sharp against my ear: "You look like you're about to strangle your husband. Keep it cool. People are watching."

My heart races as Oscar tightens his grip on my arm. Heat floods my cheeks. All I can think about are the betrayal, the lies, the way he acts like none of it happened. Like *I'm* the one overreacting.

I can't stomach his touch. The anger boils over, bitter and sharp. I grit my teeth, barely containing the snarl in my voice.

"Let. Go. Of my arm, you brute."

He loosens his grip but doesn't let go. There's hurt in his eyes, maybe confusion. Do I care? I've worn a brave face like armor for years, but right now it feels paper-thin. My pulse pounds in my ears. I want to scream the truth, tear Oscar wide open in front of everyone.

But dignity has a price.

And I'm still deciding if I'm willing to pay it.

How much harder is it when you can't even understand your feelings?

"Why are you doing this?" His voice is barely

above a whisper, laced with anger and confusion. "What have I done?"

There it goes. My eyes could almost melt metal as they bore into him.

"What have you done?" I repeat, with mocking enthusiasm. I nearly scream the question, unable to control the swirl of anger inside.

But Marie's voice cuts through the tension, saying, "Shh...not too loud...people can hear."

"I haven't seen you in a week, and this is how you treat me?" Oscar's voice carries a sharp edge, his annoyance clear. "I'm your husband. I deserve to know where you've been. And stop with this nonsense."

Nonsense? The gall.

My mother, oblivious to the tension, has her own plan. She turns to the crowd with a bright smile.

"As you're all aware, my son-in-law Oscar... where is he?" She scans the room until she spots him, then gestures for him to join her at the center stage. "Oscar, come over here!" she calls out.

As Oscar reluctantly releases my arm, I lean in close, my voice dripping with sarcasm.

"How's that fiancée of yours, huh? Surprised she wasn't invited to your mother-in-law's party?" My patience snaps, and I can no longer keep quiet. I have to expose him.

His smile slips. Just for a second. Then comes the scowl—hard, controlled. His jaw tightens, muscles twitching.

He's trying not to lose it.

I meet his eyes and don't look away. There's shock there. And something colder, like glass breaking behind his gaze. My words hit something raw.

Not a wince. I won't give him the pleasure.

He turns. Walks toward the stage. His steps are steady, but there's weight in them—anger, yes. But also determination.

He's not done. And neither am I.

My mother turns to Senator Steven Hutchins, calling him to the stage. They're cousins, bound by blood and that same glint in the eye whenever politics enters the room.

For years, they tried to pull my father into their orbit. Into speeches, campaigns, handshakes that meant nothing.

But he always declined. Always refused.

Bored by the game before it even began.

Oscar, though, he was never a hard sell. From the moment she saw it in him, my mother knew he'd run. And now, here he is, thriving in the storm, as if he was born to it.

My mom hands the microphone to Senator Hutchins, who stands tall and confident in front of the cheering crowd.

"Ladies and gentlemen," he begins, his deep, commanding voice cutting through the noise. "For those who may not know, we've been grooming Oscar to be our next governor in the upcoming election."

The audience erupts into applause and cheers, the sound swelling like a wave.

"And on this special occasion, my cousin's 60th birthday," he continues with a grin, "let's make it official and announce his candidacy."

The room buzzes with excitement as Senator Hutchins pauses, letting the anticipation build. Then, with a flourish, he declares, "Folks, let's welcome Oscar Chambers as he officially runs for governor of New York!"

"You've got to be kidding me!" I mutter under my breath, a surge of disgust twisting in my gut. My heart feels like a lead weight, pulled under by truths I never wanted spoken out loud.

I scan the room. Smiling faces everywhere. Glasses clink, laughter rolls through the air like a wave. Everyone's celebrating Oscar—his big moment, his grand reveal. To them, he's flawless. Charismatic. The perfect husband. The man who keeps his promises.

Ha! His polished charm is just a mask, carefully crafted to fool everyone around him. Only I see the truth behind it—the deceit, the lies. He's nothing but a cheat.

My thoughts drift to divorce. Maybe it's time to drop that bombshell too, I think, bitterness curling at the edges. But even as the thought tempts me, I know it won't fix anything. It won't give me what I'm really after.

I have to get out of here before Oscar finds me again. But just as I'm about to slip away, Alexi steps into my path.

"You should stand by him, like Mom said," she

insists, her tone firm.

“Why don’t you do it for me?” I snap, voice sharp with disdain. I won’t play along, not in this charade.

The words hang there, daring her to push back. But she doesn’t flinch. To my surprise, she agrees. Like it was always going to be her.

Everyone else is caught up in the merriment, showering my unfaithful husband with well-wishes for his candidacy. I don’t want any part of it.

Goodbye. Sayonara. Au revoir.

I start planning my quiet escape, hoping to slip out unnoticed, but just as I make my move, my dad grabs my hand, stopping me in my tracks.

"Not so fast, missy. We need to talk," he insists, his grip firm on my arm.

"I can't talk right now, Dad. Not here." I glance around the crowded room. "Despite my disdain for Oscar, I don’t want to cause a scene."

Dad isn't swayed. He leads me into a secluded room, shutting the door behind us with a determined click. "Now, start talking."

I hesitate, swallowing hard. “I don’t know where to begin,” I say, my voice barely steady.

My mind’s still spinning. The pictures, the headache that hasn’t let up since. A dull throb—grief, betrayal, something else I can’t name—pulsing behind my eyes.

And then Oscar. Announcing his candidacy like none of it ever happened.

"What's going on?" Dad presses, his brows furrowed in concern. My stomach chooses that moment to grumble loudly, breaking the tense silence.

"Have you eaten?" he asks, his tone softer now.

"Not really. Just coffee this morning," I reply. "I haven't had much of an appetite lately."

Dad looks at me, his concern deepening. "Stay here. I'll get something for you to eat." He knows me too well; instead of leaving, he motions to someone outside to bring in a spread of food, likely fearing I'd slip away the moment he turned his back.

He sits down across from me, his expression serious. "Tell me, kid. What have you been hiding? Are you...having an affair?" His words hit me like a slap.

My eyes widen. "Wow, Dad. Thanks! Is that what you think of me?" I snap, hurt bubbling up to the surface.

His voice lowers, demanding, his steely gaze locked onto mine, as if searching for the truth.

"Start explaining, then," he commands, his tone leaving no room for evasion.

Silence settles between us.

"Why were you hiding? And gone for an entire week?" Dad presses, his words tinged with both concern and confusion.

His gaze doesn't waver—like a spotlight, steady and searching, aimed at truths I'm not ready to give up.

"You've never acted out like this before. Not even as a teenager," Dad says, his face caught between worry and something else. "None of us knew you had it in you. Not even me."

His voice carries that strange mix—part pride, part apprehension. Like he's not sure whether to be impressed... or afraid.

I take a deep breath, the weight of his expectations pressing on my chest.

"Dad, technically, I wasn't gone," I say, my voice trembling as I try to steady the panic rising in my chest. "I called and texted you. That's not really being gone...right?"

His eyes narrow, his intense gaze cutting into me, stirring a mix of nerves and defiance. I know I can't leave without telling him the truth.

"So, are we just going to sit here all night?" he asks. His voice isn't raised, but something about it scrapes. "You're not going anywhere until you tell me, kiddo."

He says it gently. Like he's already decided what comes next.

His eyes don't move. I feel them more than see them—steady, quiet, final.

I shift. Left foot, then right. A meaningless shuffle. My hands betray me, fingers twitching.

The words are there. Caught. Not buried, just... stuck. I open my mouth. Nothing comes. Just breath and silence.

And still, he waits.

But I have to try. This is my dad, I've trusted him my entire life.

"I saw Oscar proposed to someone else," I say in a steely tone, determined not to back down. My dad's face contorts in disbelief as he processes this information.

My dad's eyebrows furrow. "A business proposal or something?"

"No, Dad, a marriage proposal," I say, my voice steady.

He lets out a laugh, short and sharp. "That's preposterous," he says, nearly choking on the word as the waitress appears with the tray.

She sets it down. I pull the plate into my lap and start eating, fast, like I hadn't noticed how hungry I was until now.

Before she leaves, I glance up and thank her with a nod. She offers her name—Stephanie—and I ask for a drink. She smiles, eager to help, and disappears down the hallway.

The food helps. Not in any profound way, just enough to steady my hands.

My dad keeps talking. Questions spill out, one after another, but I barely track them. His voice blurs, fading into the background as I chew.

Minutes later, Stephanie returns, setting down a bottle of champagne and a bottle of red wine. She explains she wasn't sure what I wanted. I nod. It's more than enough.

I thank her quietly, watching her retreat.

My father doesn't look at the bottles. His eyes stay fixed on me. "I don't know whether to believe you," he says, his voice tight, edged with something between doubt and fatigue.

"Well, then, don't!" I snap, grabbing the champagne bottle. With no glass in sight, I bring it to my lips and take a long swig, feeling the bubbly liquid burn its way down, warming my insides.

"I can show you the pictures, Dad," I say, a reckless boldness bubbling up inside me, fueled by frustration and champagne.

I'm not much of a drinker, but today's shocks leave me parched and raw. I take a sip. Then another. The cold bite of it hits hard—sharp, clean, almost medicinal.

A slow warmth spreads through me, softening the edges—pain, fear, whatever still lives beneath the surface.

For a moment, I forget. Let myself sink.

But as I raise the bottle again, something flickers, quiet, persistent. A warning I already know: You'll pay for this tomorrow.

My dad's face twists in shock as I down nearly the whole bottle. His hand jerks forward, but too late. The champagne scorches my throat, heat blooming through my limbs like fire under skin.

"Slow down, will you?" he warns, prying the half-empty bottle from my trembling grip.

Despite the shock, my dad stays eerily calm.

"How did you come by these pictures?" he asks, voice even.

But his eyes betray him. A storm brews—quiet, contained, waiting. He wears the mask well. But I see it cracking.

"I hired a private investigator," I say, skirting around the messy details of how I uncovered Oscar's affair.

“I need to see the pictures for myself,” he says, gaze fixed, unrelenting.

The intensity in his eyes makes me shift. Something crawls under my skin—heat, nerves, warning.

Desperate for a distraction, I snatch up the bottle and take another swig.

"I'm just...really thirsty, Dad," I mumble, taking a gulp. Before I realize it, I’ve drained the entire bottle, setting it back down with a dull thud.

My dad’s face stays unreadable, giving nothing away about what he really thinks of the bomb I’ve just dropped.

# 11

# Becoming a Thing

Throwing up in front of Jack Stone is becoming my new thing. Just an hour ago, Oscar found me in the back room where I'd been talking with my father. I'd hoped the flood of well-wishers congratulating him on his candidacy would keep him distracted. Shaking hands. Making promises he'd never keep. Isn't that what politicians do?

I must've lost track of time. Or maybe the champagne blurred the edges. Because suddenly, there he was.

Standing in front of me.

His face tight. Angry.

"Let's go home," he said, grabbing my arm.

I tore it back. My heart kicked against my ribs.

"Over my dead body, you cheat," I hissed. The words came out slurred, sharp, soaked in alcohol and something worse, the truth.

He blinked. Like he didn't recognize me.

The air thickened, sour with champagne, sharp with sweat, pulsing with fury.

My cheeks burned. I could've said something calmer. Something softer. The fire had already started, and I wasn't ready to put it out.

Not yet.

I knew I looked unhinged. Dramatic. Like a teenager throwing a fit.

But can you really blame me?

Sometimes the truth doesn't come out polite. It claws its way out.

From the corner of my eye, I saw her coming. My mother. Charging across the room in that blood-red gown. Anger in every step. Disappointment stitched into every thread.

"Lilanie Greta Green Chambers!"

I flinched.

My full name cracked through the air like a whip, each syllable measured, sharp, final. Her eyes burned through me. Her voice cut deeper. Whatever composure I had left scattered.

Why did they give me such a long name? Greta was too much. Too grand, too certain. Tonight, I was none of those things.

"Shame on you. Lower your voice, the entire building can hear you," she snapped. Her tone, surgical. Precise. Not loud. Just lethal. The gown swished behind her like a warning siren. "What's gotten into you?" she demanded. Her stare didn't blink. Didn't soften. "You vanish for a week without a word, and now you're back acting like some unruly teenager."

I didn't answer. What could I say? The truth wouldn't land. It never did with her.

I bit my tongue. My mind spun with the weight of

secrets I wasn't ready to share. Not here. Not tonight. Not on her 60th birthday. Not after drinking champagne like it was water.

"Wow. This is new," Marie said, her voice slicing through the tension. "I've never seen Lila drunk in my life."

She and Alexi appeared like shadows, eyes wide, voices light, soaking in the chaos like spectators at a slow-motion wreck.

My head swam. The room tilted. Faces blurred. But my tongue had plans of its own.

"Well, well," Alexi said. "What a happy little family reunion."

"Great. Just great," I muttered, clinging to what little composure I had left. But it was already slipping. Fast.

My father stood at the center. Still. Steady. He raised his hands. No theatrics. Just quiet authority.

"Enough. Everyone leave. We're done for the night."

Nobody moved.

Silence thickened.

Then Oscar stepped forward, fists clenched, jaw tight. Refusing to be dismissed.

"I'm her husband," he snapped. "I have the right. She's coming with me. We'll fix this, especially with the campaign kicking off."

I turned. Something in me lit.

"You don't get to say that," I said. The words landed slow, slurred, but sharp. "You lost the right the moment you brought someone else into our marriage."

My mother's hand flew up—stopped just short of my cheek.

Ouch.

"Be careful what you blame him for," she said coldly. "We have to protect his candidacy. No bad press."

I laughed. It came out cracked, brittle. Hiccups followed.

"You still don't get it," I said, breath hitching. "Why don't you ask him yours...yourself, Mother?"

I saw the flicker in her eye. But I didn't stop.

"Oh, wait. What's the point? You never believe me anyway."

I stared her down. No more shrinking. No more trying to earn what she never offered.

Marie clapped, slow and amused. "Bravo. I like this version of you, Lila."

Maybe it was the alcohol. Or maybe it was years of silence breaking at once.

"You've never been such a loving mother," I said, and for once the words came smooth, unbroken. Just rage.

Her hand struck my cheek. Same spot. Same sting.

I didn't flinch this time. Just tasted blood.

"You ungrateful child," she spat.

"You shouldn't talk to Mom like that," Alexi said, voice thin and cracking under the weight of it all.

"Enough!" my father's voice boomed, silencing

the room.

Oscar stepped closer.

"I'm her husband. She's coming with me."

A scream clawed at my chest. I didn't let it out, but I felt it.

The thought of going home with him twisted my stomach. No. Not now. Not ever. Just imagining it brought bile to the back of my throat.

But I wasn't finished.

"Oh yeah?" I said, voice thick with fury. "What about the woman you asked to marry on Sunday?"

The words fell out—drunken, bitter, too heavy to hold in.

Oscar blinked. "Don't be ridiculous. What woman?" His voice trembled. "I...I have a wife. Why would I ask someone else to marry me?"

A hollow laugh clawed its way up. "Look at you," I said. "Lying without missing a beat."

He opened his mouth, but I didn't let him speak.

"S...stop denying it. I s...saw you myself. On the bar. On your knees. Like some pathetic, lovesick fool." My words wobbled but hit their mark. "Even if I wanted to forget, I couldn't. It's seared into my brain. Burned in."

Oscar's eyes darted, his hands clenched. "This is madness. It's the alcohol talking."

"No, Oscar. I...it's the truth talking. For once."

I stepped closer. Hands in fists. Heat in my face. The room spinning but the betrayal sharp.

"Stop lying. I know what I saw."

Our voices cracked against the walls. The room buzzed—charged, watching, waiting.

"I can't believe you're turning this on me," he spat, false sincerity smeared across his face. "You're just drunk. Out of control. Let's talk at home."

He reached for my hand.

I slapped it away.

The sound echoed. Final.

My rage surged, alive now, his lies slicing deeper with each breath.

Around us, the silence of judgment grew louder. Eyes on me. Their daughter. Their sister. Their disappointment.

"Stop with the accusations, Lila," Alexi snapped.

I turned to her. But said nothing.

Some things didn't need a response.

But Oscar wasn't done.

His voice softened, almost pleading. "Please, come home with me, Lila. I love you."

The words twisted something in my gut. I yanked my hand back. Shook my head, hard.

Love. It rang hollow now. Rehearsed. Like he was reciting lines from an old script.

And I was close to throwing up.

Too late. I saw it all now—the charm, the mask, the performance.

"Stay away from me, Oscar." My voice came out thick, part alcohol, part fury.

I turned toward my father. Not graceful. Not steady. But determined.

Behind me, my mother stood frozen, her expression a fracture of disbelief. Her eyes flicked from me to Oscar, trying to piece it together. As if the truth didn't fit the story she'd already decided on.

"Lila, shush...you're talking like a crazy, drunk woman."

I might've been drunk. But I wasn't wrong.

Her words landed like glass in my gut, but I didn't flinch. The truth was sharp. But clean. Even if it hurt.

My father stepped forward. Calm. Solid.

"I'll talk to her," he said, voice low and steady. "But now is not the time."

Oscar moved again, too fast, too desperate. But my father blocked him, unshaken.

"Not now," he said again. Final. Like a closing door.

The room emptied. One by one. Eyes averted.

Then it was just the two of us.

He turned to me, his expression softening. The worry in his eyes had weight.

"Lila," he said gently, "why don't you come with me?"

I shook my head. Tears slipped down my face, catching the light and scattering it on the floor like broken stars.

"I can't face Mom after all that," I whispered. My voice cracked on the words.

"But don't worry. I have somewhere to go. Leo, my driver, he'll take me."

I handed him Leo's number. My hand shook, just

enough to betray me.

I smiled. Or something like it.

We hugged. Tight. No words for a moment, just the safety of being his daughter again.

When he pulled back, his hands stayed on my shoulders.

"This is madness," he said. "But if you need anything. Anything, you call me, alright kiddo?" His voice was firm. But his eyes were afraid. And full of love.

I nodded. We let go.

Each step pulled us farther from the wreckage, but something held, a thread between us. No words, just the weight of what hadn't been said.

Outside, the night air hit me like a slap. Cold. Real.

I pulled out my phone and called Detective Jack Stone.

He answered on the second ring. Tired, but focused.

"Still in the office," he said.

"I'm coming," I told him. No small talk. No space for it. "I need the rest of the file. Tonight."

There was a pause. Then a quiet sigh.

"I'll be here."

Then, hung up. And started walking

***

And now here I am, standing in front of this man, about to lose everything I've eaten and drank.

Mr. Stone moves fast. Slides a trash can in front of me just in time. No words. Just action.

On my knees. On the floor. Gripping the sides like it's the only thing holding me down in a world that won't stop tilting.

"I'm s...sorry, Mr. Stone" I mumble. My voice is shaky. Too fast. "I had... champagne."

It sounds stupid the moment I say it.

"It hit me like a bad..." I lose the sentence mid-air. "I'm not... usually, I don't drink."

A laugh slips out. Brittle. Misplaced.

"Isn't it funny," I mutter, eyes half-focused, "how people always say 'I rarely drink'—like it erases the wreckage that follows?"

I try a smile. Wobbly. Not convincing.

"But hey... I'm a writer." It spills out before I can stop it. "We get carried away. With words. With stories." A pause. "I don't usually tell people that."

Quieter now. "Please... Mr. Stone, keep it between us."

Mr. Stone lets out a low chuckle—the kind that softens a moment.

"We all have our vices," he says. "And stop calling me Mr. Stone. Call me Jack."

Then the smirk: "We really need to stop meeting like this...you throwing up, and I'm the one doing the cleaning."

I'm embarrassed. Really, I am.

I let go of the trash can and try to stand. My legs aren't convinced. So, I stay where I am.

"That bad, huh?" he says.

You have no idea.

He steps closer. The air changes.

"I need the file..." I start.

His voice hardens. "You're in no shape to deal with it. We'll talk tomorrow, when your stomach isn't staging a rebellion."

I should argue. I want to. But I can't stand. Can barely think.

"I'm sorry," I hiccup, body swaying. "I should've...not drunk all that stupid champagne."

"Stop apologizing," Jack says gently.

As I try to stand, his hand finds my waist, steadying me. The touch grounds me. And maybe it means something more.

He's close now. I catch a scent, something warm and familiar.

"What's that smell?" I blurt, leaning closer.

"Throw up," he says flatly.

"No, not that... you." I lean in, too far. "You smell like...like an aphro...aphrodisiac."

His body tenses.

"We should keep moving. You're drunk," he says, voice low.

I hold his gaze a moment too long.

Then, "I think I'm gonna be sick again."

Trash can. Fast. I grip it, head down, on my knee, skin slick with sweat. The sound of retching breaks the quiet.

Jack steps away. "Hold still. I'll get a paper towel."

He's gone. I peel off my coat. Let it fall. My gown clings like regret.

When he returns, I wipe my mouth. Then the can. The room spins. My head pounds.

I slide toward the wall and press my back to it, eyes shut.

Just breathing.

"I'm sorry," I mumble. "I promise this is the last time I throw up. Normally I have a stomach of steel. I could eat like a cow. Chug a mega pint of beer and still be fine."

I should stop talking. But I don't.

Jack chuckles. Soft. Hands me a glass of water. Then leans back, arms crossed.

"I think it's the stress," I say quietly. "Finding out my life's falling apart."

The words rush now. "I had it all. A job. A house. A husband."

My breath hitches.

"And now it's all just—slipping away."

Tears slide down. Silent. Uninvited.

Jack watches me. Something shifts in his face.

"You'll get through this," he says. Steady. Certain.

And somehow, I believe him.

He checks his watch. "Where's Leo parked?"

He offers his hand. I don't take it. Just lean harder into the wall.

Then a thought. Sharp. Clear.

"I never introduced Leo to you."

Jack doesn't flinch. "Yeah. I know Leo."

Figures. Classic.

He pulls a chair over and sits. The room smells like sweat and vomit and the end of illusions.

My head throbs. I yawn. "Mind if I close my eyes?"

I don't wait for an answer.

Before the dark takes me, I whisper, "You know ...you have really nice eyes."

I smile—clumsy. Unfiltered.

Then everything fades.

# 12
# Secrets

I jolt awake to a blaring sound, heart punching my ribs. Darkness—streaked with flashes of neon. A siren? A fire alarm?

Something drills into my skull, like a jackhammer inside my brain.

I blink—haze, pain, confusion.

Then a sting, sharp and hot, across my left cheek.

What the hell happened?

The noise cuts out. Silence swells, too sudden. A breath of relief, then the sound flares again. Louder. Closer. Inside my brain. I groan. Squint. Something's vibrating on the nightstand.

My phone.

I fumble for it, the screen slicing through the dark like a blade.

"Hello?" My voice is shredded. Barely there.

"Hey..."

A man's voice. Familiar, but not.

"Who is this?" I snap. Too loud. The words scrape my throat raw.

"It's Jack."

Like that should mean something.

*Jack.*

My brain claws for context. Comes up empty.

Then it hits. All of it. Last night, cracked open and leaking into the now.

Oscar. His grip on my arm. My mother's slap—sharp, left side, always the left. I press my fingers to the burn. The champagne. The stupid, endless champagne. I drank like it would save me. Like it wouldn't drown me instead.

My stomach twists.

"Jack?" I say again, slower. Trying to place him in the wreckage.

"I'm here with your file."

His voice is crisp. Too crisp. It slices through the fuzz in my head.

"File...file..." I repeat it, as if the word might fix everything.

Then: lightning.

Jack Stone.

I shoot upright. Bad move. Pain flares, white-hot. I bite back a groan.

"Oh. Jack..." The name falls out in pieces.

He chuckles. It shouldn't sound comforting. But it does.

"I'll be in the lobby."

Silence.

I stare at the wall, his words hanging there.

"The lobby?" My voice is scratchy. "Like...here? At the inn?"

"Yes."

No extra words. Just yes.

I didn't tell him where I was staying. Did I?

I might've. God knows what I said last night.

"Give me a minute," I mumble, and hang up.

The phone drops onto the bed.

I pull on yoga pants, grab a shirt. Doesn't matter which. Everything spins, but I move anyway.

Out the door. Down the hall.

The hangover walks with me.

Halfway down the stairs, panic grips me.

I forgot to brush my teeth.

My stomach flips. I picture Jack's perfectly carved face recoiling at the first hit of my morning breath. Disgusted. Silently judging.

I pause mid-step. Should I run back up?

My foot hovers. Then drops.

Why would it matter? It's not like we're going to kiss.

*Kiss?*

What the heck.

I shake the thought loose. Ridiculous. My brain's favorite hobby, sabotage through fantasy. I force my feet forward. One step, then the next. A slow war between vanity and urgency.

He's waiting.

In the lobby, I spot him.

Leaning against the front desk, talking with Angela like they've known each other for years. The sight jolts me. Too casual. Too familiar.

He glances over. I raise a hand in a weak wave.

His expression shifts. Brows lift. Something unreadable flickers across his face.

I feel exposed. Rumpled clothes. Hair unbrushed. Breath questionable at best.

Suddenly, I wish I had stayed in bed.

"What?" I ask, quickening my pace toward him, my cheeks warming under his scrutiny.

"Bad hair day?" he comments with a smirk.

Instinctively, I twist my hair into a bun, trying to smooth it down, and make sure there's a respectable distance between us.

"Coffee?" Angela interrupts, holding up a steaming pot.

A chorus of "Yes!" fills the air, my voice louder than intended. "I have this pounding headache..."

Jack gestures toward the inn's bar near the dining area. "Let's sit over there." I nod and follow him, my steps still unsteady, my head foggy. Angela arrives moments later with a tray—coffee, pastries, and an aspirin.

My eyes widen with relief. "You are a gift from above," I blurt, "sent to earth to cure my headache."

Angela laughs, setting down the tray. "A compliment like that might just convince me to extend your stay," she teases, enjoying the banter.

I pop the aspirin into my mouth and wash it down with coffee. Bitter, hot. Necessary. The pastry follows, sweet, buttery. But I barely taste it. Just fuel.

Jack watches me. Silent. Still.

His gaze makes my skin prickle. It's not judgmental, just...steady. Like he's waiting for something. A crack. A confession.

Fair enough. I did throw up in his office.

I take a breath.

"About last night," I start, fingers tracing the rim of my coffee cup. "I'm sorry. I hadn't had a drink in a long time and...well, you saw what happened."

The heat rises in my face. Shame always arrives late, but loud.

His expression softens. Just slightly. "It's okay," he says. "We've all been there."

A short laugh escapes me. "I highly doubt that."

I glance at him. Immaculate, Composed. The human version of a pressed shirt.

He smiles. Eyes lit with something almost kind. "Trust me, I've had my moments. But let's leave last night behind. Start fresh."

I nod. Grateful. Almost believing it's that easy.

For a second, the room feels lighter. But beneath it, something churns. That quiet, familiar dread.

Then he places the envelope in front of me.

Thick. Brown. Heavy with implication.

My eyes lock onto it. My heart ticks faster. A tightness knots my chest.

The pastry turns to ash on my tongue.

I look away. Take a sip of coffee. The cup trembles in my hand. I lower it quickly, hoping he didn't see.

"I'll take a look at this in my room," I say, voice even. Practiced. "And I'll send a check over soon."

Simple. Clean. Like I'm not unraveling inside.

I drain the last of the coffee and stand, ready to make my escape.

"Thanks for your work, Jack," I say, aiming for breezy. But my mind stays locked on the envelope. Whatever's inside is ticking.

"Sit down," he says. Firm. No room for polite refusal.

His eyes pin me in place. Like he sees more than I want him to.

I hesitate. Then sink back into the chair.

"Have you been following the news lately?" he asks.

Something in his tone twists my stomach.

"No," I say.

Jack exhales. Slow. Controlled. "Your husband filed a missing person report this morning. Claims you left days ago. That he hasn't heard from you since."

I blink. "That's absurd."

The words rush out. "I just saw him last night. We fought, sure, but—missing?"

My heart hammers. This makes no sense. None of it does.

He cuts me off, voice lower now. "He was on a morning show today. Talking about his campaign. Your absence was...noted."

He slides a newspaper across the table. I glance down. And freeze.

Oscar. My parents. My sisters. Senator Hutchins. Smiling. Polished. Staged.

And a space.

Right where I should be.

A perfect family photo with a guest—minus the inconvenient wife.

"That's impossible," I say, voice shaky. "I was at the party. I just didn't feel like saying cheese for the camera."

I try to laugh. It sounds like a cough.

Jack lifts an eyebrow. Then lets out a short chuckle. "That would explain it," he says. But the amusement doesn't reach his eyes.

I grip the edge of the table. Hard.

"I can't believe he'd go this far," I mutter. "Just to protect his image."

Jack nods. Slowly. Watching me.

"It does seem...convenient," he says. "Doesn't it?"

His eyes don't move.

He's studying me. Not just what I say. What I don't.

I bite my lip. Hard. My mind races.

Oscar is pulling strings.

But why?

And how far is he willing to go?

My mind spirals—questions tumbling fast, unformed.

Why would Oscar do this? Does he think I'll crawl back, apologize, beg?

Or is it worse? Something darker, calculated.

I don't want to be part of his political theater. Not ever.

"Well, just wait until last week's proposal hits the

news," I blurt, the words slipping out before I can catch them.

Jack shifts, leans in. "About that," he says carefully. "It was a private party. Very curated. The people there were bride's close friends and relatives. They were told not to record anything. No photos. No leaks."

He pauses. "He didn't think anyone would find out. Especially not you."

A beat. Then his eyes sharpen. "How did you get into the restaurant?"

"I used the back door," I say, keeping my voice level.

Jack frowns. "That door's locked. The manager's strict."

I shrug. "I waited. Someone came out. I offered to help carry the trash."

His expression shifts. Surprise, maybe even respect. But he masks it fast.

I shake my head. "Why pick a place that close to home? A proposal's public by nature. Wasn't it bound to come out?"

Jack doesn't answer. His silence says more than words could.

"Didn't the manager give you a heads-up?" I ask. "About the proposal or something?"

He shrugs. "I was just told to make burgers for at least fifty people. Nothing else."

He's thinking what I'm thinking. Or maybe he's not.

Maybe Oscar didn't care if I saw. Maybe he wanted me to.

Jack nods slowly, eyes still on me. Watching.

"The girl's from overseas. Her father's a billionaire," he says. "Oscar's banking on that connection—financial support, influence. She wanted the proposal close to his house. Super Bowl night. Said it felt...special."

Close to home?

Did Oscar bring her into our house? When I wasn't there?

I blink, the thought crashing in. I want to shake it loose—shake it into oblivion.

"The Super Bowl?" The words sound ridiculous as they leave my mouth. "Who proposes during the Super Bowl?"

My voice sharpens. "Does she even know he's married?"

Jack doesn't answer.

He lets the question sit.

The silence between us turns heavy. Dense. His gaze doesn't waver. Almost pitying. And that's what makes it worse. Something inside me hardens. This is no longer confusion. This is clarity. I need distance. From Oscar. From all of it.

Drained, I push back my chair and stand.

"Thanks, Jack," I mutter as I turn to leave.

But his voice stops me. Soft. Careful.

"That's not everything."

I freeze. Don't turn around, I tell myself. But I do.

I sink back into the chair. My eyes land on the

envelope—still unopened, still thick with everything I'm not ready to face.

"What?" I say, sharper than I mean to. "More bad news?"

He doesn't flinch.

I let out a loud sigh. The kind that rattles the ribs.

"How much is one person supposed to take?" The words tumble out, more to the air than to him. "One affair is enough. One betrayal should be the line. But I'm not even allowed to react without being labeled unstable. I drink a bottle of champagne and suddenly I'm the problem."

I look at him. Really look.

"Do you even know what that feels like?" I ask. "To be blindsided? To watch everything fall apart because someone you trusted turned into a stranger?"

He says nothing. Just watches.

And I know—whatever he's about to say next, it's going to break something else in me.

His voice is low, but steady. "There's more in the file. Before you open it, you need to think carefully about what comes next."

My throat tightens.

"I don't know what comes next," I whisper. "I said too much. Too loud. The champagne—I shouldn't have. I wasn't thinking."

I stop. Rambling again. I clamp my mouth shut.

What is it about him? One glance from him, and I unravel—like thread pulled too tight.

"I'm sorry. It's not fair for you to hear all that

venting. I'll stop."

I glance around. The dining area's empty. The quiet hum of the building presses in.

Just me, Jack, and the envelope between us.

"Where is everybody?" I ask, scanning the empty room.

"It's 2:00 PM," Jack says, leaning back in his chair, completely at ease. "Lunch was hours ago."

"2:00?" I blink. "I slept through the entire morning?"

He nods, amused. "You bet."

His face relaxes. Sharper up close, striking. There's something European in the bone structure, the eyes.

Desperate to shift the mood, I ask, "Where are your folks from?"

He hesitates. "Europe." Dismissive. Before I can ask more, he flips the conversation.

"So...you're a writer?"

I stiffen. Right. I told him. Or slurred it, more likely.

"Please don't tell anyone," I say quickly. "Nobody knows."

He tilts his head. "Have I read your stuff?"

"Yeah," I say, trying to sound casual.

"Confident answer." His brow lifts, teasing. "How do you know I've read it?"

"I saw it on your desk," I reply. Then I smirk. "You don't seem like the kind of guy who buys books and doesn't read them."

His eyes widen, and then he laughs. "No way...y ou're J.G. Bowler?"

"Shh—" I press a finger to my lips. "You'll blow my cover."

He leans in, voice lowered now. "Why the secrecy?"

I pause. "I didn't want anyone to know I write."

His eyes narrow, genuinely curious. "Not even your husband?"

I shake my head. I don't explain.

He grins. "You can't write that kind of stuff."

I feign offense. "Excuse me?"

He laughs again. "It reads like it's written from a guy's perspective."

"Were you convinced?"

"Oh, absolutely," he says, lips tugging into a smirk.

I relax into the moment, smiling. "You had this look—like, 'No way J.G. Bowler is a woman.'"

He shrugs. "Caught me."

He chuckles—low, warm. It echoes in the empty room. Then the mood shifts.

Jack leans in, his voice quieter. "You ought to think about your options," he says. "Divorce could be...complicated."

The words slice through the lightness like a cold wind.

"Simple," I snap. "I'll call a divorce attorney and file. How hard could it be?"

The heat flares fast. Sharp. Defensive.

Jack watches me. No smile now. His gaze cool,

unreadable. "You think he'll let you do that?" he says. "Now that he's a public figure?"

His tone walks the line between warning and dare.

He stands, tall over me. I stay seated, unsure whether I'm holding my ground or losing it.

"I'll give you the rest of the file when you're ready."

That word again.

I look up. "What do you mean? This isn't all of it?"

"When you're ready," he repeats. Calm. Final.

"I *am* ready," I say, but my voice wavers.

He nods toward the envelope. "Wait until you see what's in that one."

A chill needles my spine.

"Why?" I ask. "What's in it?"

I wave him off, trying to play it cool. My heartbeat says otherwise.

"Never mind," I mutter, but the question stays lodged in my chest.

His gaze lingers. Sharp. Too sharp.

"What?" I ask. "What's with the look?"

He tilts his head. "Do you remember how you got to your room last night?"

The memory flickers. Vomiting. Then darkness.

I blink. "Wait...how *did* I get here?"

"You passed out," he says, almost fondly. "I tried to wake you. No luck. So I carried you to Leo's car. Got you upstairs."

My face heats.

I hesitate. "Did you—sleep here?"

Jack shakes his head. "It's an inn. Angela has rooms."

Relief rushes in. Then a second wave of panic.

"Who changed me?"

He smirks, already ahead of me. "Angela. I left after she came in."

I nod, trying not to melt into the floor.

Then he winks. "Although...I wouldn't have minded."

A laugh slips out—unfiltered, unguarded. For a second, the tension thins.

"Thank you," I say quietly. "I mean...you know... not—"

He turns to leave, tossing a line over his shoulder. "Don't worry. All good."

I'm left alone with the envelope.

I stare at it, willing it to vanish.

Then his voice cuts in again—closer than I expect. "You're not going to make that thing move just by staring."

I turn my head. He's already halfway across the room, that same glint in his eye—like he knows exactly what I'm thinking.

Maybe he does.

# 13
# The Reveal

In this day and age, cell phones are a necessary evil. For me, it's both lifeline and leash. The constant buzzing, the blinking notifications—it all feels alive. A digital pulse that never stops. I hate it. But I can't turn it off. Not completely. Not when my dad might call.

And then there's Oscar.

Every time his name lights up the screen, my stomach drops. Cold dread spreads through me like ink in water.

My finger hovers over the message. Trembling. I swipe it away quick, like brushing off a spider. I can't read it. I won't. His words have teeth. They always find a way to sink in.

The voicemails pile up. I don't listen. I can't. Even deleting them feels like a kind of engagement. So I let them rot there in silence.

Avoidance is easy. Familiar. If I don't open it, it didn't happen. If I don't hear it, it doesn't hurt.

But Marie's text cuts through that fog.

Her tone has shifted. Something's changed.

I read the message once. Then again. The words feel wrong, like they're wearing someone else's clothes.

Marie: It sucks to be you. But call me if you need someone to vent to.

Marie's sudden warmth feels...off.

Too kind. Too sisterly. Too much.

Hard to believe she's being this caring—especially now. But family is family, right? Or so we tell ourselves.

She wasn't always cruel. Not like Alexi. Not like Mom. Just busy. Absorbed. There were comments—about money, inheritance. But mostly, she stayed in her lane. We never really connected. Not like sisters should.

And now here she is. Reaching out.

I don't know what to make of it.

The envelope waits on the nightstand. Thick. Brown. Heavy.

I've been staring at it for what feels like hours. If looks could burn, it'd be nothing but ash.

Curiosity gnaws at me. Pandora's box. I know better. But I can't stop.

It might just confirm what I already know—Oscar. The girl. The betrayal. But there's something else.

Something worse.

I can feel it.

My hand hovers. I pause.

I just need to open the damn envelope.

Opening this will change everything.

But maybe it already has.

So what am I waiting for?

I pick it up. The weight of it settles in my palm like a verdict.

My fingers tremble as I tear the flap.

I breathe in. And then I look.

The first few lines blur. I blink. Read again.

And then I stop breathing.

My stomach lurches. Cold spreads through my chest like ice in water.

No. This can't be right.

But the words don't move. They don't lie.

I'm not ready for what's next.

Our Maria?

The woman who cleans our house. Folds our sheets. Smiles at me like nothing's wrong.

In the next photo, she's with Oscar. At a park. Sitting close. Too close. Their eyes say what their mouths don't.

This wasn't a one-time thing. There were others.

I flip through the file. The weight of it grows with each page.

Text messages. Hotel receipts. More photos. More women.

The knot in my stomach tightens. My pulse pounds in my neck.

I can't stop. I want to. But I can't.

"What a conniving, cheating, pathetic liar of a husband," I whisper. My voice is low. Brittle with rage.

He did all this—in our home. Under my nose.

And Maria—her flushed cheeks, the way she avoids my eyes. It all fits now. Like puzzle pieces I refused to see.

There are several photos in the envelope, but one catches my eye.

My fingers tremble as I lift it out.

Then I freeze.

A woman. A face I don't recognize. No name. No date. No label. Still...something about her feels familiar. Like a dream I had once—clear for a moment, then gone by morning.

I stare at the photo. The unease crawls back in, sharper now, tightening in my chest.

I reach for my phone.

Text Jack.

> Me: Why are you not putting names on this photo. Who is the woman in the red dress with straight black hair?"

However, a few minutes later, I received a reply back from him.

> Jack: The woman in red is from Ohio. Flip the picture and you can read their names and dates.

"Ohio?" I say it out loud. The word feels strange in my mouth.

I frown, trying to place her.

Then it clicks.

Oscar's old flame.

The girl who was always *just around*—at the

Chamber reunions. Lingering too close. Laughing too loud at his jokes.

He said it was nothing. Said they'd dated in high school. Stayed friends. And I believed him.

He was honest about her, after all. That counted for something, right?

God, how naive was I?

A dull ache spreads across my chest as the truth rearranges itself into something uglier.

They'd been carrying on. The whole time.

Right in front of me.

And I didn't see it.

I think back. The glances. The private jokes. The way she'd disappear, then reappear on Oscar's arm like a ghost I was never supposed to notice.

I didn't want to see it.

My jaw tightens.

How could they? Both of them—smiling to my face while tearing me apart behind it.

My stomach twists. Grief and rage, braided tight.

I need to stop. But every page only solidifies one thing—I'm not going back to Oscar.

Me: Why didn't you give me the whole file?

Hours pass.

Nothing.

No reply.

Then—*finally*—his message comes through.

Just five words.

Jack: You can't handle the truth.

I have to laugh. Not out of joy. Something darker. Bitter. Hollow.

This is my life now.

A tangled mess of secrets and surveillance.

But I have a right to the truth. No matter how ugly.

Tears blur my vision, slide down without permission. My chest aches, but I don't shatter. Not this time.

I won't let this break me. I've been through worse. Maybe not louder, but quieter. And quiet wounds cut deeper.

Oscar's betrayal sits heavy in my gut. Like I swallowed something sharp.

But I won't confront him. Not yet.

I need to calm down. Get clear. Last night taught me that rage has a cost.

I won't make that mistake again.

Not when the stakes feel this high.

I slide the file back into the envelope. Tuck it beneath my suitcase lining. Out of sight—but not forgotten.

And just as I'm pulling myself together.

A knock.

Firm. Too firm.

Then a voice. "Housekeeping..."

I freeze.

I specifically requested no housekeeping.

And the voice, it's male. Off-key.

I move quietly across the room, bare feet silent on the carpet. My heart thuds. I peek through the peephole.

Two men. Dressed in uniform. But not the right kind. Not crisp. Not branded. Wrong shoes. Wrong posture.

They don't belong.

I don't move. I don't breathe.

They knock again. Then drift to the next door. Then the next.

Not cleaning. Just knocking. Watching.

My gut coils tight.

Oscar sent them. I know it.

They're not here for towels or trash.

They're here for *me*.

"If they're going to play the part," I mutter, "they're not doing a good job."

I step back from the door. Grab my phone.

Angela answers on the second ring. "Yes, Ms. Green. What can I do for you?"

"There are two guys knocking on my door. Claiming to be housekeeping."

A pause.

"I didn't call for anyone," I add. "And they're in white overalls."

Another pause—longer this time.

"Our housekeeping wears blue scrubs," she says. Voice tight. Alert now. "I'll call security. Don't open the door. I'll let you know once they're gone."

I thank her. Hang up.

Then I wait.

Thirty minutes crawl by. My ears track every shuffle outside the door. Every creak in the hall. My body hums with adrenaline.

Finally, the phone buzzes again. Angela.

"They're gone," she says. "Security confirmed it. I'm bringing in more staff, for extra coverage. No one will bother you again."

I nod, even though she can't see me. "Thanks."

I hang up. But the unease doesn't leave. It just settles lower.

The next morning, sunlight creeps through the blinds. I wake slowly, eyes dry, head full.

My phone buzzes.

Jack: Open CNN.

Me: I don't watch TV.

Jack: You may want to watch this one.

So, when I open the television, there I am, my face on the screen.

Me: What is going on?

Jack: Did you watch the entire segment?

Me: No, I only caught the last phrase, which was, 'If you have seen Lilanie Green Chambers, please contact this number.

Jack: They've put a bounty on your appearance.

Me: You mean...Oscar put a bounty on my head? That's insane! Shall I go there and announce I'm not missing?

Jack: I don't see that as a problem!

Me: I think I'm gonna keep hiding.

Jack: You can't hide forever.

That's right. That statement seems to resonate with the entire condition of my life. I do want to hide, especially from the spotlight. The reason why I hadn't wanted people to know about the author of the book I wrote. There's a reason why I kept my identity hidden.

I call my dad, but he doesn't answer. So, I text,

Me: Dad, what's going on?

Dad: Let's talk later. It's a circus around here. Stay hidden for now. Don't call. I will call you.

So I stay hidden.

The day drips by in a blur, slow and heavy. The memory of those two men presses against the walls. I listen for footsteps. For knocks. For danger.

Nothing comes. And yet I can't breathe.

This room, once a retreat, now feels like a cage.

I'm a fugitive in my own life. Hiding from Oscar. From the world. From myself.

I try to write. I can't. The words won't come. My mind won't hold still.

Night brings no relief. I toss. Turn. Thoughts circling like vultures. Oscar's betrayal. The file. The women. The silence outside my door.

It all plays on a loop. A nightmare I can't wake from.

By dawn, I'm exhausted. But wired.

No messages. No calls. Nothing from Jack. Nothing from Dad.

The silence is loud. Like the calm before something breaks.

I sit by the window as light filters in, pale and uncertain.

And I make a promise: I will get through this.

Somehow.

# 14

# Breaking News

The next day, just after lunch, my phone buzzes. A news alert. I glance at the screen. It's from Jack.

A link.

And a text that says:

Jack: I hate to be the bearer of bad news. But thought you should see this before it spreads.

Me: I hate bad news...

Jack: You need to be aware what's happening.

My stomach drops.

I don't click it right away. My thumb hovers. Breath caught.

Because whatever it is, t's already happening. And there's no un-seeing it.

Hesitantly, I tap the link.

A cold weight settles in my chest.

A photo of me—blown up, unflattering, raw.

Forehead creased. Nose mid-scrunch. It looks like I'm about to sneeze.

*Seriously?*

If you're going to smear my face across the internet, could you at least pick a decent photo?

I stare at it. Bitter. Angry.

Who took this? Why *this* one? It feels deliberate. Like Oscar chose it himself.

I grab the remote. Turn on the TV. Flip through channels.

There I am.

Again.

My face fills the screen, frozen and unkind.

A chill runs down my spine.

Channel 37. Missing person.

Text scrolls across the bottom: *Oscar Chambers is seeking information on his missing wife, Lilanie Green Chambers. If you know her whereabouts, please call...*

My breath catches. The room tilts.

This isn't a joke. It's war.

I fix my gaze on the screen, my heart pounding fiercely against my ribcage, a relentless fist demanding to be heard.

No more hiding.

No more silence swallowing my voice.

He's pulled me into the glaring spotlight, and now it's time to show him what happens when I stop playing nice.

I'm done merely surviving; it's time to fight back.

The sun has dipped below the horizon, leaving the room draped in shadows and silence.

I sit at the desk, surrounded by a battlefield of crumpled paper, a mug of cold coffee, and the oppressive weight of words that refuse to spill onto the page. My laptop casts a soft glow, a beacon of expectation, waiting for the words I can't seem to find. Each time my eyes drift up, they land on my phone, screen alight with unread messages.

Oscar's name flashes persistently, a reminder of what I've been avoiding. Anxiety twists in my stomach, tightening with every passing second.

I push back from the desk and begin to pace, the carpet absorbing the sound of my footsteps. Dust motes dance in the dim light, swirling in the fading remnants of daylight that filter through the window.

The walls feel tighter tonight.

Closing in.

Suffocating.

I force myself back into the chair. Hands on the keys. Eyes on the screen.

*Keep going. Don't let him win.*

But then, my phone buzzes. Louder. More insistent. A shrill, piercing sound that cuts through the silence.

I shudder. The phone slips from my hand and hits the floor.

Face down. Buzzing.

I stare at it.

Frozen.

As if reading the message might make it real.

Oscar: Come home, Lila. I know where you are. I'll give you one hour. Then I'll drag you out of that room myself.

Yeah, as if I'd come without a fight. But honestly, my hands are shaking, and my heart is pounding like a drum in my chest.

When I left, it wasn't with the intention of vanishing completely. I just needed a bit of distance, a chance to breathe freely and let my thoughts settle. I imagined us having a conversation at some point. Calm and sensible—once the chaotic whirlwind in my mind had subsided.

But then came the photos.

Now all I can think about is whether Oscar might kill me.

The fear isn't abstract anymore. It has weight. It breathes.

My heart pounds so hard I can feel it in my teeth.

I can't die. Not now. Not with so much undone. My unfinished book nags at me like a whisper in the dark. My story isn't over. And I still want a family. A real one. Kids. A house. Land. Laughter. The sound of joy echoing across a yard that belongs to me.

But none of that can exist if I go back. That dream dies with him. So I won't go back.

A knock on the door makes me jump. *He couldn't be that fast...could he?*

Then a voice—soft, urgent. "Lila...it's Angela."

I rush to the door and crack it open.

She stands there, brows drawn tight, lips a thin line. Her eyes flicker, like she's holding something back.

"What's wrong?" I whisper.

She leans in. "Remember those two officers? The ones who came before?"

I nod.

"They're back. And your husband's with them. They have a warrant to search the premises."

My breath catches.

"I don't know what's going on," she says quickly, "and I don't want to. But I'll show you a way out. They won't see you. After that...you're on your own."

I blink. "Thank you, Angela. I don't know what to say. I don't mean to sound ungrateful, but...why are you helping me?"

She pauses. Shrugs. "I don't know. Maybe it was the way Leo dropped you off. You looked like someone who needed a place to disappear."

She hesitates. Then adds, softer: "Truth is...my inn's always been that kind of place. People show up when they've got nowhere else to go."

A breath catches in my throat.

"Thank you," I say again. Quiet, but full.

"No time," she says. "Grab what you need. Now."

I throw a few things into my backpack. Phone. Charger. Laptop. Change of clothes.

"Don't worry about the rest," Angela says, already moving. "I'll take care of it."

I sling the bag over my shoulder. My heart

pounds. Every footstep in the hall feels louder than it should.

It's time to run.

I follow Angela, each step slow, deliberate.

We wind through the back hallway toward the maintenance room. She moves fast, shifting mops, buckets, and carts like she's done this before.

I help where I can, and my hands are trembling.

Behind the supplies is a door. Barely noticeable.

She pulls a key from her pocket. Unlocks it.

"These stairs lead to the basement," she whispers. "Keep going straight. You'll see another door. Use this." She presses a second key into my palm.

I nod and slide it into my coat pocket like it's made of glass.

"That door opens into a laundromat I own. Usually empty unless Jose's around. If he's there, just nod. He doesn't speak English."

She pauses.

Then, I hear footsteps. Heavy. Close.

A knock sounds down the hall.

My heart seizes.

"Go," she breathes. "Be careful. Don't lose the key. Return it when you see me again." She turns to the hidden exit, her voice lower now—deadly serious. "And this door..." She pauses. "Never mention it. To anyone."

I nod again, too overwhelmed for words.

"How can I repay you?" I ask, voice raw.

Angela looks at me, amber eyes soft. Solid.

Steady.

"Just call when you're safe," she says.

Then she shuts the door behind me. Quiet. Final. And I'm gone. Darkness swallows everything.

I pause at the top of the stairs. Cold air meets my skin like breath from something ancient. I pull out my phone, thumb fumbling the flashlight on. A narrow cone of light slices through the black. Dust drifts. The smell—wet wood, old stone, time.

One step. Then another.

The staircase groans beneath me. Each creak sounds louder than the last, like it's warning someone.

My fingers graze the wall, seeking balance. It's damp, uneven, almost alive.

Halfway down, I catch my breath. The air is thicker here.

Faded photographs line the walls—sepia-toned snapshots of the inn, the town, faces long gone. I wonder how many others descended these stairs. If they were running too.

Then—voices. Muffled, then clearer.

It's Oscar.

His voice slices through the air like a whip, louder now, closer. I freeze, crouch into shadow.

A vivid memory crashes over me like a relentless wave.

Maria. Shattered porcelain lay like jagged snow across the floor. His fury—uncontainable, volcanic—hung thick in the air.

I had once stepped between them, arms outstretched, voice calm but firm, trying to reason with a man who didn't want peace. I spoke to him like a child mid-tantrum, while Maria trembled behind me, barely breathing.

When he finally stormed out—rage still radiating like heat—Maria peeked from behind my shoulder and whispered, "Gracias...Ms. Lilli."

Her voice trembled with relief, gratitude wrapped in fear. Even in mispronunciation, it felt like a prayer.

Now, I hear that same fury echoing again. I can't let him find me.

I move. Faster now.

Machines line the corridor, hulking washers and dryers, relics of another era. At the far end, a narrow door stands slightly ajar. I reach into my pocket, the key cold in my palm. It slides in. Click.

I open the door just enough to see.

Quiet.

No sign of Jose.

Just the low rumble of a working machine. And my own breath.

I slip inside.

The air here is warmer. Fluorescent light flickers above. No shadows hiding anyone. I move across the floor with swift, silent strides, my heart racing as my fingertips graze the cool metal of the exit door, a tangible reminder of my escape.

Outside, night hits me like a slap. The wind sharp, the street empty.

No sirens. No footsteps. And that is good sign.

Just the sound of my shoes against pavement and the soft roar of my pulse in my ears.

I walk fast, almost running, past the laundromat's dim window. My reflection follows me, ghostlike in the glass. I don't look back.

If Oscar's still at the inn, I have a head start.

But I know him. And I know he never stays far behind.

As I run, I catch glances—people pausing mid-step, their eyes tracking me, lips moving in murmurs I can't hear. Maybe I'm imagining it. Maybe not. But their stares cling like static, asking silent questions I don't have time to answer.

The lights blur. Headlights slice through the dark. Shadows stutter against the pavement. The whole city feels like it's leaning in, watching, waiting.

And then, I hear it.

The low growl of an engine. Steady. Closer.

A jolt of panic seizes my chest. He found me.

My legs keep moving, but they feel like they're sinking. Heavy. Sluggish. Like I'm running through wet cement. My breath cuts in and out. My body is failing me, but I don't stop.

I can't.

The sound of the engine rises—louder, sharper now, like it's right at my back. My heart tries to outrun it.

And then, just as the panic crests, I hear my name.

Clear. Urgent.

"Lila!"

The tires scream. A car swerves and stops inches from me. My heart slams against my ribs.

"Jack?" I gasp, stumbling back a step. "Oh God. You're not Oscar."

"Get in," he says, short and steady. One hand still grips the wheel.

And he open the door.

I slide into the seat, breath shallow, limbs shaking.

He doesn't move until I buckle up. Then he glances over. "How the hell did you run that fast?"

"I run. Or used to. Before I started running for real."

The engine hums as we slip back into motion.

"How'd you find me?" I ask.

"Angela. She couldn't reach your driver."

"Leo?" My voice is tight.

"His phone's off." Jack's eyes never leave the road.

The silence settles. It's not comfort. It's calculation.

"You got a plan?" he finally asks.

That lands like a punch.

My eyes blur.

No, I don't have a plan. Not one that feels secure or even remotely mine.

"I don't know," I whisper.

"I don't even understand why I'm so scared. I just...I can't bear to see him. I can't be near him or pretend that everything is okay."

Jack nods slowly, his brow furrowing slightly, as if he's deciphering a code I haven't yet revealed.

"Is he the kind of man who could hurt you?"

He asks it plainly, his gaze fixed straight ahead, unwavering and steady, as if he's bracing himself for the truth.

And just like that, doubt creeps in, leaving me unsure of the answer that lingers just beyond my lips.

"He's never hurt me before. Physically, I mean..." I answer, unsure.

"Given from 1-10, how scared are you with your husband right now?" he inquires.

"10?"

"Really?"

"Well, not before he proposed to someone else. While married to me," I say. My voice is hollow. "So what now? What happens to me?"

Jack glances over, brow furrowed.

"I keep thinking...he'll try to shut me up. Permanently."

He doesn't say anything.

"I know how it sounds," I add, staring out the window. "But I can't shake it. If he gets me back, he'll cage me. Eyes on me all day. Every day. Especially now—he's running for governor. A scandal won't fly."

I pause. Swallow hard.

"My writing would die. I would die. Not literally, maybe. But slowly, painfully. And I don't know which is worse."

The tears are there, pressing against the edge. I blink fast. Jack says nothing. Just keeps driving.

"I can find a hotel," I say quietly. My voice betrays

me, thin, cracking.

He glances over. "You forget? There's a reward for you." A small, crooked smile. Then his eyes return to the road.

"Right." I force a breath out. "That."

I reach into my bag, fingers fumbling for my phone. I dial my dad's number. Straight to voicemail.

The silence between us grows heavier.

And for a moment, I wonder if I've already vanished.

"Daddy, it's me. Please call me back!" I hang up.

Silence beckons, and I wish I had something to say. But it's all beyond my understanding.

All of a sudden, a text from Marie pops up.

Marie: Call me, please. It's about Dad.

My heart skips—gets stuck, like a drawer jammed halfway. I call Marie.

She answers with a sound I haven't heard since we were kids. A cry. "It's Dad," she says. "I can't find him."

"What do you mean?" I press. "Have you checked the cottage?"

Silence. Then, "I've searched everywhere. Even there." Her voice is thin. "But can you check again?"

The words hit hard. That cottage, his retreat, his refuge, his whole rhythm. It's where we made pancakes and puzzles and promises we thought we'd never outgrow.

If he's not there...

"I'll try," I say, barely louder than a breath. "We'll figure this out. I'll call you later."

The call ends. I stare out the window, the road stretching on like it's mocking me. The trees blur. The sky looks bruised.

He wouldn't just disappear. Unless someone made him.

"Is something the matter?" he asks.

"My dad, according to my sister, is missing," I say.

Silence settles again. Jack drives. I think.

"Can you take me to my dad's cottage?"

He glances at me like I've lost my grip. "You really think that place is safe? It's probably the first place they checked."

"I have to see for myself," I say. "I need to find him." My voice sounds more fragile than I want it to. "What if they missed something?"

He doesn't answer. Doesn't need to. I already know the answer might be *yes*.

I stare out the window and pray—not for a miracle, just a lead. A thread. Something.

A few weeks ago, this was my life: Coffee. A morning run. A long shower.

In the basement, I would immerse myself in writing, fingers dancing across the keys until they ached from the fervor of my thoughts.

Then there was Oscar, adhering to his regimented gym routine, a ritual that defined his day.

His return home would be marked by a silence that felt heavy, and dinner would unfold like a scripted scene between two strangers, each perfectly timed yet emotionally distant.

We'd brush our teeth at our double sink, side by side like synchronized ghosts. Then lights out. A muttered "Goodnight." No kiss. No touch. Just sleep.

Looking back, I wonder—how did I survive that? That grey, empty rhythm we called marriage. And why did it take him destroying everything for me to finally want more?

The city fades behind us. Streetlights blink like dying stars. We've been driving for half an hour now—no cars, no signs of life, just the soft murmur of the tires on the road and darkness pressing in on both sides. Jack says nothing. I say nothing. It's like we're two shadows slipping across a vast, empty map.

Then he breaks the silence. "Hang tight," he says, his tone flat. "We've got company."

My head jerks toward the mirror. A glint. Headlights. A Range Rover, black and quiet and too close. Three men inside—driver, passenger, someone in back.

"It's Oscar, isn't it?" My voice is small. Fragile.

He doesn't answer but his jaw clenches.

Adrenaline hits like a punch. My breath shortens. Jack grips the wheel, knuckles pale. The car lurches forward, faster now, the road narrowing as we tear through forgotten city streets.

"What do we do?" I manage.

"We lose them," he mutters. His eyes never stop moving—mirror, road, mirror again. He swerves down alleys barely wider than the car, dodging dumpsters, skipping curbs, the city blurring past in streaks of shadow and broken light.

Then, stillness.

Jack cuts the engine and eases us into a pitch-black alley. The hum of the car fades to a whisper. He leans back, eyes locked on mine.

"We stay here. Once they realize we're gone, we'll go North to your father's cottage."

Outside, everything holds its breath. No footsteps. No engines. Just the occasional bark of a siren blocks away.

Eventually, exhaustion triumphs, pulling me into a deep slumber. I must have drifted off without realizing it. The engine hums to life once more, its low, steady rhythm vibrating through the air. I blink my eyes open, slowly coming back to awareness.

Jack glances over, a half-smile on his face. "Did you have a good nap?"

I nod, dazed. It's been nearly an hour. But with him at the wheel, that quiet confidence, I let myself believe—just for a moment—that we might actually outrun the dark.

# 15

# Cottage in the Woods

Half an hour ago, hunger won. We'd stopped at a McDonald's drive-thru. I ordered three Big Macs and a large fry. Jack just asked for a cheeseburger. Before I could even reach for my wallet, he'd already paid—flashing a sly grin like it was some kind of inside joke.

"I hadn't eaten since breakfast," I said, wiping salt from my fingers. It wasn't a lie. But I devoured those Big Macs like it was the last meal I'd ever have. The fries were gone before we even pulled out of the lot.

Since I found out about Oscar, food had tasted like cardboard. But when the hunger hit, it wasn't gentle, it crashed over me like I'd been starving for weeks.

Jack watched me as if I were some rare species. "What are you doing with the third one?"

"Saving it."

He shook his head. "Where do you even put it all? You're built like a walking stick."

"I'm not that skinny," I muttered.

He smirked. "Right. Bet there's chocolate in that

backpack of yours."

I didn't answer. People who figured me out too fast made me nervous.

He chuckled again. I stared out the window, letting the moment dissolve into the road. There wasn't much I could say anyway—not without unraveling.

Since I got married, I seldom went to fast food places, as it was one of the fights Oscar and I couldn't agree on. I asked to stop at McDonald's during our visit to Ohio to see his parents, but he wouldn't let me. He said it was "the worst thing that ever happened to America."

I replied, "It's the best thing that ever happened to America."

He went crazy and accused me of being ridiculous. He also despised food in his car. Once, when he saw me eating chocolate from my bag, he wiped it as if I were carrying a disease. He even cleaned the car to ensure it was thoroughly sanitized and reprimanded me not to eat in it again. Remembering those things made me wonder how I survived with Oscar.

So here we are at Dad's cottage, just before midnight.

I ask Jack to park a little ways off. I need to walk the rest alone. Just to see if anyone's lurking. If someone's going to snatch me, I'd rather spot them first.

I mutter a quick "thank you" and reach for the door. His hand catches my arm—firm, unhurried. He turns me toward him.

The heat between us is immediate. His

scent—clean, sharp, familiar. It pulls something loose in my chest. I pretend not to notice. Pretend I don't feel anything at all.

"So, you plan to walk to the cottage, and then what?" he asks.

"Find my dad!" I answer.

"And?" he asks again.

"And then I don't know...maybe,I... I will call Leo to pick me up if I can't find my dad or stay in the cottage for a time," I say simply.

"And what if someone is lurking around and grabs you?" he asks.

"I'll fight, kick, and then run," I answer matter-of-factly.

"Yeah, right!" He sighs and looks away, but he is still holding my arm.

"So, you're going to walk like this? In the dark?" he points outside.

"Uh-huh?! My phone has a flashlight!" I tell him. "And thank you for rescuing me. I appreciate you picking me up and Angela for the help!" I say, opening the car door. Determine to make it out to the cottage.

"You know there are...other species out there at this hour?" he says.

"Species?"

"Wolves."

I blink. "Seriously?"

He nods, solemn.

"That's ridiculous. Wolves were hunted out of New York by the 1800s. If there are any, they're upstate. North of the border. That's basic history."

His lips twitch, almost amused. "You know your stuff."

"I do."

"Have you ever actually gone out there at night?"

I pause. The door clicks shut as I ease back into my seat. No, I haven't. Not really. Dad always warned me—don't trust the forest after dark. Coyotes. Maybe a bear. Maybe worse.

I look straight ahead.

"Can you drive a little closer to the cottage?" I ask, trying not to sound like I'm pleading.

Jack starts the engine again. The trees press in on both sides of the narrow path, the headlights catching their limbs like bones in a dark X-ray. When the outline of the cottage comes into view, I point. "Here's good, right?"

He doesn't answer. Just reaches into the back seat and pulls out night binoculars.

I watch him. "Is someone there?"

He doesn't blink. "Not someone. Something."

A pause. Then, still scanning, "Coyotes. Maybe a raccoon. Skunks."

I inch closer, trying not to look like I'm inching closer. My hand tightens on the strap of my backpack.

"Can you get me closer?" I ask again, voice low.

"The cottage is just right there."

I nod, even though my throat is tight. I find the key in my bag—one Dad gave each of us, just in case. The metal feels cold and small in my hand.

I open the door before I lose my nerve.

"Thanks," I say, and step out before the car even stops.

I run fast. The kind of run that feels chased by the devil.

As I reach the door, the lock fights me. My hands are shaking. Then it turns.

I get in, slam the door, and lean back against it, chest heaving. The cottage smells like old cedar and stillness.

Safe.

Maybe.

Coyotes always get me into a frenzy. I had a disastrous encounter with them once, where they ripped my dog's leg when I was in my teens. When I tried to kick the coyotes away, one bit me, and my dad had to rush me to the clinic because my leg was bleeding too badly. It took me a while to process what had happened. Thankfully, my dog Icy survived. So, in my life experience, encountering coyotes was something I tried not to repeat.

My back still pressed to the door, I try to quiet the thud in my chest. The silence is deep and close, until it isn't.

A knock.

Sharp, deliberate.

My body jerks like a puppet tugged by a wire.

"Lila," a voice says through the wood. Calm, but not casual. "Open the door."

"Jack?" My voice breaks.

"Yeah. It's me. Open up."

I unlock it right away, and when I see him, solid, steady, familiar—I almost step into him. The outline of his body fills the frame, broad and unmoved, like he's been standing there forever.

"You didn't leave?"

He tilts his head, unreadable in the dark. "And leave a scared woman alone in the woods? And you left your burger in the car."

"Oh thanks." I say. "I'm not scared. Just... the coyote thing got in my head." I say too quickly.

He doesn't tease me for it. Maybe he sees something in my face.

I fumble for the switch, fingers finding plastic and flicking upward. The light blooms. He shuts it off immediately.

"If you don't want them to know someone's here, don't light it up like a Christmas tree."

"I can't see," I mumble.

"Use this."

A small flashlight presses into my palm. Warm from his pocket.

"You staying?" I ask.

A pause.

Then: "Yeah. For a bit. To make sure everything's okay."

The relief is immediate. Heavy, and strangely tender. I didn't know how badly I needed someone to say they'd stay.

I walk deeper into the cottage, the narrow beam

of light dragging memories out of the dark corners. The furniture's still where it was last summer. The smell of pine. Of dust. Of something else, more metallic.

"No sign of your dad?"

"I haven't looked yet," I whisper. "But this place feels...empty."

I set my backpack on the couch, its soft thump echoing too loudly. I head for the kitchen. My shin collides with the coffee table. Pain shoots up like a flare and I curse, half falling onto it.

"Stupid table," I mutter. Then, quieter: "Sorry."

"You okay?" Jack calls from somewhere near the fireplace.

I nod, even though he can't see it. The pain throbs like a pulse.

"I'm fine," I say. "But my knees aren't. Neither is my ego."

I scoop up the flashlight and limp toward the kitchen. The place is too quiet. If Dad were here, the air would be heavy with coffee. He always had a pot going, morning to night. But the counters are wiped. The sink's empty. No half-read newspaper. No clutter. Just silence.

Still, if coffee's on my mind, I might as well make some.

I find the grounds, the filters. Fill the reservoir, press the button. The machine clicks on, humming low. I lean against the island, arms crossed, the flashlight resting beside me like a useless talisman.

Thoughts pile up—Dad, my novel, Oscar. The ache in my knee. The ache in my chest.

"Hey..." Jack's voice breaks the stillness. And made me jump.

"I hate darkness," I say, too fast, too sharp.

"Coffee at night?" he asks, stepping into the edge of the kitchen.

"It's basically my emotional support beverage," I mutter, half-laughing.

"You want some?" I reach for a second mug without waiting for an answer, pouring rich, steaming liquid into the cup, fingers brushing a cold creamer pack from the fridge.

"I prefer something stronger," Jack says.

"Behind you," I say, nodding toward the liquor cabinet. "That's where my dad keeps the good stuff."

Jack moves in the dark, a quiet silhouette. We look like two strangers breaking into someone else's life. Fumbling for comfort. Or something like it.

"You sure you don't want any?" he asks, his voice low, frayed at the edges.

"No," I say quickly. "My last drink ended with a trash can and a detective. I think I've met my quota."

He doesn't laugh, but I think I hear the corner of a smile in his breath. Or maybe that's just me needing the moment to soften.

Fumbling in the dark, careful not to drop the mug, I pull out a chair and sit. The legs scrape against the floor—too loud for the hush that hangs over the house. Jack takes the chair across from me. The air between us holds a kind of truce.

"I'm sorry you got dragged into this," I say, my voice quiet, roughened by guilt.

He doesn't speak. Just grunts, as if he's too tired for comfort, too wired for sleep.

Outside, the forest presses in. Inside, it's just us and the coffee and the ache of not knowing what comes next.

Silence settles. Heavy, like fog in a sealed room.

"I think I'll sleep here tonight," I mutter, eyes fixed on nothing. "Maybe I can sleep off the thoughts—my dad, my marriage...everything."

I hesitate. "If you want to stay... there are bedrooms upstairs and two down. Pick one."

A pause. Then: "Are you asking me to stay?"

I offer a half-smile. "Am I that obvious?"

I stand and take my mug to the sink. Rinse. Breathe. The ache behind my eyes tells me sleep is the only thing left.

"If you decide to leave...wake me first, okay?" I say quietly.

Still nothing from him. Just his presence, steady and unreadable.

I yawn—loud, exaggerated, unconvincing. "Good night, Jack."

"You just had coffee," he says. "Isn't that supposed to keep you up?"

"I'm immune," I reply. "It's like water at this point."

I turn to go. "I'm sleeping downstairs. Left room." Another yawn. Then I hit my head on the door jamb.

A curse slips out. I apologize on instinct.

Behind me, Jack chuckles. Then presses the flashlight into my hand. "You'll need this."

I nod, grab my backpack, and disappear into the dark hallway.

The bed welcomes me like it remembers me. I barely touch the pillow before I'm out.

Then—howling. Low. Somewhere beyond the window.

Coyotes, I think.

But if it's wolves...Lord, have mercy.

I blink into the dark, reaching for the lampshade. My fingers brush its base before I remember—I'm not supposed to turn it on.

What time is it?

My phone's in the backpack. Dead. I never charged it. Too tired. Or careless.

I lie still, listening. The house holds its breath. I shift, feeling around the bed for the flashlight. Nothing. Just blankets, a wrinkle in the sheet, the cold edge of the mattress.

I sit up.

The phone charger is in the side pocket. I fish it out, careful not to make noise. My fingers move slowly along the wall, searching for the outlet. I know it's here—I've slept in this room more times than I can count. Summers, holidays, storms.

My fingers find the socket. A rush of relief.

I plug it in, whispering a prayer I don't finish. The silence tightens again, and I lie back, watching the phone screen glow faintly to life.

Four percent.

Not enough. But something.

The howling continues nearby, and I don't recall hearing anything like it in my younger years.

Lying back down, I think about Jack. Where is he sleeping? Or did he leave?

I rise, one hand trailing the wall. The floor chills my feet. The air feels different now—still, but watching.

At the window, I check for headlights. Nothing. Just trees standing guard and the soft hush of night.

He's gone. Or hiding.

I cross the hall.

This room is darker. Deeper. Not even a thread of moonlight to catch the frame.

I ease the door open, slow. Listening.

No sound.

I step in. Fingers searching. Sheets—wrinkled, still warm. Then, something solid. A body.

My hand stills.

"Jack?" I whisper.

No answer. Just silence, thick and waiting.

Then—a shift. Sudden. Two hands find me. One at my waist, the other across my back.

I'm pulled down—weightless, breath caught—onto the mattress. His body presses into mine. His breath grazes my face.

I don't move. I can't.

My arms stay limp. My voice won't come.

The dark folds around us like a question no one dares to ask.

I ask again, softer this time. “Jack?”

A breath. Close enough to feel.

Then his voice—low, gravel-thick. "Of all the things, Lila, you shouldn't touch a man while he's sleeping!" he scolds.

He doesn’t move. Neither do I.

Something hangs between us—more than darkness. Weight. History. Possibility.

I turn my face toward him, just enough to whisper, "I'm sorry!" I whimper, feeling embarrassed.

He's still holding me, his body pressing so close, and I can smell his manly scent.

"Jack...," I whisper his name again.

"Do you have clothes on?" I ask.

"No."

"You sleep naked?"

His hold on me tightens, and his breath is so close to my lips. My world stands still, and then I hear his grunts. He releases me, moving to the side. His presence beside me and his sexy grunting add to the palpitating heartbeat that consumes me.

"What are you doing up?" he asks, his voice gruff.

In the darkness, I touch him softly.

"If you care about your reputation tonight, please get your hands off me!" Jack warns, and he groans.

I quickly withdraw my hand and whisper, "Jack..."

"Yeah," he replies, his breathing labored.

"Is that coyotes outside howling?"

"No. By the sound of it, they're probably wolves!" he answers.

"Wolves? You're joking, right?" I whisper.

"Maybe I am!" he says.

"Don't joke like that?"

"Go back to sleep, Lila!" he retorts.

Silence. But I stay. Not ready to move. Not ready to be alone in my own thoughts.

“Can I stay? Just...for a bit?” I ask, voice nearly gone.

He doesn’t answer.

I pretend to yawn and lie still. Listening. The howls go on, like something coming undone in the dark. I edge closer to Jack, and he says, “Don’t...”

His voice is a grunt, rough and frayed at the edges.

Somewhere between fear and comfort, I drift—half-asleep, half-waiting.

Morning comes. Pale light filters through the curtain.

Jack is still beside me. One arm thrown over the sheet, breath quiet. His chest rises and falls with a kind of ease I don’t remember ever having.

I watch him. Too long.

My hand drifts toward him before I can stop it—slow, uncertain, as if it belongs to someone else. The curve of his chest, the faint line of his torso, it draws me in like warmth on a cold morning.

His eyes open.

Sharp. Awake.

I draw my hand back, fast—cover it with a yawn I

don't feel.

We don't speak.

But something shifts.

I rise without looking at him. "Morning, Jack," I say lightly, already halfway to the door.

In the hallway, I mutter to myself. "You're still married. Act like it."

In the kitchen, I dump the cold coffee from last night. I grind fresh beans and start again, my hands in my hair, the silence thick around me. I stand there, waiting as the coffee begins to burble.

The floor creaks.

I glance up—Jack.

Framed in the doorway like some half-formed sin. Bare chest. Low-slung jeans. Hair mussed just enough to look accidental. A shadow of stubble softens the sharp line of his jaw.

He walks toward me—or maybe toward the coffee. Hard to tell. Then he leans in—slow, unhurried, his arm grazing mine as he reaches past me for the mug.

The contact is brief. Barely anything.

But it sparks.

A flicker.

A low hum beneath my ribs.

He doesn't speak. Just stands there. Still. Too close. Like the moment belongs to him now.

I'm caught between him and the counter. One breath away. Lip caught between my teeth, like that might steady me.

His scent reaches me first—earth, cedar, and something darker. Masculine. Unrushed.

Then, finally, his voice. Low. Casual. Dangerous.

"Coffee?"

"Y-yes."

It barely comes out. My throat's too dry to lie. And I just stand there. Blank. Frozen. As if desire stole all the commands from my brain.

He pours. One mug. Then the other.

He takes his black.

He remembers mine—two creams. Of course he does.

He hands me the mug.

His fingers brush mine—just enough to jolt something I wish would stay buried.

Then he leans in, mouth near my ear. Breath warm. Voice almost a smirk.

"Don't drop the mug."

And just like that, he's gone.

Leaving behind the scent of him, the echo of his voice, and a pulse I can't calm down.

# 16

# Chase Me Away!

After my coffee, I head for the shower. But just before stepping in, I pause—drawn to the window like it's part of the ritual. Maybe it's habit. Maybe instinct.

My gaze drifts over the dock, the tree line, the pale shimmer of water.

Still. Too still. As if the world is holding its breath.

The lake glows in the early light. Pale, quiet. Hush, then hush again.

My father used to say the stillness here could fix a person. Even if the fish didn't bite. He bought the cottage for that. My mother never understood. She came once, angry and certain I was hiding.

I draw the curtain and undress. The water hits hot. Too hot. I let it. It strips away the chill, the static, the ache beneath my skin.

I hum—low, broken. A sound to keep the silence from closing in.

Steam fills the room. My breath settles. And for a while, I let it hold me.

I don't think about Oscar. And how he complicates my life.

As I shut off the water, silence creeps in, enveloping the room. I drape a towel over my damp hair, another around my body, their cotton a weighty comfort. The mirror is shrouded in mist. With the towel's edge, I clear a small circle, revealing my eyes. They look back, weary yet strikingly lucid.

Then the knock.

Sharp. Sudden.

A sound too loud for this quiet place.

And just like that, the calm is gone.

My heart jolts at the knock. Then Jack's voice—urgent, low, almost swallowed by the wood between us.

"Lila, we need to leave. Now."

Panic licks at the edges of my calm. "I'm not dressed," I call back, gripping the towel tighter, water still trailing down my legs.

"Open the door."

Something in his tone, tight, strained. It cuts through me. I crack the door.

He's there. Wide-eyed. Breath unsteady. Not his usual calm.

His gaze flickers—my wet skin, bare shoulders, the towel. I see it register, then vanish. Still, heat blooms under my skin.

"What is it?" I ask, swallowing the lump in my throat.

He blinks hard, then: "Someone's outside."

A beat of silence. Just long enough for fear to dig in.

"Who?"

"I don't know. But we're not staying to find out." He grabs my wrist—not rough, but firm. Urgent. "We'll take the back."

I resist, my voice sharp. "Jack, I'm not *dressed*."

"You can dress in the car," he says, already pulling me through the hallway. "We need to go. Now."

My breath snags. "Wait, I need my things."

"I'll get them. I parked just behind the trees. Go."

I hesitate, one barefoot step after another, towel clinging to my skin, heart pounding like it knows something I don't.

My heart hammers as I call out, "Don't forget my phone."

Jack nods and veers into the bedroom.

I make for the back door, the towel clinging to me like it knows this isn't right. Before I can reach the handle, he's already there. Of course he is, pulling it open with one sharp motion.

"Hurry," he says.

"Who is it?" I ask, breath catching, following him into the shadows.

"Three of them," he says. "Same ones from yesterday. I'm sure of it."

His voice is flat. Focused.

Mine isn't.

The air outside bites at my skin. Goosebumps rise. Bare feet on cold stone. Running in a towel wasn't on my bucket list—especially not commando. This isn't adventure. It's madness. Absolute madness.

And still, I keep running.

We bolt for the car. Jack throws open the back door without a word, and I dive in, clutching the towel like it's armor. He slams it shut behind me and climbs into the driver's seat, engine roaring to life in one breathless motion.

"Keep your head down," he snaps.

I drop low, but not before catching a glimpse. Two large men, sprinting toward us. One of them I recognize. NYPD. Oscar's friend.

My chest tightens. Jack punches the gas.

And then, a gunfire.

Four sharp cracks tear through the air.

I scream. My hands fly to my ears. My heart beats so hard it hurts. Outside, the world blurs past—trees, gravel, the glint of something behind us. I lift my head just enough to see it.

Oscar.

Standing back. Watching.

"What's happening?" I cry, voice cracking. "Why are they shooting?"

Jack doesn't answer. His focus is absolute. The car jolts hard to the right, then lurches again as he takes a narrow bend too fast.

I'm tossed sideways, half-naked, still trying to stay down, stay conscious, stay sane.

"Hold tight!" he shouts over the wind and chaos.

I do.

Because what else is there?

In the chaos, I fumble with the towel, trying to

wriggle free and get dressed, only to find—nothing.

"Did you grab my clothes from the bed?" I ask, trying to keep the edge out of my voice. Gratitude, I remind myself. Gratitude, not panic.

"Sorry, no time," Jack says, eyes fixed on the road. "Just your phone. It's in your backpack."

Of course. My backpack. My phone. Not the cotton underwear or the jeans that don't ride up. Not the shirt I actually like.

I spot a gym bag in the back. Jack's, probably. I lunge for it, careful not to lose the towel barely clinging to dignity. Inside, thank God, a gray shirt and a pair of gym shorts.

The shirt's soft, worn-in. The shorts, huge. I yank the drawstring tight and knot it twice. No bra. No underwear. Just borrowed clothes and adrenaline.

My life, clearly, has chosen its downhill path.

I toss the towel from my head, fasten the seatbelt with shaking fingers, and force my eyes to the road ahead. My heart won't stop pounding. The question circles like a vulture.

Why are they shooting at us? I understand the chase—but shooting? Does Oscar want me gone?

The thought chills me more than the towel ever did.

"It suits you," Jack says, eyes flicking to the rearview, lips twitching at the corners.

"Well," I mutter, managing half a smirk, "this is better than being half-naked in a moving target. First time going commando. Might as well make it count."

He laughs, rough and surprised. I let myself join him, for a breath, maybe two.

Then his face shifts.

"They're here," he says.

His voice goes flat.

"Hold on. Stay low."

And just like that, the laughter dies.

My phone vibrates, and while trying to duck, I manage to grab my phone from my backpack.

I notice several missed call notifications: ten calls from Oscar, five from my mom, and twenty-five from Alexi.

I search for messages or missed calls from my dad, hoping for a clue. But there's nothing.

Just then, a message from Marie catches my attention. It reads,

> Marie: I can't find Dad. I checked the hospitals—nothing. Do you know any of his friends? Maybe he went into hiding after all the pressure Mom and Alexi put on him when you left. Call me.

The worry in her words wraps around my own. Tightens it. I text back with fingers that won't stop trembling.

> Me: We'll find him. I'll try. But Marie… do you know why Oscar's men are shooting at me? Am I wanted or something?

Three dots appear.

Disappear.

Then the reply:

Marie: What?? Be careful.

Marie: Mom and Dad had a big fight at Mom's party after you left. Dad left deranged. Mom and Alexi stayed with Oscar. Whatever you do, don't get caught. I heard Oscar saying, 'Once he gets his hands on you, he will lock you up.' I don't know if he was serious or not.

Marie: Whatever happened between us before, please know you are still my younger sister and part of my family. I don't like what Oscar is doing to our family.

That text from Marie seals it. Confirms everything I've feared but couldn't say out loud.

Jack punches the gas. The engine growls—raw and angry. Wind howls through the barely sealed windows.

Déjà vu.

We're being chased again.

"There are three cars behind us," Jack mutters, eyes locked on the road. "And judging by the way they're moving, they're pros."

"Pros?" I echo. "Pros at *what*, exactly?"

Tires screech somewhere behind us. I twist around, heart in my throat.

Three black cars. Gaining.

"Are we...dangerous people now?" I whisper. But the adrenaline makes it sound louder. Bitter.

My fingers dig into the seatbelt. Out the rear window, the cars fan out, coordinated. Predatory.

"They're closing in," I say, barely breathing.

Jack's hands grip the wheel tighter. "I'm not sure I can lose them this time."

The road ahead is long and narrow, flanked by thick, shadowed woods. No turnoffs. No cover.

Just us.

And the hunt.

The cars don't let up. They follow like shadows—tight, silent, relentless.

My pulse slams in my chest. My mind is a tangle of fear and questions I can't untangle fast enough. Why is Oscar doing this? Why send people to kill—or capture—me?

These are his men. Loyal. Trained. And terrifying.

A shiver runs the length of my spine.

In a panic, I dial his number.

The line clicks alive.

"What are you doing?" I shout, voice cracking. "Your goons are shooting at us!"

Oscar's voice comes through low, steady. Too calm.

"It's too late, Lila. You're not getting away from me."

My throat goes dry.

"Are you insane?" I choke out. "They could've

killed me."

"They're doing their job," he says, cold as steel. "Tell your driver to stop the car. Then they'll stop shooting."

His tone is flat. Unbothered.

Like my life is just another inconvenience he needs cleaned up.

One car cuts ahead, slicing through the highway like it owns it. Another veers close on our right, hugging the line, too close, too deliberate. The third shadows behind, mimicking every move. We're boxed in.

Trapped.

The black cars are silent monsters—windows blacked out, bodies gleaming like predators. They weren't built for speed. They were built for damage.

Then the lead car surges.

Gunfire erupts.

A hail of bullets screams from the windows, shattering air and reason. Jack yells something—"Duck!"—just before a brutal crunch sounds behind us. Metal groans. Our car jerks hard, spins. My body slams into the door.

The world blurs.

My stomach drops.

Oscar is trying to kill me.

"Oh my God," I scream, raw and shaking. "You want me *dead*!"

Rage erupts in my chest—hotter than fear, louder than the gunfire.

"Stop the car," Oscar says over the phone, his

voice like ice.

"You tell your *goons* to stop *shooting*," I scream back. "If I survive this—I swear to God, Oscar—I'll kill *you* myself."

And for once, I mean it. Every word.

The phone slips from my hand—gone, like everything else I can't hold onto. The world blurs. Then—silence.

And then—

Impact.

We crash through the trees. Metal screams. Glass explodes. The car spins—once, twice—everything weightless, then crushing. My body jerks, slams, twists. The seatbelt digs in, a cruel tether. My head hits the windshield with a crack so loud, it silences the world for a second.

Somehow, the car stays upright in the end. But it's wrecked—crumpled, smoking, groaning like it's alive and dying all at once.

I don't pass out.

I wish I did.

I'm still here—dizzy, blood roaring in my ears. The jungle presses in from every side. The wreck creaks around me like it's still alive.

*I'm going to die.*

The thought loops.

*I'm going to die. I'm going to die.*

The only sound left is destruction—settling metal, dripping fluids, a distant hiss like the forest is holding its breath.

And me.

Still breathing.

Still trapped.

I blink through the blur, trying to orient myself. Then—Jack.

His face, ghost-pale in the fractured sunlight.

Eyes closed. Blood streaming down his temple. Hands still clenched on the wheel like he's bracing for impact that already came.

"Jack..." My voice is a whisper, broken by shock. He doesn't move.

Panic spikes.

This isn't his fight. I'm going to kill Oscar. For real.

I fumble with the seatbelt until it gives, then kick at the door with what little strength I have. It won't budge. I kick again. This time, it opens. The air stinks—gasoline and smoke, sharp and rising.

I crawl—every limb screaming—toward the driver's side. The door won't budge. Locked.

Hands trembling, I lurch into the backseat, reach across the console, and fumble blindly for the latch. My fingers find it—*click*. It gives.

I haul myself up, dizzy and breathless, urgency dragging me forward. No time to think. No room for pain.

Flames crackle at the hood, growing louder, closer. The fire wants in.

Beyond the wreckage, figures emerge. Guns drawn.

Oscar's men.

No time.

I reach for Jack's seatbelt, fingers slick, shaking. It won't give. I yank harder.

"Come on, Jack...please..."

His body slumps, heavy, unyielding. Dead weight.

But he's not dead.

He can't be.

Not yet.

I can't give up now.

Something primal kicks in—a wild survival instinct that overrides everything else.

Adrenaline roars through my veins like a tempest, numbing the searing pain, sharpening my focus to a razor's edge.

I grip Jack under the arms, feeling the full dead weight of his body, and start dragging him slowly away from the mangled car.

The heat slams into my face, licking at my skin with fiery tendrils—an ominous warning that we're seconds from catastrophe.

Thick, acrid smoke fills my lungs, each breath a struggle. But I pull. Harder.

One step. Two. The fire advances with a sinister hiss, as if it's a living predator on the hunt. I can't fathom how I manage it, given his weight and the chaos surrounding us.

My muscles scream in protest as I haul him farther, inch by painful inch, then, in a violent crescendo, the car erupts into a fireball.

The explosion throws me backward. I hit the

ground hard. Dirt in my mouth. Smoke in my throat.

The wreck blazes, flames tearing through what's left.

Jack lies still. Too still.

I crawl to him, cradling his head in my lap. My fingers shake as I search for a pulse. Then—there. Faint but steady.

Relief floods through me like oxygen.

We're not dead yet.

The noise around us sharpens, shouts, screeching tires, a blaring horn, and then, a siren. Distant. Piercing. Hope.

I turn.

But it's not rescue. Not yet.

Oscar's men.

They emerge from the tree line, guns drawn, shadows of menace. My stomach knots.

"Jack... Jack, wake up," I whisper, tapping his cheek. Nothing.

"Give it up, Mrs. Chambers!" one of them yells. The name doesn't fit. Not anymore. I'm not Mrs. Chambers.

Then, another siren. Louder. Closer.

A voice cuts through the madness: "Police! Drop your weapon!"

Oscar's men freeze. The moment fractures.

They scatter into the woods, ghosts disappearing into green.

I exhale a jagged breath.

The ground trembles beneath us as a second

explosion rocks the air, louder, deeper. Debris rains from the trees. I curl over Jack, shielding him with what little strength I have left.

And then, he moves.

Just a twitch of his foot. But enough.

His eyes blink open. Dazed. Alive.

"Oh, thank God," I whisper, brushing hair from his bloodied forehead.

And then, finally, my body surrenders. The world tilts.

And everything fades to black.

# 17

# Escape From Hell

*A billowy sea of white encircles me in the surreal landscape. My Dad's warm and gentle voice washes over me like a wave as he calls my name. "Lila... wake up. We have something to do." His figure emerges from the mist, and I see his familiar face. He grins, his eyes twinkling with amusement. "You still owe me a book, remember?" "Dad?" I call out, reaching toward him. But he turns away, his figure fading into the distance. "Dad," I plead, confusion growing. "Where are you going?" The next moment, I find myself standing in my basement, where I used to write. My Dad stands before me, a playful smirk on his lips. "So, this is where the excitement is happening? Oscar doesn't know about it?" His laughter rings out in the air, almost as if he's sharing a private joke. "He gets what he deserves." With those words, I realize what we have to do. Then, like a dream, he vanishes.*

I come to slowly, surfacing like something drowned.

My eyes flicker open. I search the room for Dad. But the mist is gone, and so is he.

A voice cuts through the haze. Bright. Too cheerful.

"Well, look who's decided to join the living. Welcome back, Mrs. Chambers!"

The name lands wrong. Like something forced into place.

My throat burns as I try to speak. My lips barely move. The room shifts around me—white walls, beeping machines, sterile light. My head pulses with a low, relentless throb, like distant drums. I can't feel my limbs. Everything is numb, hollowed out.

"My...head," I manage, my voice sandpaper.

"You have a concussion, Mrs. Chambers..." the nurse says gently. "the painkiller should kick in soon."

*Mrs. Chambers.*

Why do they keep calling me that?

I remember we were in the car. Then—impact. Screeching tires. Gunfire. Jack.

I wrench upward, try to sit. The nurse presses a hand to my shoulder. "Lie back. You're only hurting yourself."

Panic claws its way in.

"The man with me—Jack—where is he?"

"He's in the next room. Minor concussion. Forehead laceration. He's stable." A pause. "But... he's under surveillance."

I stare at her.

"Surveillance?"

She nods, her tone soft but firm.

"Your husband said, the man who brought you

in...kidnapped you. He's been here since the ambulance arrived. Waiting for you to wake up."

*Kidnapped me?* The words echo, weightless and absurd.

I try to speak, but nothing comes.

Just the sound of my heartbeat. Fast. Frantic. And somewhere in the hall—Oscar is waiting.

"Oh God, no...no—*not* my husband. Not Oscar," I gasp. "I escaped him. He's lying. I wasn't kidnapped—Jack was helping me—"

But the words unravel, slurring at the edges. The room tilts. Everything softens, melts. A thick fog rolls over my thoughts.

"What...what did you give me?" I ask, struggling to keep my eyes open.

The nurse's smile curls at the edges—sweet and venomous. Her voice, too soft to trust.

"Don't worry, Mrs. Chambers. You're in safe hands now. We'll make sure your 'kidnapper' never sees you again."

The black scrubs she wears feel like a warning. Not care. Not comfort. A uniform for something else entirely.

"You're not listening," I whisper. "Please...don't let Oscar come. Don't let him—"

"I think you hit your head badly. You need to relax. I will tell your husband that you have awakened and fall back to sleep again." The nurse says.

"No...no...no...please, don't let him come near me."

I feel the tears in my eyes, and when she wipes them, she says, "Don't cry, Mrs. Chambers. Everything's going to be alright. You'll see. He knows what's best for you."

The nurse's words echo—blurring into the throb behind my eyes. I tried to speak the truth, but it drowned in protocol, in Oscar's charm, in whatever they pumped into my veins.

Of course he's twisted the story.

Of course they believe him.

As sleep drags me under, one thought clings: He won't stop. And maybe I'll never get out from under him.

Next time I surface, I don't open my eyes.

But I *hear* them. Voices. Movement. A soft clink of something metallic.

Oscar's voice cuts through first—calm, composed, in control.

"I've made arrangements at Harmony Mental Health Center in Uptown," he says. "The director assured me they can accommodate her by tomorrow. All the paperwork's signed."

*Harmony Mental Health Center?*

The words claw at my brain.

*He's committing me.*

My heart races, trapped beneath stillness. I force myself to stay limp. Silent.

Then—Alexi.

"I mean...what if she wakes up?" she asks. Her voice wavers. Nervous.

Alexi?

She's here?

*Is she part of this?*

I lie there, eyes shut, breathing shallow. Panic curls inside me, slow and tight.

They're moving pieces while I sleep.

Oscar's voice lowers, a shade darker now—smooth, cruel, calculated.

"No, she won't. I've instructed the nurse to keep her dosage high until the transfer. She'll be unconscious until then."

A chill spreads through me. Every word lodges like a splinter. I want to run. Scream.

I lie still, forcing each breath to stay slow, even. It takes everything in me to keep my body limp, to silence the fear hammering in my chest.

Then Alexi, quieter.

"Do you think she'll figure it out?" she asks. "That we're the ones putting her there?"

*We.*

The word slams into me.

They're in this together.

My sister.

And my husband.

My body doesn't move. But inside, something breaks.

Another voice enters—cool, composed. Familiar.

"No, she won't. But honestly...who cares if she does? I *am* her mother, after all."

My blood runs cold.

"It was my idea," she continues, calm as tea. "She needs to be locked up. We'll stage her as unstable—emotionally unfit for public life. Once she's in, we control the narrative. It's the only way to protect Oscar's image."

*My mother too?*

She's in on it too.

Is everyone?

A heaviness fills my chest. The room tightens, thick with knowing. They're not just letting this happen. They're planning it.

*Oh God...*

My own family is willing to bury me alive. And I'm still lying here. Pretending not to know.

I need to escape.

Their voices, their plans—fuel something hot and wild inside me. Plotting my disappearance like I'm nothing.

*Over my dead body.* I can't let them win.

Then Alexi again—this time, a tremor in her voice.

"Don't you think she could hear us?"

Oscar scoffs. "She's heavily sedated. Don't worry."

"But the man she was with?" Alexi presses. "Wouldn't he go to the police?"

Oscar lowers his voice, but I hear it anyway. Every word lands like ice down my spine.

"Don't worry about him. We have ways of handling that. Once Lila's in the institution, he's no longer a problem."

Jack.

Don't you dare touch him. He isn't part of this.

Jack... oh God, not Jack.

They're not just erasing me.

They're going after him, too.

And if I don't find a way out soon, neither of us *will get another chance.*

Alexi's voice murmurs something—low, anxious.

Oscar cuts in, smooth and practiced, always the politician, even now.

"Listen, Alexi, don't worry about it. Your mom and I worked this plan out so your sister wouldn't be a problem anymore. We've dealt with her long enough to know exactly what needs to be done. Once she's in the Center, she's out of our way. And most importantly, she won't be able to file for divorce."

He pauses, like savoring the cruelty. "She gave me enough headaches running off. I don't need her stubborn streak screwing up my campaign."

There's a silence, then Alexi sighs. "You're right. Lila's been a thorn in your side. I just don't want her ruining your chances in the election. Once she's gone, we can finally focus."

Oscar chuckles, then softly: "That's my girl."

*My girl?*

The words hit like a slap.

*Oh God—*Is Alexi sleeping with Oscar?

I feel bile rise in my throat. My body still. My pulse erratic.

How deep does this go?

Then my mother's voice—cool, resolute.

"I agree. We've come too far. We can't let anyone jeopardize Oscar's image now. I didn't know Lila had it in her—to just run. She used to be the pushover. Like a doormat. We'd tell her to do this, to do that, and she'd do it. I don't like what she's becoming. We need to step in. Steer things back before it gets out of hand."

A pushover? No. That's not fair. I stayed. I helped. I kept quiet. That's not the same. They talk like I'm property. Like I'm inconvenient. But I'm still here. Still listening. Still fighting.

And I swear, I will not disappear quietly. And I will rise up. Watch me.

Realizing that my mom and Alexi are behind this plot to lock me away and helping Oscar is a heavy blow.

"Mental hospital? Oh God, please! Have mercy!" I plea.

"I will be here tomorrow. I will make the transfer smoother," my mother says.

I hear the door creaks open.

"I need to check on the patient. Make sure her vitals are good," a new voice says—calm, clinical.

A nurse.

I freeze. Not visibly. Just inside. My performance has to be perfect now. Every breath measured, every muscle still.

I keep my eyes shut, my face slack. I imagine sleep—deep, heavy, drugged. I let the illusion sink into my limbs.

She moves beside me. I feel her presence before her touch—cool hands, efficient fingers. She checks my pulse, the machines, the numbers that determine whether I stay free or disappear.

"How is she doing?" my mother asks, her voice a syrupy lie.

The nurse answers without pause.

"She's stable. The sedation is holding. She should remain asleep for a while. We'll monitor her closely."

I stay still, but inside, I'm screaming.

Keep talking. Stay distracted. Don't see me.

Because the second they believe I'm truly unconscious—Is the second I can start planning how to *get out.*

Beneath the covers, I clench my fists. Nails pressing into my palms. The nurse's words confirm it—I'm trapped. For now.

I can't move. Can't speak. Can't scream the truth.

Not yet.

She finishes her assessment. The machines continue their quiet hum. But no one leaves.

The silence is thick. Smothering. And in it, my resolve sharpens.

They want to bury me alive in some institution, like I'm a threat to their convenience. Like I'm in the way of Oscar's ambition, Alexi's comfort, my mother's warped sense of loyalty.

But they're wrong.

Listening to them talk like I'm already gone only hardens me. This is no longer just about escape. It's about divorce. About freedom. About justice.

How dare they.

How *dare* they.

Did they think I'd never learn the truth? That I'd sleep through their betrayal?

God is not sleeping.

And neither am I.

Two people I try to love—my own family—plotting my erasure. Treating me like a problem to solve.

I'm not a pawn. I'm not theirs.

Every human being has the right to live freely. To choose. To fight.

And I will.

But right now...I need them gone. I need quiet. I need a crack in their plan.

And I need You, God. Please. If You're listening—Show me the way out.

I'm not sure when they finally decide to leave. The minutes bleed together. I only catch fragments—Oscar saying something about stopping at the nurses' station.

Then the sound I've been praying for.

Doors opening. Then closing.

I wait.

Still.

Breath shallow. Muscles coiled. Eyes shut.

Then—nothing.

I crack one eyelid. Just enough to scan the room. Empty.

But I don't move yet. I can't. There's still a chance

someone comes back.

And I'm right.

A soft click. The door opens again.

Footsteps. Slow. Deliberate.

I freeze, body limp, willing my heartbeat to go silent.

Oscar's voice. Close. Too close.

"Maureen, make sure she's heavily sedated. I'll make it up to you. What do you want?"

A woman answers—light, flirtatious.

"I told you, Oscar, I don't want money. I want *you.* Your time. It's been so long..."

I clench my fists beneath the sheets. *Another woman.* Cheating bastard. How many?

"She's still out," Maureen says, casual. "I'll be back later."

"I have to go," Oscar replies, voice low and final. "Make sure she doesn't wake up until she's safely inside the institution."

"I got it, don't you worry," Maureen assures him.

A beat. Then: "Don't forget tonight...at my place."

A chuckle. "You bet."

The door closes again.

And I know now—they've sealed my fate.

Unless I undo it myself.

A few minutes pass after the door shuts.

I exhale slowly and peel open my eyes, inch by inch. The room stays still. No movement. No watchers.

Time is bleeding out.

I reach for the IV and yank. Blood wells up

instantly, warm and red, but I barely register the sting—just a dull pulse, distant, irrelevant.

The door stands closed.

I have to move. *Now.*

But everything spins. I crashes like a freight train, dragging the floor out from under me. My vision warps, limbs trembling as if made of paper. I fall—hard—hitting the ground in a heap of dead weight and panic.

The drugs haven't worn off. Not nearly enough.

Still, I crawl.

I grip the bedframe, hauling myself upright with shaking arms. Everything inside me screams to stop. But I can't. I won't.

I have to find Jack. Before they take him. Before they vanish *me.*

Each step is war. A breathless fight. But I drag my body hard. It takes everything just to reach the door.

I open it a crack.

Footsteps.

Voices.

I freeze, pulse hammering.

Then—laughter, fading away.

Not the nurse.

I close my eyes, whisper a thank you to God, then ease the door open again.

The hallway stretches ahead—too bright, too long. I step in, one hand on the wall to steady what's left of me. I wobble, then drop. But I rise again, gathering what little strength and will I have left.

Every step forward is borrowed time. And time's almost out.

The nurse said Jack was in the next room. But which next room? Left...or right?

I hesitate for a second, then turn right, praying I guessed correctly. My legs barely cooperate—each step slow, unsteady, like walking through water.

Please let it be the right one.

I reach the door and press down on the handle, careful not to collapse. Just getting here feels like a small victory.

I ease the door open.

A soft hum greets me. Medical machinery. Steady. Alive.

Someone lies on the bed.

I move closer, cautious, breath held, heart rattling in my chest.

Please be Jack.

"Jack...?" I whisper, then louder—urgently—"*Jack, wake up... we have to go.* Jack!"

I shake his shoulder, lightly at first, then harder. No response.

Panic claws up my throat.

I reach for the IV and rip it from his arm. His body doesn't flinch. I tap his face, gently then harder, trying to rouse him. Nothing.

He's out cold.

They sedated him, too.

I glance toward the door, heart racing. Every second counts.

I need a wheelchair. Something. Anything to move him.

And I need to pray the nurse hasn't returned yet—because if she walks in now, it's over.

I lean closer, whispering like a promise:

"I'm getting you out of here, Jack. Just hold on."

I search the room—frantic, wild—but there's no wheelchair.

Nothing. No way to move Jack.

This plan collapses without one.

My heart pounds as I slip into the hallway, barely upright, legs shaky, mind locked on one thing.

Find that wheelchair.

The corridor is dead quiet.

Too quiet.

Good. I need quiet.

Each step is fragile, my balance off, vision still swimming. I scan the hall—left, right—for movement, for help, for threat. Just a chair. That's all I need.

I turn a corner. There it is. A wheelchair. Parked like it's waiting for me.

Then, movement.

A woman in scrubs. Mid-hall. Head down, thumbing her phone.

She doesn't see me yet. Please don't see me.

She turns. Walks away. Never looks up.

Thank God.

I move fast. Quiet, shaking—grabbing the wheelchair, dragging it toward me like it might vanish if I wait too long.

This is it.

Now or never.

My hands tremble as I wheel it back to Jack's room, every turn of the wheels echoing in my ears like a countdown. I pray no one sees me.

He's still unconscious.

I slip inside, close the door, and move fast. My heart pounds. Lifting him is nearly impossible. His weight folds against me, dead and heavy—but adrenaline takes over. I grit my teeth, hook my arms beneath him, and wrestle him into the chair.

He doesn't stir.

I barely catch my breath.

Now or never.

I glance down at the hospital gown clinging to me. No way I'll make it far in this. I need to look like I belong. There are cameras everywhere—I just pray no one's watching too closely.

As I push Jack into the hallway, I spot it—a small door marked Maintenance. Not far.

I retrace my steps, wheels whispering against the floor. My head swims, but I press on. I can't afford to fall now.

Inside the maintenance room, I dig through shelves and hooks. No scrubs. But there—a navy-blue uniform. Baggy. Functional. A matching cap on a hook.

Good enough.

I strip fast, pulling the overalls over my hospital gown, tucking everything in, zipping it shut. I jam the hat on my head. My reflection in the dusty glass is almost unrecognizable.

Perfect.

I whisper a prayer. Just one.

Please, let us make it.

We reach the elevator.

I hit the button hard, tapping my foot, pulse pounding in my ears.

Seconds stretch like hours.

Behind us—nothing yet.

But I know it's coming.

I pray the elevator is empty.

It is.

I wheel Jack inside, breath hitching. Just as the doors begin to close, a voice calls out—too close.

"Hey...hold the elevator for me, please!"

I mash the *close* button like a panicked child, jabbing it again and again.

The doors slip shut just in time.

*Thank God.*

I press *L* for lobby. We descend.

I can barely stand. My legs tremble, my vision swims, but I force myself upright. Leaning against the railing, I grip the handles of Jack's chair tighter.

The sense of doom hasn't left. It hums beneath my skin like static.

The elevator chimes.

The doors slide open.

And there he is.

Oscar. Back turned, leaning on the front desk, charming the nurse with that smooth, practiced laugh.

Flirting like the world owes him its attention.

*Flirt away*, I think, fury cold in my chest. Soon-to-be ex-husband.

He doesn't see us.

Neither does she.

Flirting takes focus.

With slow, deliberate steps, I steer Jack out of the elevator, past the edge of their attention. I don't rush. That would draw eyes. I just move.

Then—*hiss*—the sliding doors open.

Like heaven itself is holding the door. Thank God. We walk through.

Not fast.

Not free. But through.

# 18
# Push It Through

I grip the wheelchair tight, my fingers aching, bloodless. The hospital fades behind us. A gust of night air hits my face—sharp, sobering. We're out.

Jack slumps forward, sedated and silent. His head bobs with each bump in the sidewalk. He doesn't stir. I wish he would. Just a word. A glance. Anything to remind me I'm not alone in this.

The city stretches before me, a glittering map of unknowns. Every streetlight hums like a warning. Every shadow watches.

I push faster.

The wind is colder now. I should have brought a jacket. Or a plan.

No phone.

No money.

No car.

No one.

What's the use of a million in a bank account when, right now, I'm penniless and powerless? Rich on paper. Stranded in reality. Just a wheelchair, a sedated man, and the weight of a city that doesn't care.

I stop beneath a flickering light. My breath slips

out in curls, pale as smoke. Jack's still out cold. I rest a hand on his shoulder, not sure if it's for him, or for me.

I need to think.

I need to move.

I need to go somewhere safe before someone realizes we're gone.

And still, nothing but the steady hum of the city, and the weight of the night pressing in.

The idea of stealing a car crosses my mind, but I've never done it before. It might seem cool on TV or in books, but in real life? Ha! Breaking into a car would take time, and I need to weigh the risks and consequences. My determination would have to be strong to consider stealing someone's car.

Oh God, I need help. Please, help me.

I can't ask Marie, they might be tracking her. Angela? Maybe. But the inn's not an option. Oscar and his goons were already there. And I won't drag Angela into this.

Leo. I need Leo.

I memorized his number by heart, before everything started falling apart.

With clenched teeth, I shove the wheelchair forward. The wheels catch on every crack and uneven seam in the sidewalk. Each jolt rattles Jack. His breathing grows louder, shallower.

A neon sign flickers up ahead—a convenience store, its light twitching like a nervous tic, not a welcome.

I don't stop.

My arms ache. My palms sting. But I keep going. Stopping isn't a choice.

I can't bring Jack inside. A man slumped in a wheelchair draws questions. And I can't afford questions. I scan the alley beside the store—partially covered, mostly hidden. Some old crates. A vending machine with a sign out of order.

It'll have to do.

"I'll be right back," I whisper, though Jack can't hear me. Still, I say it—for me, not him.

I ease him into the shadowed stall, then pull my hat low. My face has been on screens lately. Too many. For reasons I don't want to remember.

The bell above the store door chimes. Fluorescent light floods my eyes. The air smells like cheap gum and burnt coffee. Behind the counter sits a man in his late sixties, skin paper-thin, eyes dull. He doesn't flinch.

I step forward. Calm. Careful. Controlled.

"Excuse me," I say, voice low, rehearsed. "Could I borrow your phone? I just need to make a quick call. I just need someone to pick me up."

A beat. A pause.

I wait, hoping help doesn't look too much like a lie.

The store owner stares at me, his eyes dark and sharp, like he's scanning for lies. I feel exposed, as if the harsh fluorescent lights have peeled back every layer of disguise.

He doesn't blink. His face is unreadable—serious, set, the kind of face that doesn't tolerate nonsense. His accent is thick, his voice sharp.

"You one of those kids who fake being lost just to steal?" he says, waving a hand toward the door. "Go. Go away."

Before I can respond, he gets up, reaches, and gives my shoulder a shove—light, but enough. Dismissal, not violence. But it stings just the same.

"I'm not—" I start, but the words die. He's already turned his back, muttering in another language, shaking his head.

I stand there, stunned. Humiliated. The moment stretches. My mouth is dry. My heart pounds, not from the rejection, but from the clock ticking on Jack. On us.

I step back into the night, the bell above the door mocking me as it chimes again.

As I turn to leave, the door half-open, a voice stops me. Kind. Firm. Unapologetic.

"Come on, Dad," she says, not scolding, just steady. "Don't be like that. She might actually need help."

I freeze.

From behind the counter, a woman steps into view. Mid-thirties, maybe. Calm eyes, soft smile. Her presence diffuses the tension like a warm current. Chinese, like the man—but lighter somehow. Less guarded.

She gives me a quick once-over, then offers her

hand. "You can use my phone, Miss..." She lets it hang, an open door rather than a demand.

My throat tightens. Relief comes fast and foolish, like it doesn't know better. I nod, swallowing back something grateful and fragile.

"Thank you," I say, stepping toward the counter once more.

She pulls a slim phone from her pocket and offers it without hesitation.

I dial Leo's number with shaking fingers, sweat slick on my brow. The phone rings. Once. Twice.

"Come on, Leo," I whisper. "Pick up. Please."

A click. Then, "Leo's Limo Service. How can I help you?"

"Leo..." His name spills out, tangled with shock, relief, and the threat of tears. "It's me. Please...Jack's not well. I need help. Can you come get us?"

The words tumble out in a rush, tripping over each other. I don't even know if I'm making sense.

There's a beat of silence. Then his voice. Steady, familiar, warm like an old song. "Where you at?"

I blink, glance around. "I...I don't know. Wait. Let me ask."

I turn to the woman behind the counter, the phone pressed tight against my ear. My breath hitches.

Leo speaks again, voice lower now, calmer. "Take ya time, alright? I ain't goin' nowhere. You just breathe."

His voice is a tether in the storm.

I turn to the woman, hands trembling. "Could

you...I need the address. My friend, he's coming to get me."

She nods, calm as ever. "You're in Middletown, New York," she says, already reaching for a pen. "Here, let me write it down."

Relief floods me. I take the note like it's a passport. "Thank you," I breathe, more than once, then press the phone back to my ear.

"Leo," I say, my voice steadier now. "It's Middletown. Corner of Lafayette and 116th."

"I'm on my way," he says without pause. "Stay put."

Then, before the line clicks, his voice drops, gentle but firm. "Find a place to hide till I get there. Might take a minute. Just... breathe, alright?"

I nod, even though he can't see me. "Okay. Thank you, Leo."

I turn to the woman again. "Thank you. Truly."

She gives me a soft smile, then turns back to her counter like none of this ever happened.

I rush out into the dark, heart thudding, air colder now.

I round the corner, and stop.

The alley's too quiet. The wheelchair is empty. Jack is gone.

Fear slams into me like a fist. I stumble forward, my breath caught—half-scream, half-prayer.

"Jack?" My voice cracks. "Jack...oh God, no. No, no."

Tears sting. The alley spins. I whip around, scanning crates, shadows, anything that could hide a man too weak to stand.

"God, please," I whisper. "Haven't they done enough?"

"Jack!" I call louder now, voice bouncing off brick and night. "I'm so sorry. I shouldn't have left you alone..."

A rustle. Then a voice, low, hoarse, rising from the concrete.

"Lila...?"

I turn fast. And there he is—half-slumped against the wall, eyes dazed, legs folded beneath him like he'd tried to move and the earth gave out.

"Jack!" I drop to my knees beside him, brushing his hair back. "Oh thank God. Are you hurt? What happened?"

He seems just as confused as I am. "Beats me... why am I in a wheelchair? Where am I?"

The answers are coming at me too fast, crashing into each other. I can barely think, let alone explain.

"Oh God... I can explain," I stammer, crouched beside him. "I...I smuggled you out of the hospital. They found us, Jack."

He stares, still foggy. I push forward.

"My husb—"

I stop. The word catches like glass in my throat.

Not now. Not anymore.

"Oscar," I say instead. "And my mom. Alexi. They showed up. I didn't know what else to do."

The words tumble out, clumsy and too fast, but it's all I have. All I can offer him in this moment of wreckage and truth.

I wheel the chair beside him and crouch low. "Sit down... here. I'll help you. You're gonna feel unsteady. I did too. They sedated me, but you..." I pause, adjusting the brakes. "You got a much heavier dose. I tried waking you, Jack. Over and over. You were out cold."

He doesn't answer right away, just breathes in—deep and rough, like every inhale takes effort.

"Man..." he mutters finally, settling into the chair with my help. "I've always stayed away from that crap. Hate the way it makes me feel—numb. Like my body's here but I'm not."

His voice is quiet but solid. A flicker of the old Jack, just beneath the fog.

I nod, swallowing the guilt lodged in my throat.

"I'm so sorry, Jack." My voice breaks as I steady him in the chair. "This is all my fault. I got you involved."

He exhales, slow and measured, still groggy.

I keep talking, the words tumbling out. too fast, too much, but I can't stop.

"The nurse... she said you were my kidnapper. They were going to keep drugging you, Jack. I heard them."

His head lifts slightly, eyes narrowing with dawning clarity.

"They want to put me in a mental hospital," I whisper. "Can you see how twisted this is?" I swipe at my eyes. "God, why did I ever marry Oscar? What did I ever see in him?"

Tears well and blur the edges of the alley, but I blink hard, forcing them back. No time for a breakdown.

Jack settles deeper into the chair, sighing like his whole body just remembered how to breathe. "So," he says, with a faint smile, "how'd you pull it off?"

"I don't know," I admit. "I just...couldn't leave you there. I couldn't live with it. I didn't plan it. I just moved."

The words hang between us—messy, breathless, true.

"But what were you doing on the ground?" I ask, the question hitting me again now that the panic's eased.

Jack gives a soft laugh, sheepish. "Honestly? For a second, I thought someone had kidnapped me."

I blink.

"Yeah," he continues, rubbing his temple. "I came to, tried to stand, and my knees just said 'nope.' Next thing I know, I'm crawling. Then I hear your voice, and I think—am I dreaming? Hallucinating? Or just finally gone crazy."

His tone is light, but there's an edge of disorientation that hasn't fully faded.

"The last thing I really remember," he says, more slowly now, "was the hospital. You passed out, they swarmed you. I don't remember anyone else coming in after that. Later, they moved me to a room. Said they had something for the pain, I declined."

He pauses, frowning. "But I guess...I must've drifted. And now—" he glances around at the dark alley, the broken vending stall, the chill biting at his skin, "here I am."

A shiver rolls through him. "Damn. It's cold out here."

"Yeah, spring nights are usually this cold," I say, rubbing my arms for warmth. I notice Jack shifting uncomfortably in the wheelchair and add, "I wish I had something to keep you warm while we wait for Leo."

"You called Leo?" Jack asks, his brows lifting.

"Yeah," I nod. "I had to borrow a phone from someone inside."

He exhales, the corners of his mouth tugging into something like a smile.

"I'm so sorry, Jack," I say, my voice quieter now. "This whole mess...it's my fault. You could've walked away back at the cottage. But you didn't. I don't know how to repay that."

He watches me, eyes steady, saying nothing at first.

Then he shivers.

"Do you want me to warm you up?" I offer, half-serious, half-nervous. "I mean—human heat's the number one source, right? I could sit on your lap and give you a hug."

His expression shifts, blank for a second, then deliberate. Serious. And then: "That's...not a good idea."

I frown. "Why not?"

He meets my eyes, voice low, dry. "Because I'm still a man, Lila. Sedated or not."

I blink, then laugh. "I meant it platonic. My intentions are pure."

He smiles, finally. "That's what makes it worse."

The lap idea dies a quiet death in my mind.

Instead, I move behind Jack's wheelchair and lean in, wrapping my arms around him from behind. My hands rub gently along his arms, slow and warm. I feel him gasp—just slightly—then exhale, the tension melting from his body in a soft, contented sigh.

I rest my cheek against the back of his shoulder.

"I'm truly sorry I brought this on you, Jack," I whisper. "My life...it's spiraled into seven layers of insanity."

He doesn't speak. Just listens. Breath even. Still grounded.

"Just a month ago, I was an ordinary wife. Mundane. Predictable. Then I walked into your restaurant—and saw what Oscar did. Everything changed."

I pause, the air tightening around my ribs.

"I can't go back," I say. "I can't unsee all his lies. I won't live in that version of myself anymore."

I almost mention my mother. And Alexi. The twisted truth hiding behind their perfect façades.

But that's another layer. And I'm not ready to peel it open.

Not yet.

A warm smile spreads across my face as Jack speaks.

"Hmm. How many times you gonna say sorry?" he says, voice low but steady. "You saved me twice now, first from burning alive, then from being trapped in that hospital."

He turns slightly, just enough for me to catch the weight in his eyes. "You could've left me, Lila. But you didn't."

We fall quiet, peering into the night like it might give something back—clarity, courage, a way forward. The silence holds us for a moment.

Then the sirens start.

Distant at first. Faint, but rising. Like a warning winding its way toward us.

"I think they just realized we're gone," I whisper, glancing over my shoulder.

A new sound follows, tires on loose gravel. Fast. Too fast.

My breath catches. "Leo has to get here before they do," I murmur. "I'd rather freeze out here than let Oscar find me, again."

My fists clench. My pulse pounds so hard it rattles my ribs. I try to breathe through it, but it's like the air has teeth.

Jack reaches over and grips my arm, firm. "I'm not letting you face them alone."

His words land like shelter. My chest aches with something that feels like gratitude, maybe even trust.

"Thank you," I whisper.

We dock into the shadows of the recessed entry, crouching beside a newspaper rack and a vending machine taped with a crooked *OUT OF ORDER* sign. The city's noise blurs behind us. Darkness closes in, not as threat, but as cover. As quiet mercy.

Minutes crawl. Then, headlights.

A black sedan glides down the street, slow and smooth. My heart surges, almost too fast to track. The car coasts to a stop. The engine hums low.

I rise halfway, hands trembling. "This has to be Leo," I breathe.

I wave, fast and sharp, praying it's him and not a trick, not a trap.

The driver's door opens. A figure steps out. Tall, familiar, broad-shouldered. Leo.

His eyes lock onto mine, and his face splits into a wide, unmistakable smile.

"Bout time," he calls, striding toward us.

That smile, solid, unshaken—feels like a lighthouse cutting through storm.

We're not safe. Not yet. But we're no longer alone.

# 19

# Face it Or Not

The scent of polished leather fills the air as I slide into the backseat beside Jack. His head leans against the seat, eyes closed, fingers seemingly massaging his temple. The door shuts with a heavy thud.

Leo climbs into the front. The limousine starts with a low purr, smooth as breath. Like a lion settling in the dark.

"Apologies for the delay," he says, eyes scanning the mirrors. "They've set up a roadblock. Stopped every car matching your description."

My stomach knots. A checkpoint. I hadn't realized Oscar had that kind of reach.

"Do you think we'll make it?" I ask, my voice barely audible.

Leo nods once. "I know another way."

In the rearview, his eyes flick to Jack. Quick. Calculated. Unreadable.

Jack stirs beside me. His eyelids flutter open, slow and uncertain. Shadows bloom beneath his eyes, and his hair's a quiet tangle. The hospital gown hangs loose on him, thin fabric, thinner strength.

"I don't know where to go, Leo," I whisper. The

words scrape out. Uncertain, hollow.

Leo doesn't answer right away. The engine hums. The road stretches ahead, blank and black.

He replies, "I do. I know just the place."

I meet his eyes in the mirror.

There's something steady there, anchored. A quiet promise, not spoken, but remembered.

My mind drifts to the first time I fled to this car. The way his silence wrapped around me like safety. The way I curled into the leather seats and let the world fall away.

And that night, the one that changed things.

The one I never talk about. But now, in the low hum of escape and memory, it comes back. So does the trust.

"You'll never know how much your help means to me, Leo," I murmur. "I owe you more than I can say."

His eyes meet mine in the mirror—warm, steady, no performance in them. Just presence. His smile is slight, but real. Somehow, that's enough. He doesn't need to speak. He never did.

Silence falls again, padded and heavy, until Jack breaks it.

"What's your next plan?" he asks, voice thin, uncertain.

I don't answer right away. My forehead leans against the cool window, and I watch the city pass, street lamps bending into gold ribbons, storefronts glowing like distant promises. The world looks soft, surreal. As if I'm watching it from the wrong side of a dream.

I close my eyes.

That question has stalked me for weeks: *What must I do?*

The truth blooms in the quiet. No more running. No more hiding in borrowed shadows.

“I have to face him,” I say, eyes still closed.

The engine hums. The lights blur.

“I can’t disappear forever. I have to fight back.”

A chill slides down my spine, not from fear, but from the weight of what comes next.

“I need a lawyer,” I add, opening my eyes. The words feel heavy. Real.

Images flash unbidden; Oscar’s threats, the way the backpack detonated like a warning. My ID. My documents. All gone.

Jack turns slightly, his voice steadier now. “I know some of the best. I’ll make a call.”

I nod, grateful, but my thoughts race. Without ID, I’m no one on paper. I can’t reclaim my life if I can’t prove it’s mine.

The car rolls on, and outside, the city doesn't know what it's carrying.

But inside, something’s shifting.

Resolve, raw and rising.

My eyelids grow heavy. Exhaustion pulls at me, slow and steady, like the tide. I yawn, jaw cracking with the stretch—and sink a little deeper into the seat.

Leo glances back. “Rest,” he says softly. “We’re almost there.”

His voice stirs a question that's been flickering in the back of my mind since we pulled away from the curb.

"So..." I mumble, yawning mid-sentence, "where are we going?"

I lean my forehead against the windowpane. The glass is cool. The streetlights blur and swim.

But the answer never comes.

Sleep takes me before it can.

Wrapped in motion, in silence, in something close to safety, I drift. Held not by certainty, but by two near-strangers who feel more like home than anyone I've ever known.

*As I drift off, I find myself in my usual spot with my Dad – an old, run-down diner. We sit together at the corner table, and he seems so natural that it feels like a normal conversation. But as he speaks of life lessons and stories from his past, his voice grows quieter until it fades completely. The diner starts to spin around me faster until everything turns into darkness. All of a sudden, I am back in my basement. I am so focused on typing away at my laptop that I don't hear the steps coming softly down the stairs. When I look up, I see my Dad with a wry smile. I am startled, and he steps forward, hands in his pockets. His eyes roam the room and settle on me. "So, this is where you spend your time?" He gestures to the dimly lit room with a playful grin.*

Jack lurches forward, his hand gently shaking my shoulder.

My eyes fly open. My heart races. *Did I dream about my dad again?*

Jack's face hovers close, his voice low. "We're here."

I blink, disoriented, then glance out the window. We've arrived. And before us stands a house so beautiful it takes my breath. Grand, but rooted. Like something from a dream that never dared to wake.

"Wow," I whisper. "This is incredible." A pause, then, " I dream of having a house just like this. But... on a farm."

Jack turns, brow raised. "On a *farm*?"

I nod, smiling, soft and a little wistful.

"Yeah. One day, if I'm lucky enough to find a husband after divorcing Oscar—I want this. A house like this. A yard full of chaos. Kids running wild through fields. Laughter everywhere. In a big land."

The words hang in the air between us. And for the first time in a long time, they don't feel impossible.

"Children?" Jack asks, curious. "How many are we talking here?"

I smile, the idea wrapping around me like an old, soft blanket. "Four? Five? Maybe half a dozen."

His eyes widen. "Seriously? That many?"

I shrug, still smiling. "Why not?"

He pauses, then asks, "And what if you never find someone to marry again?"

The question lingers.

My smile fades just slightly. "Why? You think I'm not desirable enough? That no one will have me?" The words slip out before I can stop them, my insecurity rising to the surface.

Jack leans in, eyes locked on mine, his voice low and syrup-smooth.

"Oh, don't get me wrong," he says with a sly grin. "With just one glance, men will line up for a chance. Beg, even."

My pulse jumps, heat rising to my face. There's a pull in his tone I can't ignore.

"Are you... making fun of me?" I ask, half-teasing, half-defensive.

His grin deepens.

"Not at all," he murmurs. "Just speaking the truth."

And in that look, just a flicker longer than necessary, something shifts. With my brow furrowed, I study Jack's face, trying to read past the charm, to whatever truth lingers behind his eyes.

And then it dawned on me.

I come with baggage. A failed marriage. Complications. History I didn't ask for, but can't pretend away. So I answer, not with apology, but with resolve.

"Well...then I'll just adopt all six of those kids myself," I say, a wry smile tugging at my lips. "I'll make it happen. My money. My dream. My vision of a beautiful farmhouse like this." I glance at him "Men are just a bunch of headaches anyway."

Jack laughs. "*All* men?"

I let it it go. Some things need no reply.

I walk toward the house, letting my gaze linger on its quiet grandeur, the intricate trim, the weathered porch, the kind of charm only time can build.

Leo waits on the front porch, his stance easy and confident, like he's been expecting us all along.

"So... it's more about having kids than a husband?" Jack asks behind me, curiosity tugging at the edges of his voice.

"Huh?" I keep walking, eyes on the porch. "Well, if the next one's anything like Oscar?" A dry laugh slips out. "I've kissed my romantic life goodbye."

Jack laughs. Harder than I expected.

"Don't get your hopes up," he says, more serious now. "Most agencies won't even consider a single person for adoption. Let alone someone aiming for six."

His words land with weight, half realism, half regret.

Then he adds, winking, "Your best bet is to get the man *first.*"

"Seriously? You're kidding, right?"

I stop beneath the shadow of the porch, fingertips brushing one of the ornate columns. "Whose house *is* this, anyway?"

Jack trails after me. But instead of answering, he asks, "That dream of yours, about the kids. Did you ever tell your husband?"

I glance over my shoulder. He's not looking at me.

"Oh yeah," I say, my voice quieter now. "At every opportunity. But Oscar's always two steps ahead. He knows how to shut things down before they begin." I pause. "Who knows? Maybe he already has kids with someone else."

The thought chills me.

Then I turn to Jack, catching his silver gaze.

"Wait—have *you* told me everything? Is there more to this case? Are there kids involved?"

He looks away, jaw tightening.

"It's cold," he says. "Let's go inside."

He doesn't answer. And that silence says more than any yes.

We're greeted by a man in an impeccably tailored black suit, his face unreadable. Mid-fifties, maybe. He bows, measured and precise. When he speaks, there's no mistaking it. His accent is not American.

"Good to see you again, Jack. Your aunt will be down shortly. In the meantime, may I offer either of you something to eat?"

My stomach answers for me. Loudly. The sound echoes in the quiet hallway. My cheeks flush.

The man raises an eyebrow. "You must be Mrs. Green?"

"Please, call me Lila," I reply, shaking his hand.

"My name is Everest," he says, with the kind of calm that suggests nothing ever surprises him.

Then, footsteps. Quick, deliberate.

A tall woman appears at the top of the staircase,

gliding down in a long maroon nightdress that flows like silk water. She moves like someone who's used to being noticed.

"Angela?" I blurt, eyes wide as I glance at Jack.

He nods, casually. "Yes. Angela's my aunt."

"Is that so?" I manage, trying to steady my voice. "Would've been nice if you'd mentioned that earlier."

Jack grins. "You never asked." And winks.

Angela reaches the bottom step and takes in the scene—Leo, Jack, and me. Like pieces falling into place. Her expression softens.

"Leo called on the way to pick you up," she says, gently patting their shoulders. "I told him to bring you here."

Everest steps forward. "I was about to tell the cook someone needs food."

A *cook*. Of course!

"Yes, please, Everest. Thank you," Angela replies, smiling.

"So...Leo will stay?" I ask.

Angela turns to me, warm. "Yes. It's far too late to head back to the city. He and his wife are dear friends. They always have a room here."

Then she steps closer, her tone softening. "Now, back to you. I'll show you your room. You need a long shower, or a bath, whichever you prefer."

I open my mouth to thank her, but she holds up a finger, silencing me.

"No need for words now," she says. "Tomorrow will take care of itself. Tonight, you need a warm meal, and real sleep."

Later, in the quiet of my room, after stepping out of the shower, I devour the hearty meal she left for me. Simple. Rich. Comforting. On the bedside table, a new toothbrush and a travel-sized tube of toothpaste.

After brushing, I slide beneath crisp white sheets, lavender curling into the air like a lullaby.

And finally—the warmth, the stillness, the bed. Sleep takes me. Not peacefully, but deeply. And with it, a fitful dream.

> *I find myself at one of Dad's famous parties, where coworkers and clients all laugh and joke around him. But when Mom taps his shoulder, something changes - his face darkens, and his eyes harden. But my mom laughs, laughs, and laughs. Suddenly, I was no longer at the party but in our family's basement. I step slowly down the stairs, a muffled moan coming from the bathroom ahead. As I open the door, there is Dad - bound and gagged. He makes eye contact with me, and his gaze pleads for help. "Dad...?" I scream.*

Jack's hands grip my shoulders. Warm, steady. Pulling me out of the dark.

"Lila...wake up. You're having a nightmare."

His voice is low, urgent. My eyes snap open, breath coming fast. The room is too still. Too quiet. I sit up, heart hammering against my ribs.

"My father...I need to find my father," I whisper, already halfway out of bed.

The floor is cold under my feet as I race toward the door, instinct leading the charge. Something's wrong. I feel it in my bones. In the way the picture formed in my mind. In the echo of his voice lingering in my dreams.

The clock flashes **1:00 AM**, red and unforgiving.

I reach for the doorknob.

Jack steps in front of me, blocking the way like a wall of calm steel. "You need rest," he says. "We'll deal with it in the morning."

"No," I push, frantic now. "They have him. Somewhere underground. I saw it. I keep seeing it. He's gagged, tied up, trying to tell me something."

My voice cracks. The tears are already falling.

Footsteps above. Angela and Leo appear at the landing, eyes clouded with sleep. Everest behind them, composed as ever.

"I have to go," I plead, glancing at all of them. "I think he's in a basement. Maybe Oscar's. I need to start there."

Jack studies me. "Do you know for sure?"

I shake my head. "No. Just...I know I won't sleep until I try."

Then I turn to Leo. "Please. Let me borrow your car. I'll buy you a new one if I wreck it..."

Leo's soft chuckle cuts through the tension. "You're not buying me anything," he says. "I'll drive."

The relief crashes over me, sharp and overwhelming. "Thank you," I whisper, voice breaking.

Jack steps forward. " Alright...I'm coming too."

"No, you need sleep. The meds, your injuries..."

"I'm fine. I had worse..." he says, though he winces slightly. "I'm fit as a bull." It's a lie. But it holds.

Angela folds her arms. "Both of you, go upstairs. Get dressed. I'll bring coats."

We don't argue.

"I'm very sorry to disturb your home like this," I say. "I have no control over my life right now, but I promise to get back to you. And thank you. Thank you so much for helping me. You've been a light in all this."

Angela gives the slightest nod. "No worries. Now go."

We pile into Leo's black limousine once we're dressed and ready to go. The engine hums to life. I glance at the center console and ask Leo if I can borrow his phone to call Marie.

She answers on the first ring.

"Lila?"

"Yeah. It's me. You still up?"

"I couldn't sleep," she says. "I've had this awful feeling...about Dad."

I close my eyes. "Me too."

She exhales sharply. "Alexi said you were kidnapped, in a car crash, maybe dying. What's going on?"

"Don't believe anything she says," I murmur. "Or

Mom. Their stories never match."

"I stopped believing them weeks ago."

I nod, grateful for her steadiness. "Listen...I've dreamed about Dad three times now. And every time it ends in a basement. He's...trying to reach me. I'm heading to Oscar's place first. If he's not there, I'll keep looking. Basement by basement."

A long pause. "Marie?"

"I'm here." Her voice is barely audible. "How far are you?"

"Two hours, maybe less."

"I'll meet you there. Or halfway."

"What about Oscar?" she asks, her voice tight with dread.

"I'm not going in alone."

Another pause.

"So you really think your dream means something?"

"I don't know," I admit. "I just...need it to. You think it's crazy?"

There's a rustling on her end. Then, "Lila, even if it sounds crazy...I'll take crazy. If it gets us to Dad."

The line goes quiet. Then she hangs up.

I stare at the phone and feel the weight of hope settle like fog. Not sharp, not bright. But there.

Heavy. And real.

# 20
# Daddy!

We turn onto my old street.

Familiar red brick. Narrow sidewalks. Trash cans tucked too neatly. The townhouse is still there. Five stories, quiet, watching. I used to call it home.

I dial Marie. No answer. Then I try again.

"I used to run here," I say softly, almost to myself. "Every other day. For five years."

Neither Jack nor Leo responds. They've learned to let my thoughts drift.

The security camera on the door is fixed in place. Small, dark, always watching.

"We shouldn't park in front," I murmur.

Jack nods once. His gaze sweeps the street. Quick, trained, not casual.

A silver car rounds the corner. My pulse kicks.

I call Marie again.

"Are you in the silver car?" I ask.

"Yes."

"Don't stop near the house. There's a camera. Park further down."

I hang up.

The silence inside the car sharpens. Outside, the house doesn't move. But it sees. And I can feel something tightening. Something old. Something waiting.

As soon as Marie steps out of the car, I rush forward and wrap my arms around her. No words. Just the weight of relief, familiarity, and something that feels like home.

Then I notice the man stepping out of the driver's seat. Tall. Lean. Confident in that quiet way some men carry without trying. He moves to stand beside Marie, hands in his pockets, a trace of a smile already forming.

Marie's eyes sparkle. She beams. "Meet my fiancé, Alden!"

I blink.

"Get out of here..." It's all I can manage. Half shock, half joy.

I reach for his hand, shake it, then pull him into a hug that feels surprisingly easy.

"I'm thrilled for you," I say, meaning every word. "And it's great to meet you, Alden."

I glance at Marie, eyebrows raised. "When did this happen? And why didn't you say anything on the phone?"

The questions come fast, but underneath them, I'm happy for her. I really am. Even if the timing feels like something I wasn't prepared to carry. Still, in the midst of all the family drama, there's a kind of celebration wrapped around it, and that counts for something.

Then, Jack exits the car, catching Marie's attention. Noticing her curiosity about his identity, I quickly give a brief explanation of my chance encounters with Jack. Marie evaluates Jack for a moment, then says, "Well, everyone needs a hero." A small smile tugs at the corners of my mouth as we share a laugh.

The unexpected connection between Jack and Alden piques both Marie's and my interest. Our eyebrows raise in unison as we ask simultaneously, "You two know each other?"

Intrigued, I inquire further, "Where did you two meet?"

"In Quantico," Alden responds with a hint of mystery, unraveling a shared history between the newfound friends.

"Wow, is that where FBI training takes place?" I ask, my fascination evident.

Jack replies cryptically.

Marie, already aware of Alden's involvement in the FBI, nods in affirmation.

"Yes, I knew," she confirms.

"But did you have any inkling about Jack?" Marie questions me.

I shrug and smile mischievously.

"The man is an enigma," I declare.

"I've heard that before," Jack chimes in with a slight smirk, adding another layer of intrigue to his persona.

Marie's voice reverberates through the silent night, her words lingering in the air.

"So, what's the plan?" Marie asks.

“We go through the back,” I say. “Basement door. The spare key’s still under the pot. Once we’re in, we’ll need to kill the alarm.”

My heart is pounding. My voice stays level.

“Okay,” I add, “but here’s the real problem. What if Oscar wakes up?” I pause. Then ask it straight. “Who’s going to knock him out?”

The question hangs there, heavy.

No one answers.

Marie is the first to react. She shakes her head hard. “Definitely not me.”

Alden raises a brow. “You’re okay with him getting hurt?”

I exhale, slow and tight. “The man has made my life a living hell,” I say, low and clipped. “I don’t want him dead. I don’t even want him broken. But if it comes down to it, I want the right to shut him down. Just long enough.” I look at them both. “Unconscious. That’s it. No blood. No drama.”

A beat. “Anyone have a way to do that?”

The wind shifts. No one answers. But now they’re listening.

Both Jack and Alden chuckle.

"Let's hope it doesn't come to that," Jack interjects.

The three of them trail behind me, guided by a lamppost near the corner and a single porch light, flickering like it’s losing its nerve.

We reach the gate. Old, swollen, permanently stuck. Still stubborn after all these years.

Without a word, I climb over, landing hard on the other side. I crouch, feel for the latch from inside.

Jack's voice cuts through the dark.

"What are you doing?"

"Opening the door," I say quietly. "It's the only way it's ever worked." "I need to unlock it from this side. Don't worry, I've done it countless times," I reassure him. Once I unstick the gate, I let them in.

We reach the door. I kneel by the clay pot, brush aside the dead leaves, and lift it. Beneath, just like always. In a Ziploc bag. Inside: a single key and a slip of paper with a code taped to it.

I hand it to Jack. He doesn't speak, just shows it to Alden, who gives a slight nod.

"Ready?" Jack whispers.

I take a breath, deep and shaky. My heart's pounding like it wants out. I nod.

Jack fits the key into the lock. Slow. Precise. Time bleeds out around us.

Thirty seconds. That's what we'll have.

The lock clicks.

Alden moves fast, his fingers punching the code into the keypad just inside the frame. One beep. Then silence.

The alarm is down.

Jack's voice cuts through the stillness, low but sharp. "Move."

Marie and I rush forward, still amazed at how fast the two of them move. The chill of the basement wraps around me like a warning.

The door closes behind us with a soft thud.

Dim light spills from a nearby appliance. The fridge, maybe. Or, the air conditioner. I move toward it, drawn more by memory than sight.

Each step deliberate.

Each breath held.

My father's voice echoes somewhere inside me. Keep going. Don't stop now.

Jack, Alden, and Marie fall in behind me. The basement is colder than I remember.

We move slow through the dark. Without a word, Jack and Alden each pull out small LED flashlights. They'd come prepared. Of course they had. Their beams slice through the gloom, casting long shadows that twitch across the walls like something alive.

I offer a quiet, automatic thanks. No one answers. No one needs to.

The air thickens as we press forward. Damp. Still. A sharp undertone of old paint rises from the floor and stings my nose.

I flinch. Wrinkle it. Keep going.

"What's that smell?" Marie asks.

"Sorry about the smell," I murmur, the words barely louder than the creak of the floor beneath us. "There's a lot of paint in here. I called it my pretend project."

I glance at the wall, half-covered in faded strokes, some colors bleeding over each other like bruises.

"Oscar hated this room," I add. "Couldn't stand that something this...uncontained existed under his roof."

Marie's voice floats in from behind me. "Since when do you paint?"

I pause. "It's a long story." A beat passes in the dim light. "I'll tell you later."

Even moving cautiously, I hit my knee against something solid. Metal, maybe. The pain blooms sharp and immediate. I try to swallow it down, but a low curse escapes before I can stop it.

"You okay?" Jack asks, voice low behind me.

"Yeah," I breathe. "Me and darkness...we don't get along."

I keep moving. The throb in my leg dulls to a background pulse. The air wraps around me. Cold, close, almost sentient.

"In my dreams," I say, eyes locked on the far door, "Dad is in the bathroom. Lying there..."

But I can't finish. The words hang. Then fall. Silence answers.

Jack. Alden. Marie. Frozen. Watching.

Then, "Did you hear that?" Marie's voice is thin, barely above a whisper.

She raises the flashlight. The beam stutters, quivering as her hand trembles. It throws uneven light across the walls—edges flickering, growing, collapsing.

No one breathes.

Even the air has gone still.

Like the house is listening. And remembering.

"Where is the bathroom?" Marie queries.

“This way...” I murmur, nodding toward the door on the right.

Alden moves first. Marie follows close behind.

My pulse quickens with each step.

She reaches for the handle. A soft click.

Then silence. Marie gasps.

“Oh my God...Dad?”

Her voice cracks. The flashlight lifts, catching the edge of his face. Still. Pale. Slumped on the tiled floor like something forgotten.

“No... no... Daddy, please wake up...” she whispers, cradling his head against her. “Who did this to you?”

The words echo, unraveling in the dark.

I can’t breathe. The room tilts. My father, my father...is here. But not.

My knees give. Jack’s arms close around me, grounding me before I fall.

“Breathe,” he says, voice low at my ear. “You’ve made it this far.”

Tears blur my vision. I blink hard. The smell of mildew. Paint. Faint cologne still lingering in the air.

I draw in one breath. Then another.

And I stand. Because I need to.

“Dad? Dad...” I call him. My voice breaks as I fall to my knees beside him. Heat floods my face. I reach for him, but my hands shake.

“Is he breathing?” I ask, desperate, my words catching in my throat.

Marie leans in close, two fingers pressed gently to

his neck. "His pulse is weak," she says. "But it's there."

Relief and terror collide inside me.

"We have to call 911," I say.

Jack and Alden move without a word. Jack crouches low, assessing the angle, then gathers my father into his arms like it's instinct. I can hear his breath hitch under the weight, but he lifts him with control—shouldering the burden like he was made for it.

We head for the basement door. Quiet. Urgent. Focused.

Then, click. A switch. The room floods with light.

Everything freezes.

We are no longer in the dark. And someone else is here.

"What's going on here?"

Oscar's voice cuts through the air, sharp and loud, from the top of the stairs. He's backlit by the hallway light. His shadow spills down the wall.

Marie straightens, her voice tight. "You...what did you do to Dad?"

He ignores her. His eyes find me.

"Lila," he says, too calm. "What is this?"

I hold his stare. "We could ask you the same."

Oscar descends one step, then pauses.

Alden speaks, "Mr. Chambers, I'm going to need you to come with us. We have questions."

Oscar squints. "Who the hell are you?"

"Alden Escalante. FBI." He flashes the badge.

Oscar's face falters. His mouth opens, then closes.

A flicker of something. Not fear. But recognition.

We reach the door. Then the sound: sirens. Close. Loud. A firetruck. An ambulance.

I glance at Alden. "Who called 911?"

"I did," he says. "And backup."

He doesn't elaborate. Doesn't need to.

Oscar stands frozen, watching everything slip from his hands.

# 21
# Saving Grace

The sirens grow louder, then stop. Red lights dance across the house as the ambulance and fire truck come to a halt.

Two paramedics move fast, stretcher between them. Jack helps guide my father onto it. The man's weight seems heavier now, like something already letting go.

One paramedic presses two fingers against his neck. His brow tightens. The other sets up oxygen, dextrose—hands practiced, voice low and measured as he explains what's happening. A mask slips over my father's face. Tubes hiss. Velcro straps bind him to the stretcher.

Marie and I don't speak. We watch.

A call is made to the hospital. Vitals are read off. Time is logged. My father is dying in bullet points.

I cover my mouth with both hands. The sob slips out anyway. Quiet, but enough to shake me.

They lift him into the ambulance. Metal doors gape open like a mouth waiting to close.

A paramedic looks down at us, one hand on the handle.

"Anyone riding with him?" he asks.

The air holds still, waiting. Marie's sob echoes mine, a cracked mirror of grief. She wipes at her cheeks, trying to steady her breath. "Just... give me a second," she whispers.

Jack nods gently. Leo steps closer, a quiet presence beside her.

"We've got her," Jack says to me. "Go. Be with your father."

My gaze flicks to Alden, who hasn't moved from Oscar's side. His posture is all duty now, firm and alert. "He'll need to answer some questions," Jack adds, eyes narrowing toward Oscar.

I open my mouth to say something. Anything, but the words won't come. They clog my throat, hot and useless. So I just nod. One, slow, fragile nod. My legs feel brittle as I walk. The pavement dips, shifts beneath me. I reach the back of the ambulance, hand gripping the cold frame of the door.

Then a voice cuts through the weight of it all, firm, clinical.

"We need to go, Miss."

I climb in. The door shuts behind me with a hollow thud, sealing us into the blur between fear and hope.

The ambulance hums around us. Steady, enclosed, too bright. My father lies still beneath the harsh white light, his chest rising only because of the oxygen. Machines beep. Plastic crinkles. The air smells like antiseptic and plastic and metal fear.

A woman crouches near his head, hands working with practiced urgency. Olive skin, dark hair pulled into a tight bun. The other, pale, with red hair clipped short—stands by the monitors. His eyes flick to me, then back to the screen.

"Is he breathing?" My voice barely escapes.

"He has a pulse, but weak, " the woman says without looking up. "That's a good sign." Then her gaze meets mine. Calm, and clear. "I'm Candace. This is Greg."

"Lilanie," I say. The name feels foreign in my mouth.

They glance at each other. A flicker of recognition. Then Greg studies me, his forehead creased with a memory surfacing.

"Wait... I think I saw your picture on the news," he says. "You were the missing wife of Oscar Chambers, right? The one running for governor?"

I nod once. Small. Tired.

Greg scratches at his chin. "They didn't do you justice with that photo," he adds, almost as if it were casual. "You're beautiful in person."

His words thud in the air, sharp and misplaced.

I don't respond. Just look away. The silence in the back of the ambulance folds over me again. Thick, unwelcome, and pulsing with everything I haven't said.

Candace doesn't look away from me when she speaks. "Forgive my colleague," she says, voice low but firm. "He forgets his manners sometimes."

Greg shrugs, unbothered. "What? It's true."

I manage a brittle smile, the kind that doesn't reach my eyes. "It's okay."

But it's not. Not really. There's too much else pressing down.

I shift my focus, steering us away from the weight of compliments that don't belong in the back of an ambulance. "Do you think my dad will make it?" I ask, voice small, hands wringing in my lap.

Greg glances at the monitor, then at my father's face; too pale, too still. "We're doing everything by the book to stabilize him," he says, tone suddenly measured. "At this point, it's up to your father. His will to fight." He offers a faint smile. "But let's all pray for the best."

I nod slowly, eyes fixed on the rise and fall of my father's chest, each breath mechanical. My prayer is silent. Wordless. A quiet ache pulsing inside my ribs.

The hospital swallows him whole.

Sliding doors part, then close again, sealing off the stretchers and shouts, the monitors and fluorescent light. I'm left standing in the corridor, arms limp at my sides, as if something in me has been cut loose.

A nurse, not young, not old—places a steady hand on my shoulder. Her voice is low, practiced. "Stay here, Miss."

I don't respond. Can't.

She softens. "Grab a coffee or something." Her eyes hold mine. "We'll do the best we can."

The bench beneath me is unforgiving, metal, cold, meant for waiting. I stare at the emergency doors as if watching them long enough might make them open again. It doesn't.

A hand on my shoulder. I flinch, then turn.

Marie. Jack behind her. His eyes catch mine. Cool steel softened by something warmer. I want to collapse into him, to let the ache drain out. But I don't. I offer only a faint smile, and he answers with a quiet presence. He sits beside me, his hand finding mine like it's always belonged there. No words. Just weight, warmth, and witness.

Marie stands in front of us, arms folded tight. "Shall we inform Mom?"

The word *Mom* lands like a stone in my gut. I feel it before I speak.

"No." My voice doesn't shake. "I think she's the reason Dad's here."

It's not rage. Just clarity.

Marie doesn't argue. She just nods. Maybe she's known it too. Maybe we both have, for a long time.

"What about Alexi?"

"She'll find out eventually," I answer.

The clock ticks without mercy. We're still waiting. A vending machine hums behind me. Still no word. No one has come out.

I say a silent prayer for God to stay with my dad. Not to take him.

Not yet.

Across the room, Jack leans against the far wall, tall and still, his silhouette cast long in the fluorescent wash. He's holding a paper cup of hospital coffee, steam curling near his chin. He looks like he belongs nowhere and everywhere at once—watching, waiting, anchored by presence more than purpose.

I walk to him, quiet footsteps on waxed linoleum. "Jack..." My voice is low, careful. "You can go if you want. You need rest."

He lifts his gaze and tries for a smile. It falters. "I'm alright," he says. "I've had worse."

"You always say that. Are you sure?" His eyes don't waver. "Do you want me to stay?"

Something in me softens. Or maybe collapses. I nod. Not dramatic. Just enough. Just real.

"Coffee?" he asks, offering the cup he's holding. I take it and drink, the warmth grounding me more than I expected.

After long hours of waiting, the emergency room doors burst open. A woman in a wrinkled white coat strides out, coat flaring like wings behind her. Her hair is pulled into a haphazard bun, strands clinging to her temple. She moves fast, scanning the hall, the tension in her shoulders mirroring ours.

"Are you his family?" she asks, patting her coat for a stethoscope she doesn't seem to need.

Marie and I step forward. We nod.

"He's stable," she says, the breath catching in her throat before she lets it go. "Thank God."

Her voice lands like a thread stitching us back together.

It takes me a moment to place her. But then I see it, behind the exhaustion and the urgency. Dr. Jane

Rosenberg. My father's physician. She was the one he trusted, the one I used to sit across from in cold exam rooms, swinging my legs, pretending not to listen.

She meets my eyes. I think she remembers me, too.

Dr. Rosenberg is tall and wiry, yet her presence fills the room with an aura of strength that only decades of experience can provide. Her gaze meets mine, and something in her eyes tells me she shares my relief at seeing him survive.

"Thank you, Dr. Rosenberg...," I say through tear-stained cheeks, admiration for her skill oozing from my voice.

"Don't be thanking me yet; thank God or your father, he's' too stubborn to die." Rosenberg says.

My heart swells within me, and I breathe a sigh of relief. "He's in the recovery room. The nurse will guide you." She adds.

A few minutes later, a nurse appears, Filipino, maybe mid-forties, with gentle eyes and the kind of smile that steadies you without trying. Her name tag reads *Gina*. Her blue scrubs are freshly pressed, her dark hair pulled back in a tight bun.

"You can see him now," she says softly. "But just a few minutes. No physical contact, please." Her voice is kind, but practiced. She's done this before.

Marie and I nod, murmuring our thanks.

Jack steps back. "I'll stay by the door," he says quietly. "In case Oscar gets bold."

The hallway falls away as we step inside.

The smell of antiseptic hits first. Clean, sharp, inescapable. Then the light, too white, too loud. Everything sterile. Everything humming just beneath the surface.

And in the middle of it all, Dad.

Lying still. Eyes closed. Tubes tracing the map of his body. But his chest... it rises. And it falls. A rhythm. A lifeline. A miracle.

It's the most beautiful thing I've seen.

Marie doesn't speak at first. Just stares, frozen at the threshold.

Then, barely above a whisper, "Dad..." Her voice cracks.

And the room, for a breath, feels like it might break open with the weight of that one word.

Dad's eyelid flutters. Just once, but it's enough.

Marie gasps. Her whole face softens, tears tracing paths down her cheeks. She leans in, whispering something only he can hear. Something tender and broken and full of belief.

I step closer, the air thick with hospital quiet. My throat tightens, a lump forming behind it. Hope is heavy. Heavier than fear.

Five minutes pass. Maybe less. Time bends in rooms like this.

I slip out first, the weight on my shoulders shifting. Not gone, but lighter. Like something cracked open inside me and let the light in.

Jack is on the bench outside, same place as before. Still. Waiting. I sit next to him. The bench is cold.

His hand is warm. He doesn't speak, just turns his palm up for mine.

I take it. Squeeze it.

"Jack," I say. My voice barely there. "Thank you."

He gives a small nod. The kind that means more than words. And I know this moment won't last. Oscar is still out there. Still watching. Still capable of stealing this quiet if we let him.

Jack releases my hand, slow and silent.

And the silence between us grows. Not empty, but loaded. Like we're both bracing for the next break in the peace.

I stare at my sneakers, their laces tangled like the thoughts in my head. My fingers twist around each other, small anxious knots.

"Jack," I murmur. "I'm sorry for keeping you here like this. Please don't feel obligated to stay. If you have somewhere else to be..."

He grins. Not the full, charming one. But a tired, real one. The kind that still reaches his eyes and makes the lines around them crinkle.

"I'm free until next week," he says.

Relief slides through me like a breath I didn't know I was holding. I let it out with a soft smile.

"But," he adds, leaning back slightly, his voice dry with just enough humor to steady me, "since your... hus—Oscar—has already accused me of kidnapping you, maybe it's best if I stick around for a bit."

I huff a laugh. It escapes before I can help it. A small, startled sound.

For a moment, the tension lifts. Just enough to feel human again. The air between us feels lighter as we laugh at the absurdity.

"Were you saying you want to suggest a top-notch lawyer for me?" I ask after a pause.

"Yeah, but do you need to rush into it?" Jack replies, scratching his neck.

"Maybe I could call, introduce myself, see if they respond," I suggest. "Do you know them?"

His eyes gleam with recognition as he nods. "Yes, I used them when I divorced my ex-wife two years ago."

His words hang heavy.

My interest sharpens. "You're divorced?"

He nods, eyes crinkling with faint amusement.

"Why? How?" I push, curiosity flaring.

He laughs softly, rubbing his chin. "Like your situation, I found out she was unfaithful. She resisted signing the papers, so the lawyers pressured her. Eventually, she caved."

My eyes widen. "Why was she so resistant?"

Jack sighs, his head leaning against the cold wall. "She claimed she made a mistake, wanted to work on it," he says, disbelief in his voice. His fingers twist, a furrow deepening between his brows. He crosses his arms, as if holding himself together. "She suggested therapy, all that," he continues, bitterness lacing his words. "But I can't stand cheating. Trust is hard to regain." His eyes drop, shoulders sagging under the weight.

It's the first time Jack has opened up to me about

his life, and I don't take it lightly. There's a quiet weight to his honesty, and it stirs something in me.

I stare past him, lost in my own storm. Oscar wants me back. Not out of love, but fear. Fear that the fallout from our crumbling marriage will cost him the election.

A heavy sigh slips through my lips. If only things had gone differently. If only love had been enough.

Nerves coil in my stomach. I take a shaky breath and fidget with my hands, searching for steadiness.

"Do you think Oscar will give in?" I ask, barely above a whisper.

Silently, I pray—not for Oscar to change, but for a way out. For a miracle that doesn't come wrapped in conditions.

Jack's shoulders tense, and when he looks at me, there's a flicker of something. Guarded, and uncertain. He hesitates, then slowly shakes his head, lips pressed into a tight line.

"It's hard to say," he murmurs. "Your situation's... complicated. Politics changes the rules." He pauses, then softens his tone. "But let's stay hopeful. The right lawyer can make a difference. We'll make sure you've got the best."

The silence that follows isn't heavy. It's steady. A quiet understanding. And in his eyes, I catch a glimpse of something rare: sincerity... and just enough hope to hold onto.

# 22

# The Battle is On

Marie asks Alden if he knows someone. Someone who gets things done. Someone who can make sure no one gets into Dad's room. He nods once. That's all.

Two hours later, they arrive. Two men. Hulking. Silent. Arms folded behind their backs like they were sculpted that way. They don't speak. Don't blink. Muscle and stone. No one gets in unless we say so.

Marie walks ahead, her shoulders squared, the air around her shifting. Her voice is low, deliberate. She hands over the visitor list like it's an order. Not a request.

Inside dad's room, the air is still. Our father sleeps. When his eyes open, he scans the room, then land on us. A slow smile spreads across his face. Peace settles on him.

We speak in quiet tones, catching him up on small things. Marie, ever practical, ever tender, asks the question I wouldn't.

"Do you want to see Mom?"

His smile fades. He turns his head toward the window, away from us. The silence stretches.

The chill moves in without a sound.

"No," he answers in a firm voice.

After she's talking to Dad, she turns to the guards, voice steady, eyes sharp. "Mom's not allowed in," she says, and hands them a photo. Small, worn, our mother's face looking somewhere else, as if she already knew.

The guards take it without a word, their expression unchanged, stone to the core. When Mom finds out, it's like lighting a match near dry grass. She marches down the hall with her chin high, fire in her eyes, ready to go through them if she has to. The guards don't flinch. They don't need to. Their silence is a wall she can't scale. And for the first time in a long time, she's the one on the other side of the door. Powerless. Watched.

"Do you know who I am?" my mother hisses, sharp and low, the kind of voice meant to draw blood.

Her face glows with rage. Controlled, but only barely. When the guards refuse to step aside, something beneath the surface buckles. She doesn't raise her voice. Not exactly. But every word that follows lands like a slap: clipped, venom-laced, precise. Her hands move in wild, furious gestures, punctuation for the storm she's trying to contain.

The sound isn't volume—it's intensity. Tension sharp enough to wake the entire hall.

I hear her before I see her, my mother's voice cutting through the air as I head back to Dad's room, coffee in hand. I turn the corner and freeze. Then slip back into the shadows.

Watching. Waiting. Wondering how much damage she'll do this time. From the shadows, I watch the storm take shape. And I feel it again. That low, familiar dread blooming in my gut. The kind I've carried since childhood. Her fists are already clenched, arms tight at her sides, pacing in agitated loops before the hospital room door.

"What madness is this?" she mutters, voice like gravel under pressure. "Why can't I see my husband?"

Her jaw barely moves, but her eyes betray her. Wild with fury, glazed with disbelief.

The guards don't flinch. They don't have to. They step forward with quiet authority, guiding her away from the door, down the hall.

That's when the dam cracks.

The tirade that follows isn't loud but it's laced with venom. Unfiltered. Precise. No audience. No restraint. Just fury, sharp and breathless. It's not the volume that turns heads. It's the tension in her voice, so tight it could cut glass.

Later, I find her voice waiting in my new voicemail. I'd lost my phone in the crash, but I bought another. She calls me ungrateful. A traitor. Blames me for everything. Then, just before the message cuts off, her voice drops—lower, colder.

She says Oscar will never let me rest. That I'll regret all of it. That she hopes I rot in hell.

Click.

Silence.

But her voice lingers. Like smoke. Like a curse.

Ouch, that hurt.

A mother shouldn't say things like that. Not to her daughter. Not ever. But she did. And she meant every word. It wasn't the first wound. Just the most recent.

Growing up, she wasn't there. A nanny taught me how to tie my shoes. How to hold a spoon. How to stop crying without asking for comfort. My mother was elsewhere, always just out of reach. She missed every recital. Every timid bow onstage. I danced well, they said. People clapped. But the seat I searched for stayed empty.

Some absences leave more than silence. They leave shape. A hollow that keeps its form, even when you grow around it.

Now she's trying to claw her way back into my father's life. He won't see her. Won't even flinch when her name is mentioned.

She blames me for that too. And for Oscar, his falling numbers, his fading influence, his desperation. She says I've ruined everything.

Maybe she's right. Maybe I shattered something she was still trying to hold together. Or maybe I just stopped playing the pawn—stopped being the pushover they named me. Either way, there's a strange peace in knowing the storm has a shape now. And this time, I won't be the one sinking in it.

Victoria Pratt, my lawyer—the one I hired to push through a speedy divorce—called. Her voice was calm, deliberate. The kind of calm that makes you listen harder. She said the documents hadn't reached Oscar yet.

"They're set to land on his desk Monday," she said, pausing just long enough to let the weight settle. "Hours before the debate."

I didn't respond right away. Not because I didn't understand. But because I did. Too perfect. Too sharp. The kind of timing that doesn't happen by accident. It won't just rattle him. It will expose him.

And in politics, blood in the water is an invitation. Too close. Too pointed.

If anyone on that stage wants blood, they'll mention it. A pending divorce. A fractured image. A man who can't keep his house in order.

The timing isn't subtle. It's surgical.

The night we found Dad in the basement, the lights sliced through the dark like blades. Harsh. Unforgiving. The kind of light that doesn't hide anything. The medics moved fast, but the reporters were faster. Flashbulbs before questions. Headlines before breath. By morning, the opposition had already carved a story out of it—weakness, scandal, a family unraveling in shadows.

Before that incident, Oscar was golden. Leading in the polls. Filling arenas. The kind of man who made promises sound like destiny. And I was the quiet trick. The one who vanished. The wife he claimed to miss. The one he kept framed in grief.

New York fell for it, the story of a strong man broken by love. A husband in search of a missing wife.

Now, they'll see what's beneath the surface.

The divorce.

The father-in-law found in a locked basement.

The illusion cracking at the edges.

The headlines won't ask why. They'll only measure how far he's fallen. And nothing draws blood like a break, right before the debate. The night the FBI, the media, the ambulance, and a firetruck all showed up at Oscar's house, his numbers collapsed. Polls don't lie. Not when the sirens are that loud.

The footage looped for days—agents at the door, stretchers wheeled out, lights strobing across stone walls. The public didn't blink. They turned. A wave of headlines followed. Dark, relentless. Oscar went from front-runner to cautionary tale in a matter of hours.

He tried to control the damage. Sat in front of cameras with his hands folded and voice low. "I had no idea he was in my basement," he said, brows drawn together just enough to look human. It almost worked. He almost looked like a man blindsided by chaos.

But when Marie and I spoke to Dad, the truth landed quiet and heavy. He didn't want to press charges. Didn't even want his name in the papers.

"It'll stain the family," he said. "Let it go."

He'd rather swallow the whole thing than watch us come undone in public. That's the kind of damage Oscar doesn't understand. The kind that doesn't show up in polls.

On the last day of our dad's hospital stay, Alexi comes to visit Dad. Standing in the hallway and talking to the guards, her facial expression shows frustration.

I hesitate at the edge of the hallway, tucked back in shadow, waiting for Marie to arrive and take the lead. But it's too late. Alexi sees me.

Her eyes narrow, her voice rising before I can speak. "Why can't I be with Dad alone? Did you and Marie set me up? You turned him against me, didn't you?"

Her frustration spills over, flushed across her cheeks. She's not crying. Not yet. Just trembling with the kind of anger that's built over years, not days.

Marie's voice slices through the air behind me, calm and cold. "Stop being paranoid. Grow up, Alexi. Be grateful you even get the chance. Or else—"

"Or else what?" Alexi snaps, turning toward her.

Marie steps forward, slow and sure. Her smile is too pleasant for the words she's about to say. "Or else you end up like Mom. On the list."

She laughs, light and dismissive, then throws me a wink like we're in on some private joke. But there's no joke. Not really. Just tension stretched thin and a family that's learned how to weaponize love.

Marie leans in close, her breath warm against my ear. "Bad news alert," she whispers. "Oscar and Mom are downstairs. Lobby."

A shiver skims my spine. "Thanks," I whisper back, pulse picking up.

She touches my arm. "Is Jack coming?"

"He'll be here soon," I say, giving her shoulder a quick, reassuring squeeze.

Then, Alexi's voice cuts through the air like a blade. "What are you two whispering about?"

Her eyes flick between us, sharp with suspicion. She's always been good at sniffing out secrets. Mostly because she assumes everyone's keeping one from her.

Marie and I share a glance. We don't answer. We don't need to. We walk past her and push open the door to Dad's room.

"Dad," Marie calls out, hesitation lacing her voice. "Alexi's here."

The words barely land before Alexi brushes past. At his bedside, her composure unravels, quietly, quickly.

She takes his hand. Her eyes brim, spill. "I'm so sorry this happened," she says, her voice splintering. "How...how did you end up in a basement?"

The question doesn't land. It drifts. Hangs in the stale hospital air, untouched.

Dad doesn't answer. Instead, he runs his hand along her back, slow and rhythmic, as if memory can be soothed away.

He's always known where her loyalty lies—closer to Mom, even now. Still, he holds her.

His face stays unreadable. A still lake, hiding its depth. But the silence is loud. Something fractured. And though he's back, he's not entirely here. Whatever happened in that basement, he's keeping it buried. And the grief of it, the not-saying, the not-knowing—seeps into all of us.

Marie approaches quietly. "Are you okay?" she asks.

He nods, *yes*. But the word stretches longer than it should. Tired. Threadbare. The look in his eyes says more: *I've had enough.*

"Girls," he starts. He's perched on the edge of the bed, shoulders rounded, thinner than I remember. He rubs his palms together, old calluses, pale scars. Like he needs to remind himself he's still here.

His eyes sweep across us, Alexi, Marie, me. He looks like he's searching for a way to ease into it. There isn't one.

"Since I've got you all here," he says slowly. "And I don't know when I will again..." He pauses, fingers cracking at the knuckles. "There's no right time to say this." Another pause. "But now." He exhales through his nose, eyes dropping to his hands again. "I know it's not easy to hear," he says. "But I'm divorcing your mother."

Alexi's breath catches, short, sharp inhales as tears rise. She doesn't speak, just crumbles quietly beside the bed.

Marie and I stay still. Neutral. But inside, something loosens. Relief, maybe. Maybe now he'll stop hurting. Maybe now he won't have to walk on eggshells.

Still, the question curls at the back of my mind: What did Mom do this time?

Marie breaks the silence. Her voice is calm, but edged. "It took you long enough, Dad."

Alexi recoils. "Marie," she snaps. "Don't say that. That's cruel."

Marie scoffs, arms crossed. "You know how Mom treats him."

Alexi's eyes go wide, her voice breaking as she turns to our father. "But Dad... you always said divorce was wrong. That we fight to stay. Why now?"

He shrugs, barely a movement. "I thought it was wrong too," he says quietly. "Turns out, I was wrong about a lot of things."

It's strange how things arrive in pairs. Dad divorcing Mom. Me leaving Oscar. A matching set. Two parakeets in separate cages, flapping against the bars. Maybe this is what freedom looks like. Not one clean break, but two. Two chances. Two paths. Diverging quietly toward something better.

I've decided to stay with Dad until he's well enough to return to work. He hasn't said anything, but I can tell he knows. Marie and I exchange glances, equal parts disbelief and resignation.

Then, suddenly, Marie tells me, "I think I'll surprise Dad. Tell him I'm engaged."

I blink. "He doesn't know?"

She smiles, but there's sorrow in it, like something cracked behind her eyes. "He disappeared the night Alden proposed," she says. "I never got the chance."

Three hours later, after the final signature and too many nods from nurses, Dr. Rosenberg appears.

"You're free to go, old coot," she says, a hand on Dad's shoulder. "Don't be too hard on yourself. You're lucky. Most men don't have daughters like these."

Dad just nods, eyes on the floor.

We step into the lobby. And there they are.

Mom. And, Oscar.

She spots him first, Dad. Her eyes flare, sharp and bright, and she starts toward him like a storm uncoiling.

"Jeremy... Jeremy!" she calls. Her voice cuts through the lobby.

Dad steps back instinctively, shoulders tightening.

Two security guards intercept her. "Ma'am, please step aside," one of them says, calm but firm.

Everything stops. People look. Time freezes under the harsh lights. The waiting room stills, breath held.

Oscar doesn't move. He watches me, unwavering. Like I'm already his again. Like this mess doesn't matter.

But Jack stands just behind me. Close. Still. Unmoving. Not saying a word, but present in a way that steadies me.

Alexi hovers near the corner, arms crossed, eyes fixed on the floor. She's already begun the act of disassociating, pretending she's not one of us. And maybe right now, none of us want to be.

Mom strides forward, her voice climbing with each step. "What are you doing?" she snaps at the security guard. "That's my husband. I have a right to be with him!"

Marie catches her arm, tugging gently, urgently. "Please, Mom...don't."

But Mom pulls away, and turns toward me.

The fire in her eyes doesn't dim. "What have you been telling your father?" she spits, closing the space between us.

Her fingers twitch—that familiar flick, that awful pause before the strike. The same motion from her birthday.

I don't flinch this time. I just stare. But the blow never lands. Dad steps between us, his hand clamping around her wrist mid-air. The grip is firm. Controlled. Just enough pressure to stop her. His eyes are steady. Angry, but contained. The kind of anger that makes people stop moving.

"Enough, Edwina," he says, voice low. "You've done enough."

She opens her mouth, but he cuts her off.

"You'll hear from our lawyers soon." It's quieter, just for her. But final.

For a second, she just stands there. Shocked. Speechless. The silence stretches. Then something in her face crumples, and she steps back, slowly, wordless.

Dad leaves her standing there, stunned, still processing what he just said. I watch him go and wonder. What did she do to break him like that? What choice, what final act, made him walk away?

As I turn to follow, Oscar grabs my wrist. His grip is firm. Possessive.

Jack steps in instantly, the space between us closed in a blink. Solid. Protective. Ready.

I place a hand on his arm, grounding him. "It's okay, Jack."

Dad hesitates at the exit, casting a quick glance back. I catch Marie's eye and nod. "Can you help him to the car?" I ask gently.

She understands. She goes.

Now it's just me. Oscar. And the weight of everything unsaid.

Jack doesn't move far. I feel him nearby—his presence, his steadiness. I inhale deeply. The air is thin, but it fills me.

"Thanks, Jack," I say, my voice low. "I'll talk to him. Once and for all."

I meet his gaze. There's no fear in it. He nods once. Silent, sure. Like a promise.

Oscar's eyes flick to Jack, measuring him. There's a flicker of unease. He straightens, trying to reassert control.

"She's my wife," he says, voice low but laced with disdain. "You have no right to be here. No right to be with her."

Jack doesn't flinch. His gaze stays level, solid, still. Oscar looks away first. His edge dulls. Something falters. When he turns back to me, his tone shifts. Softer. Almost pleading.

"Lila...come home with me."

I shake my head, the weight of it slow and final. "After all you've done?"

His eyes search mine, blue and desperate. He steps closer.

"Why not? We had a life. Would you really throw it away?"

The words land with a thud. As if *he's* the one being left. As if he doesn't see the irony. I blink. Is he serious? He's the one who broke it. Split the life he's now asking me to salvage. And yet, he's the one asking for mercy.

"Are you for real?" I ask, voice low but cutting. "You think I could trust you after everything? The cheating. The crash. Trying to have me institutionalized?"

My breath catches, but I don't flinch. "You sent men after me, Oscar. You wanted me gone."

"I didn't tell them to shoot," he says. "They acted on their own." He tries to soften his voice. "Can't we just move on? Start over?"

"So you admit the cheating?"

Silence.

He shifts his weight. Looks away. The silence says more than anything he could've confessed.

"What would it take for you to be with me again?" he asks.

I laugh. Bitter, tired. "Nothing, Oscar. The damage is already done."

"Please...Lila."

I meet his eyes. Hold them. Inside me, a knot of anger coils tight.

"Then tell me the truth. Look at me. Did you ask

someone else to marry you?"

His eyes dart. His hands twitch.

"Of course not," he says with a forced laugh. "That's ridiculous."

"Liar," I whisper. "I was there, Oscar. I saw the whole thing. Don't deny it."

His eyes dart. His hands twitch.

He falters. "It was supposed to be staged," he says weakly. "A stunt. No one was supposed to see."

"Staged?" I scoff. "What, you're rehearsing betrayal now? Playing games inside our marriage? I can't forgive you for that."

He steps closer, his hand landing hard on my shoulder, fingers digging in. "Don't be too high and mighty, Lila. You'll come back to me. You always do, and we're not done, Lila," he growls. "I know you've been using cash. Living like a ghost. But you'll come crawling back. Once your little escape burns out."

I yank away from him. Turn. Walk.

He lunges again—but Jack is there, between us. A wall.

Oscar's face tightens, a flicker of annoyance breaking through his calm. Then he sees Jack's arms around me.

"Get your hands off my wife," Oscar says, his voice low and firm.

But Jack doesn't budge. He stays right where he is, determined to protect me.

But Oscar isn't backing down. "What are you going to do, huh?" he sneers from behind me. "Go get a job? You've never worked a day in your life." Then louder, angrier: "You can't divorce me either. You have nothing."

I stop. Turn back.

"Why not?" I ask.

His smirk returns.

"You'll get nothing," he says. "You signed a prenup. The house. The accounts. Everything. It's mine. What do you have, Lila? Your daddy? There's nothing left."

My stomach tightens.

"What do you mean?" I ask slowly. "What happened to dad's money?"

He smiles. Cold. Confident.

"Your mother drained it. Said I needed the funds for my campaign." He shrugs, like it's a joke.

A chill runs down my spine. Is that why Dad changed? Why he never wanted to see mom?

Then the memory returns, my father in the basement.

"What was he doing down in your basement, Oscar?" I ask, my voice hardening. "Did you have something to do with it?"

Oscar's expression flattens. "Don't be ridiculous," he snaps. "Why would I risk my candidacy? Invite scandal?"

He's good at lying. I know it. Except, not this time. His eyes don't blink. His voice doesn't waver.

"Then who?"

There's a pause. Just long enough.

And then, quiet. Certain.

"Ask your mother."

She marches toward us, eyes narrowing, jaw tight.

My voice trembles. "What did you do, Mom?"

She stops. Her stare sharpens, lips curling. "Stay out of it," she hisses. "It's none of your business."

The hatred isn't subtle. It never is.

I step closer. My chest rises and falls with every breath "Did you have anything to do with Dad being in the basement?"

Her eyes shift. Not toward me.

Away.

The pause is too long. The silence, unbearable.

My breath catches. I step back.

"You did," I whisper. Then louder: "You almost killed him."

She doesn't deny it.

"How are you capable of something like that?" My fists clench at my sides.

I push forward, the words catching fire as they rise. "You tried to institutionalize me. You'd do anything to get what you want. You're cold. Ruthless."

She doesn't flinch, but her jaw tightens.

"You dare speak to me like this?" she spits. "I need you to come home. With Oscar."

There it is.

"Make me," I say, voice flat.

"You disrespectful child,"

Her hand flies up. But this time, I catch it mid-air.

"Stop with the hand, Mother," I say. My grip tightens around her wrist. "You can hit me, scream at me, call me whatever you want. I'm not going back to Oscar. I'm not staying near him."

Tears sting the corners of my eyes, but I don't let them fall. "I'm glad Dad left. You drove him to it. You drive everyone away."

I let go of her wrist. She doesn't move.

"I spent years hoping we'd fix things," I continue, voice softening. "But you never wanted that. Nothing I did was ever enough for you."

I pause.

"And now, I'm done."

Her silence is the coldest thing in the room.

"I hope when the silence finally catches up to you," I say, "when the house is empty and no one answers your calls, you remember us."

Then I turn. She calls my name. Her voice rises behind me, shrill and wordless, but I don't stop.

It's over.

I feel it in my chest. A loosening. Like a thousand thorns pulled free.

Oscar follows. Of course he does.

I stop. Turn slowly to face him.

My voice is calm. Almost quiet. "Thank you, Oscar. For the prenup. And wait for those divorce papers on your desk."

A beat.

"You've made it so much easier to leave you."

A hollow laugh escapes, dry, empty. Just air. Then I walk away.

And this time, no one follows.

Except Jack, who's walking beside me.

# 23
# Cottage Life

After two hours of winding roads, the car drifts beneath tall pines and cliffs sharp as teeth. When Jack eases to a stop, Dad steps out and inhales. The air is sharp with pine. Below, the lake glitters. Wide, still, and waiting.

The cottage sits just above the slope. Weathered, quiet. Right where it always was, even in his mind.

A second car pulls in, Mr. Flemming, Agosto, and Rainer. Dad's oldest friends. Uncle Robert arrives not long after, parking crooked in the gravel, already waving.

Dad lifts a hand in return, the corners of his mouth turning up. Something in his chest eases. He doesn't say a word. He doesn't have to.

Jack and I leave Dad surrounded by voices louder than ours. Laughter, a familiar cadence of old friends. He barely notices us slip out.

We carry his things in silence. The cottage swallows our steps.

Once everything is in place, Jack checks his watch. "I've got to head to the office," he says, voice low.

I nod. But something in me resists the moment ending.

"Thank you," I say, and my voice is too soft, too small for all it's trying to hold. "For...everything. I don't know what I would've done without you."

Jack's eyes meet mine. Still, and steady. A flicker of something passes between us. Maybe understanding. Maybe the quiet cost of loyalty. Then he turns to go.

But I move, quick, without thinking. My arms wrap around him from behind, my forehead pressing into his back. He doesn't speak. Doesn't move. Just breathes.

"Really... thank you," I whisper.

His body stills. Then he turns, his hands brushing my arms as if I'm something fragile. He holds me there, but not tightly. Just enough.

"You've thanked me enough," he says. His smile is there, but faint, like a promise fading into morning light.

I search his face. "Will I see you again?"

He chuckles, a low sound, intimate. "You won't get rid of me that easily."

Then, tilting his head, he adds, "Besides...if you ever need someone to investigate something, I doubt you'd settle for three stars."

I laugh. Loud. Too loud. But it breaks the heaviness.

As he walks out the door, I stay still, watching. I'm not sure what we are. Client and investigator, technically. But there's more in the pauses, the glances, the way silence sometimes settles between us like a shared secret.

He hasn't said anything. Maybe that's for the best. I'm still married, after all, even if it's just on paper and old promises. I don't want to add another layer to the mess. Not yet.

So I let it be. One day at a time. When the truth of my feelings demands a voice, I'll meet it then.

I lean against the doorframe, arms folded tight, as he strides toward the cluster of Dad's friends. They welcome him easily—handshakes, smiles, the kind of laughter that echoes like home.

Dad looks up, grinning at something Jack says. There's a question, an answer, another burst of laughter.

Then Jack glances up toward me. He lifts his hand, waving casually, but there's a flicker in his eyes I can't name. A glint of something...knowing. It brushes against my chest, light as breath, then drifts down like a feather I can't catch. Then he turns. Walks toward his car.

I stay in the doorway, still leaning, still unsure. But smiling.

Dad, Uncle Robert, and the others talk about everything but business. Their voices stay light, laughter easy. Not once do they mention the days he was gone. But I know they all remember. They were the ones who searched. It's as if silence is their pact.

In the morning, one by one, they hug him goodbye. No speeches. Just firm embraces, quiet words. Their eyes are bright, not from denial, but from something harder to hold onto. Hope, maybe. Or the ache of borrowed time.

They leave with promises to meet again. No one says *if.* Only *when*.

"Are you sure you don't want me to stay?" I hear Uncle Robert ask as he is the last one to leave.

"Nah, I'm okay. I bet Susan and the kids are waiting for you," Dad says.

"I can just call and let them know I'm needed," Uncle Robert replies.

"Go..." Dad gently pushes Uncle Robert away. "Lila is here, and she'll make sure I'm well taken care of," Dad explains.

Uncle Robert, towering over me, says, "You better call me if something happens, or you'll get a sermon from me with no end," he warns.

I smile and reassure him.

After a few more minutes coaxing Uncle Robert to leave, Dad slips into the shed. The creak of the old door. The soft clatter of tools shifted. He emerges with his fishing rod in hand, an unchanged quiet ritual.

Then he walks the path to the dock, alone.

Four weathered Adirondack chairs wait at the edge, their backs to the world, facing the water like sentinels standing guard. We used to sit there back when we were teens: Dad, Marie, Alexi, and me. No one talked much. We didn't need to. We just watched. The sun would vanish behind the hills in slow motion, and the lake would catch the last bit of light— hold it for a moment, like something sacred. Then let it go.

One by one, the stars came out. We never spoke of them, but we watched—always together. The waves lapped softly beneath us, a rhythm that felt like breath. Safe. Familiar.

Mom never came. Not once.

Dad always had a reason.

"She's with friends."

"She's having dinner with friends."

"She running an errand."

Excuses, polished and effortless. As if he was protecting her. Or protecting us from her absence.

But now, she's out of the picture. At least for a while. And I wonder what that means for him. For his future. For the house. For the money he never talks about but I know he worries over.

I won't bring it up. Not yet. I'll wait until he does. If he does.

The ticking of the grandfather clock presses against the silence. Each second loud and steady. A slow, deliberate countdown. Marie and Alden will be here soon. They're going to tell him. About the engagement. And everything might shift, again.

His shoulders slump in that way that says more than words ever could— not tired, exactly. Worn. Fractured. Hollowed out in places no one sees. He tells me he needs to be alone. So I don't sit beside him. I don't speak.

I just watch.

Maybe he doesn't know. Maybe he does, and chooses not to meet my gaze. Either way, I stay. Because something in me won't let go of the sight of him like this. Still, silent, unraveling beneath the surface. And I can't stand the way it feels. Like he's drifting just out of reach, and I'm the only one who sees it.

I go to the bathroom for a moment, and when I get out, I hear Marie and Alden arrive. Marie's voice carries through the hallway, "Where's Dad?" My stomach drops at the familiar question.

"By the docks!" I say, pointing my finger in the direction of the waterfront. But as Marie and Alden follow my outstretched arm with their eyes, there is no sign of life on our way to the dock. My heart begins to race as fear begins to set in. I start sprinting, desperation fueling my every step.

"Dad...?" I scream out into the empty harbor, my voice echoing off the surrounding forest.

The sun has just risen, and Dad's fishing rod is lying on the docks.

I fling myself into the lake. The shock hits instantly, ice biting through my clothes, turning fabric into weight. Still, I push forward, arms slicing through the water, searching for him.

I've known this was coming. Felt it tightening around the edges of yesterday, in every glance, every silence. I've been watching him like a hawk, waiting for the moment the surface breaks, and takes him.

And now, it's happening.

I don't shout. There's no time for sound. Just motion. Just breath and fear and the ache of cold closing in.

Marie's voice is a desperate plea, "Is he there?" As I breathe for some air.

I plunge again, the cool rush swallowing me whole. My legs kick hard as I cut through the water, heading toward the deep end. A sudden splash beside me. I glance over, Alden.

He's swimming fast, harder than I've ever seen. Each stroke drives him deeper, farther. He vanishes for a second beneath the surface, then resurfaces, then dives again.

My lungs tighten. The burn creeps in fast, urgent. I flip onto my back, gasping, throat raw with the sudden need for air. My chest heaves, heartbeat thudding like a warning. I blink water from my lashes.

He's still going. Too deep. Too far.

As I am about to go back into the water, Alden rushes up, and Dad in his arms.

Marie stands nearby, her face streaked with tears as Alden gently places Dad onto the dock.

"Call 911," Alden snaps.

Marie fumbles for her phone, yanking it from the pocket of her brown parka. Her fingers tremble as she dials.

Alden's hands are already on Dad's chest—pressing, counting, pressing again. His movements frantic, controlled only by instinct and desperation.

I stand frozen, lips moving in a prayer I can't form into words.

Then, a gasp. A cough. The silence breaks. Dad lurches, sputtering, water spilling from his mouth.

Marie drops to her knees beside him. Her body curls inward, shaking with sobs. Relief. Shock. Grief that came too close. Just the echo of breath returning.

"Why did you do that, Dad?" she screams through sobs. Her accusing glare pierces my heart as deep guilt surges through my veins. "We just saved you from dying! Why would you do something like this again?" Her voice is laced with accusation.

My dad slowly sits up, his gaze filled with a mixture of regret and guilt. He reaches out across the waves of Marie's emotions and says in a low voice, "I'm sorry, Marie. I lost it. I wasn't thinking. All I wanted was to swim, but something held me back from swimming back to the surface. I thought of going deeper and just letting go of it all."

Marie's sobs seem to shake the dock. Even Alden is moved by his fiancée's tears.

Marie grabs our father's hand, tears flowing freely down her face. Her voice catches in her throat as she pleads and screams at the same time, "Whatever Mom did to you, Dad, it's not worth your life. Who would walk me down the aisle if you're not here? Who?" She collapses on the dock, her emotions seemingly drained.

My dad's eyes widen in surprise, and his mouth opens slightly. He coughs and blinks a few times before finding his voice. "What? You're getting married?" His expression softens, becoming more hopeful.

"I didn't want you to find out this way," Marie says. "This is my fiancé, Alden."

Alden extends his hand for a shake and smiles confidently as he says, "How do you do, sir?"

My dad shakes Alden's hand firmly before looking back at Marie with a proud smile, with water dripping down his face. He then, squeezes Alden's shoulder and offers him a half-smile. "Thanks for saving me, son. You'll find out soon enough why we're made of family drama," he jokes in his attempt to lighten the mood.

My laughter fills the lake, joined soon after by Marie's. His face breaks into a relieved smile, and his shoulders relax as if all the tension has drained out of him.

"Now, this is a call for celebration!" he exclaims. "Do we have any champagne?"

"I brought some, just in case," Marie forces her smiles.

"I invited Alexi too," Marie says, her voice trembling slightly.

"Did you invite your mom?" Dad's face changes, his brow furrowing in concern.

"No? Do you want me to?" Marie asks hesitantly.

"Nope." The word comes out with a finality that makes it clear this is not an open discussion.

The ambulance arrives at the cottage ten minutes later. Dad and Alden speak to the paramedics as one of them checks Dad's vitals.

Later that day, we begin to build a fire while Marie receives a text from Alexi saying she can't make it due to Mom being drunk and indisposed.

After dinner and the clinking of glasses, with Dad asleep for the night, we find ourselves in the kitchen, loading the dishwasher, when the conversation turns to Mom.

“Mom’s been drinking?” I ask, the shock slipping out. “And she got arrested?”

Apparently, she harassed a waitress at some bar.

"Yup, sometimes life throws us unexpected curveballs," Marie replies. "Isn't it strange that we don't feel Mom's presence in this cottage?" she muses.

"That's because she hardly ever comes here, except that one time when they thought I was missing!" I explain.

When Alden steps outside to answer a phone call, I tell Marie everything I know. Her expression shifts from shock to deep thought as the reality of the situation dawns on her. "That's why Dad wants to end things with her?" she mumbles.

Marie stares out the window, her jaw clenched in frustration. "I can't believe Mom did this to us," she mutters.

I sigh and look away. "She overdid it this time," I say quietly.

***

Monday morning seems to arrive too quickly, with Victoria's gentle reminder that the court papers have been served. Then my new phone buzzes in my pocket, and I see a text from Oscar,  his words glaring up at me in all bold letters:

Oscar: YOU BITCH. YOU CAN'T DIVORCE ME."

I ignore the first few buzzes. But the phone won't stop. Finally, I pick up. Of course, it's my mother. She's already mid-sentence—shouting, cursing, her words crashing over each other so fast I can't catch them.

I don't respond. Just wait for a breath. "Goodbye, Mom," I say.

And I hang up.

Jack appears at the edge of the path, dragging my suitcase behind him I left at the inn. The envelope is clamped under his arm, edges curled with sweat. His shirt clings to him, creased, damp, shaped to his body like it remembers the heat.

At the door, he pauses, catching his breath. I open it before he knocks.

"Hi," I say, too quickly. My voice cracks.

His silver eyes lock on mine. A smile. That smile. My stomach flips, traitorous.

Behind me, Daddy sits by the fireplace, still as stone, and reading the newspaper. His hands tremble just slightly at the corners.

Jack's voice is quiet, but it lands like thunder.

"Have you seen the news?"

"Why?" I whisper, each beat of my heart threatening to break through my ribs. "Is there something wrong?"

Daddy lowers the paper. His eyes, usually soft, are hard now—dark. Measuring.

Jack steps forward, unsure. His voice catches. Nothing comes. Daddy clears his throat, breaking the silence with a question that hangs in the air like smoke. "What news?"

"Lila filed for divorce against Oscar. It's all over the news."

I watch my dad closely, noticing a tiny hint of satisfaction on his face that only I can detect — the way his lips turn upwards ever so slightly as he mutters, "Serves him right."

Daddy turns to me, eyes lit with something boyish. "It's about time, kiddo."

He gets up, reaching for my head—then pauses, clocking the new hair. A chuckle rumbles up from his chest. I can't help but smile.

He heads for the door. "I'm going fishing," he calls out, full of the same misplaced confidence as always.

I stiffen. Last time didn't end well.

But he must sense it. His hand lingers on the doorframe. "Don't worry, kiddo," he says, softer now. "Nothing will happen this time. Future looks promising to me." His grin is wide, easy. Too easy.

Then he glances back at Jack. "Stay, young man. Stay." And he's gone.

Jack asks if everything is okay, and I tell him what happened. When he sees me sitting by the window, watching my dad's silhouette as he marches down the cobblestone path toward the docks, Jack understands that I will be there until my dad returns.

So, he sits next to me, feeling relaxed. I ask, referring to the news, "Is it bad?" I ask him tentatively, "What does he say?"

I usually stay away from news reports and online articles, knowing how depressing some of them can be. Too much bad news is always a quick way to ruin my mood and give me unnecessary anxiety.

"He seemed pretty angry when someone interviewed him, but he didn't make any comment at all." Jack's voice is low and strained. I look at him and smile. And forget about the news that spreads.

He holds an envelope tightly in one hand and slowly places it on the chair between us. His face is expressionless as he looks at me with hooded eyes.

"I came for this too," Jack says, voice low. There's a bitterness to it, like he's been holding it in too long.

He lifts the envelope, weighing it. "You might not want what's in here."

The air feels heavy, as if even my thoughts are afraid to move. "This is the last one," he adds. "But it may sting more than the rest."

He starts to rise. Without thinking, I reach for his hand. "Will you stay?"

The question hangs between us, bare and exposed.

I try to soften it. “Only if you’re not busy. I know you probably have—”

“I’m free all day,” he says, not looking away. A smile edges in. “I’m all yours.”

Relief blooms in my chest. I bite my lower lip, willing my face not to give me away.

# 24
# Truth Sucks!

I bite my lip, hands clenched tight. My brow furrows as I glance up at Jack. The question hangs between us like smoke.

"Do you think I should find out the truth... or let it stay buried?"

He doesn't answer right away. His gaze drifts to the lake. Dark. Still. Then back to me. His eyes hold something I can't name. Not pity. Not hope. Something harder.

"It's hard to say what you should do," he says quietly. "Truth hurts. But if you're content living with a lie... that's yours to carry. Just know, truth has a way of surfacing. Sooner or later."

The wind shifts. A bird calls somewhere in the trees. Everything feels too quiet.

His words make sense. They always do. But I still grip the illusion. I've lived inside it so long, it feels like home.

I've wanted to know. Ever since I learned who Oscar really is. But now, standing at the edge of it, I hesitate. This feeling, the slow ache of avoidance. The safety in not knowing.

How long can I keep walking blind?

I already know about the affairs. Each betrayal etched in me, like bruises I've learned by heart. But when Jack said this last one might cut deeper, I believed him. And the truth is, I don't know if I'm ready to bleed again. However, I have to face it, no matter how much it drags me through the dirt.

My hand trembles as I reach for the envelope, my fingers fumbling to open its flap.

Son of a gun.

Alexi and Oscar?

Inside the envelope, I find a photo. Dimly lit, too intimate for friends. They're seated close in a restaurant, leaning in, faces soft with something that looks like love. My chest tightens.

I turn the page.

A newborn. Wrapped in a striped hospital blanket. Eyes closed. Fragile. Real.

The dam breaks. Tears fall fast, hot and unchecked. I blink hard. But the image stays, blurred now, but burned into me.

I lift my eyes to Jack. My voice barely comes. "Since when?"

He doesn't answer right away. His jaw tenses. His silence is answer enough.

The memory hits like a punch. On my wedding day, she said she was sick. Pale. Quiet. I'd believed her. Was she really sick or already pregnant then?

"They have a baby?" I ask, the words warped by disbelief.

Jack doesn't speak. He just looks away, and something in his face folds in on itself.

I steady my breath, forcing the next question past the lump in my throat. "Where's the child now?"

I try to keep my voice flat. Controlled. But it trembles at the edges. Even if it destroys me, I have to know. I can't keep living in the dark. The sad truth is etched across his face like scripture—no need for words. But then he gives them anyway.

"They put her up for adoption," he says softly. His grey eyes meet mine and hold. Unflinching.

My stomach drops through the floor. Lands somewhere far below the earth, buried in something cold and irreversible. It feels like concrete settling inside me. Heavy. Permanent.

"A girl?" I whisper. The word tastes like ash.

I start pacing. My pulse pounds—steady, insistent. Each thought crashing into the next. My sister loved him first. Quietly, maybe. But it was real. She smiled. Encouraged me. Handed me over like I was borrowing something she'd already lost.

What was she thinking?

A tear slides down my cheek. I wipe it away, angry at myself. Angrier for not seeing it then. For believing her love just...disappeared. Like that happens.

Oscar's betrayal doesn't scream. It seeps. Slow. Venomous. A heat that never cools. And Alexi. God, Alexi. Will I ever forgive her? I'm not sure.

But I know this, something inside me broke clean. And I don't think it's coming back the same.

My father's footsteps echo against the floor. Measured, heavy. He stops just inside the doorway, his gaze locking onto mine. Reads the room instantly. The silence between Jack and me. My posture. My face. He knows something's wrong.

His brows pull together, worry already forming before a word is spoken. I want to shield him. But it's too late for that. My hands tremble as I reach for the photo resting on the wooden bench. I don't speak. Just offer it to him.

He takes it slowly, as if bracing for impact. A sharp inhale. Then stillness. He stares at the image. At the child, and something in him falters. His guard, usually ironclad, fractures in the quiet.

At first, he's gentle. Confused. But the confusion curdles. His eyes sharpen. His jaw sets. The lines in his face deepen with something darker: not just shock. Not just hurt. But the cold, steady rise of betrayal.

He doesn't look at me. Just keeps staring at the photo, as if it might answer the question we're both too afraid to ask out loud.

"What is this?" he asks, voice low but rising. Confusion laced with something harder. Dread. I can't answer. My throat closes around the words.

Oscar. Alexi. My silence says everything. The photo trembles in his hand. His eyes flicker from the image to me, searching for a version of this that could make sense. There isn't one.

All the years I let Oscar pretend all the moments Alexi smiled too easily, lingered too long—they snap into place now like a cruel puzzle I never meant to solve.

Jack steps in, voice quiet but firm, slicing through the stillness. "The baby in the photo...it's Oscar's. And Alexi's."

No one breathes. The words don't fall. They land. Hard. Final.

My father doesn't speak. Not right away.

He stares at the child. His grandchild. Born of silence, secrets, and betrayal. And I feel it then, like a wire pulled too tight: grief, shame, rage. All of it braided into the air between us.

"Son of a..."

Daddy's voice breaks off, the rest swallowed by silence. His fists curl tight at his sides.

I feel it too—the fracture, the shift.

My heart doesn't just ache. It feels crushed, stomped flat, scattered in pieces I no longer recognize.

Five years married to Oscar. Five years blind. All while he slept with my sister. And worse, they had a child. They gave it away. Tucked the truth behind their polished smiles.

How did I not see it?

My father looks between us. Me and Jack. His eyes flicker, searching. Then he turns to me, quiet now. "What are you going to do?"

I shake my head. No words come. Just the churn of everything. Rage, grief, humiliation, the kind of sorrow that doesn't cry, just burns.

He places a hand on my shoulder. Warm. Steady.

“You’ll get through this,” he says.

And for a moment, I almost believe him.

His voice carries conviction despite the tears glistening in his eyes.

"I don't know, Dad," I reply between sobs.

"I'll talk to her," he says.

"And what would you say, Dad? She's spoiled. A brat and always gets what she wants," I respond.

The muscles in his jaw clench as he considers my words. He walks toward me. Trying to give me comfort. His hands, warm and comforting, cradle my face, forcing me to look into his intense eyes.

"I'll tell her the damage she's done to the family," he says in a measured tone, a hint of anger in his voice that I have never heard before. "I'll make sure she comprehends what she's done, how she has damaged not just you but all of us."

I sniffle. The tears won’t stop. I nod, slow and heavy, the hollow in my chest widening. The thought of facing her, it hurts in a way I can’t name.

Ours was never a strong bond. More vine than root. Thin. Brittle. And now, it snaps.

Dad’s hand lingers at my cheek. His thumb catches a tear before it falls. “I know it’s hard, kiddo,” he murmurs. His voice carries a sadness I rarely hear. “But we can’t ignore this. Not anymore.” He draws back, jaw clenched, eyes alive with something fierce. Still, there’s a tremble at his mouth. “And maybe...” he says, barely audible, “maybe she’ll come to her senses. Maybe she’ll ask for forgiveness.”

His words hang in the room like smoke. But I don't breathe them in. Not yet.

"I'm not sure," I tell my dad. "She's incredibly self-centered and spoiled." But I know I need to confront her at some point. I turn to my dad and say, "I'll decide when the time is right to confront her."

My dad nods in understanding.

His lips pursed at my words, and his expression was serious and thoughtful. He nods slowly in agreement before turning to Jack. "Do you know where the child is now, and how old?" My dad asks.

Jack's eyebrows furrow, and he pauses, squeezing his eyes shut before finally speaking: "The last record was five years ago. She's probably five now." Dad's face contorted with sadness as the realization of how Alexi's selfishness has torn our family apart sinks in. I feel the tears gathering in my eyes but harden myself against them.

Then, my phone buzzes, and Oscar's name flashes across the screen. I don't bother to answer. He leaves a voicemail and then quickly follows it up with a text.

Oscar: Let's sit down and discuss this like adults. Do you really want a divorce? You don't have the means to support yourself financially; how will you manage?

Me: THAT'S THE LEAST OF YOUR CONCERNS.

Me: Maybe it's time for you to take care of Alexi for good and focus on her instead.

Oscar: What do you mean?

Me: I know all your secrets, Oscar: Not only that girl in the bar, but also your high school sweetheart in Ohio, Maria, our cleaning lady, and now my sister? Do you think you can fool me now? Your days of deceit are over. I can't stand being with you any longer.

Oscar: I am still not signing the papers.

Me: We'll see about that.

As Jack settles into an armchair, his eyes distant, as if his thoughts are miles away. Dad takes the seat beside him, and I notice the subtle exchange of glances between them, a silent understanding passing through my father's hazel eyes, which sparkle with a hint of anticipation. He clears his throat, breaking the silence. "We were thinking of watching the debate in a few hours," he says.

Jack shifts slightly, running a hand through his tousled hair. His silver-grey eyes stay locked on mine, a trace of uncertainty flickering in them. "If you want to, that is," he adds softly.

I pause, debating whether or not I want to watch my soon-to-be ex answer questions about our divorce during the debate. This could be an interesting way to see how Oscar would handle the situation.

Finally, I give them a weak smile, "Alright, what time?"

"In two hours.." My Dad replies. He enthusiastically claps his hands, attempting to lighten the atmosphere. With his eyes sparkling joyfully, he says, "That's the spirit!" It's clear he's trying to bring some semblance of normalcy into my day.

Two hours later, he turns on the device, and we huddle together, united against the storm unfolding before us. A shadow falls over us as Oscar's face appears on the screen during the debate, ready to defend his political propaganda. When he is asked about our failing marriage, my curiosity is sparked.

The air in the room feels heavy as Oscar continues to lie. His words are like daggers, cutting deep and stirring anger and sorrow within me. I feel Dad's hand move through my hair, his fingers tracing soothing circles; Jack's firm grip on my hand keeps me grounded. As the debate continues, the stress weighs on my shoulders, a burden that threatens to overwhelm me.

# 25

# Trial for Freedom

Tristan Coumelly, Oscar's running opponent, a man with tousled look hair and an air of superiority, tries to discredit Oscar by attacking his personal life. He sneers in front of the cameras, "How can we trust a governor who can't even make his marriage work?"

With his falsely calm demeanor and unflappable confidence, Oscar brushes off Coumelly's accusation without hesitation. He knows this is just a cheap shot, a last-ditch effort to discredit him in the eyes of the public. Oscar is no stranger to such talk and seems to know how to handle it with grace. In a falsely humble response, he says, "It's true that I haven't seen my wife for a while since she ran away from home..."

The crowd erupts. Applause swells like a wave, drowning out Coumelly's scowl. Oscar stands tall, soaking it in—shoulders back, face composed, charm weaponized. He smiles.

"As for my wife," he says, "I love her with all my heart. And though I gave her everything I thought a woman could need...I can't stop her from looking for it somewhere else."

That son of a gun. I watch, frozen. The debate blares from the screen, but all I hear is the blood rushing in my ears.

He's done it. Twisted the truth until it bleeds. Now I'm the one who ran. The ungrateful wife. The liar. The adulteress.

Oscar fielded every question with slippery grace, offering half-truths, dodging the rest. Not a flicker of guilt on his face. No shame. Just performance. Each heartbeat slams against my chest, furious and helpless. Each breath a silent scream.

That son of a gun.

I watch the debate in horror as Oscar twists the truth, smooth as silk. Now I'm the unfaithful wife. The runaway. The villain.

My heart pounds, each beat a furious protest. I want to scream, but there's no room for my voice in his story.

Then Coumelly strikes. He narrows his gaze, sharp as a blade. Brings up the time my father was missing.

The air shifts. The crowd leans in.

Oscar, ever composed, answers with maddening calm. "I may appear to be harboring my father-in-law in my basement," he says, almost amused, "but I assure you—I didn't know he was there. It's my house, sure, but someone clearly planted him to discredit me."

He gestures like it's obvious. "The man's alive. Unharmed. And I'm not the villain here."

The audience claps again. Coumelly's face darkens. Disbelief written all over it.

And me? I can't breathe. Because now the truth isn't just lost, it's buried beneath applause.

The public starts to believe him. His lies morph into a new story that swings in his favor, and soon enough, he is at the peak of his popularity.

Fury bubbles up inside me, a relentless tide of frustration that I can't seem to quell. The truth has been distorted. I have no way to fight against him since I don't like to be on camera. It feels as though I have already lost the battle.

He takes to the talk shows like a man born for the stage. Same lines, same charming delivery. A web of untruths, spun with just enough plausibility to catch the unsuspecting.

He plays the victim now. Targeted. Misunderstood. A good man caught in a smear campaign.

And the more they believe him, the more he believes himself.

Each appearance feeds his control. Each headline deepens my erasure.

The world tilts. Slow, cruel. And I feel it, he walls closing in.

Then, one afternoon, my phone buzzes.

A text.

Oscar.

Just his name on the screen is enough to freeze my breath.

I open it. And whatever illusion of safety I've built begins to fracture.

> Oscar: People believe me, Lila. No one will believe you. You'd better come back to me. Where else would you go? Huh?"

He's delusional. My hands tremble as I force myself to ignore his text, my resolve hardening with each ignored message. As the court date looms, I brace for the inevitable clash.

On the morning of the trial, my hand shakes as I clutch my coffee mug, nearly spilling its contents when Arabella appears at the cottage door. Her unexpected arrival startles me.

"What are you doing here?" I ask, my voice faltering.

Arabella's wide smile pierces through my tension, her eyes sparkling with warmth. "Don't you think you need a best friend by your side at a time like this?"

"Oh, Arabella..." I pull her into a tight embrace, my tears soaking into her shoulder. "You have no idea how much this means to me."

As I finally pull back, my cheeks wet with tears, I ask, "How did you know?"

"Your dad called me," she says, her tone steady but kind. "I'm glad he did. Otherwise, I wouldn't have known what's been happening."

"I didn't want to interrupt your work in Nepal," I admit, my voice catching.

"But after playing best-friend for you today, I'll need to head back." She says.

We settle into the cozy warmth of the cottage. As I pour out the details of the past months, Arabella listens intently, her brow furrowed and her eyes reflecting a deep concern.

Two hours later, Victoria strides in, briefcase in hand. She reviews my case one last time, her focus unwavering. Her team's meticulous preparation has one goal: ensuring I have a fair hearing.

The clock ticks toward the trial. As we exit the car, a blinding flash of cameras greets us. Reporters' voices merge into a cacophony of questions. Oscar's supporters brandish signs, their chants piercing through the noise. "Cheater! Cheater!" The words echo, but I hold my head high, Arabella's supportive arm steadying me. Dad and Jack flank us as we step into the courthouse, a wave of relief washing over me as the door shuts behind us.

But then I remember my conversation with Oscar, he insisted on televising our divorce, claiming the public had the right to know.

> Me: "Are you out of your mind? You and my mom tried to keep our separation a secret from the start. So why make it public now? If you do this, it'll be your undoing."

I tried to make him see reason, but his reply was as stubborn as ever.

**Oscar:** I have nothing to hide. Whatever lies you spin in your head, no one will believe them. People love me here in New York. I'm willing to give you another chance if you return to me – all my anger will dissipate, and I'll welcome you back as my wife.

Me: You seem to have forgotten. Camera or not – truth never lies. So, think better of it.

Oscar: You are a helpless woman Lila. You still have time to reconsider your decision and tell your attorney to back off. The world will know what a liar you are.

Me: Stop this. No camera.

Oscar: Everyone knows you cheated on me. The public should know. And they will love me more…

Unbelievable. The truth has a way of revealing itself, no matter how desperately one tries to hide it in the shadows. I can feel its weight looming over us, ready to expose all of his carefully constructed lies at the perfect moment.

Me: Do you really believe that? But I warn

you, I have nothing to lose. But once your dirty laundry is out in the public, you will lose this election.

**Oscar:** Stop being a nuisance. You should be supporting me, not going against me. After everything I've done for you, this is how you repay me? If you don't get back in line, I will make your life a living hell.

Inside the courtroom, my pulse quickens and sweat begins to form on my brow.

This is it.

On one side of the room: Oscar, my mother, Alexi, and Oscar's mother, Brenda.

Brenda's face is carved in stone—lips tight, eyes sharp. That same look she gave me on my wedding day. Like I was never good enough.

It cuts, but I don't flinch. Not anymore.

Funny how we've arrived at this moment—divided, almost formally. Sides drawn without anyone needing to say a word.

Marie had texted me earlier. *I'm not showing up on camera, but I'm rooting for you, especially if you land one square on his smug face.*

God, I love her.

"Order of the court," one of the judge's staff announces. "Honorable Judge Perry presiding."

The courtroom stills.

Judge Perry enters, flanked by bailiffs, her robe

sweeping the floor like a shadow. She moves with quiet command, a woman in her late fifties who needs no gavel to summon order—her presence does that on its own.

Everyone rises.

Everyone stands in acknowledgment, and as she takes her seat, she nods, signaling for everyone else to be seated. Her eyes sweep the room. Cool, sharp, unflinching.

They pass over my trembling hands, linger briefly on Oscar's smug smile, then move on.

She sees everything. She misses nothing. The weight of this moment settles into my bones. I try to steal a moment to compose myself, but time seems to be moving at an unforgiving pace.

I glance across the aisle. Oscar sits like he belongs there. Tailored suit, every hair in place, the perfect portrait of the wronged husband. His attorney, all polish and pretense, leans in and murmurs something. Oscar smiles. Not kindly, not nervously but with practiced confidence.

That smirk twists in my gut. The audacity of it. To sit there, cloaked in lies, pretending innocence while I'm the one bleeding. I steady my breath.

Victoria leans closer. Her voice is quiet but firm. "You can do this."

I look at her. She means it. And for a moment, that's enough to hold me steady.

Judge Perry clears her throat.

"This case concerns allegations of marital infidelity by the defendant, Mr. Oscar Chambers," she begins, her voice steady. "It is also alleged that he has refused to consent to a divorce filed by his spouse, Mrs. Lilanie Chambers."

She pauses, letting the words settle.

"The evidence will be examined carefully. Both parties will be given the opportunity to testify."

Then she looks directly at Oscar.

"Mr. Chambers, can you explain to the court why you've refused to consent to your wife's petition for divorce?"

Oscar straightens in his seat, smoothing his tie. "Your Honor, if I may—I'm simply looking out for her best interest."

Judge Perry tilts her head. Her voice remains calm. "So, to clarify—you believe withholding divorce is in her best interest? Could you explain how denying her legal separation supports her well being?"

Oscar opens his mouth, but nothing coherent comes out. Instead, his lawyer leans in, whispering. Oscar nods, says nothing more.

She shifts her attention to me. "Mrs. Chambers, have you made use of your husband's financial resources since leaving the marital home?"

I rise. "No, Your Honor."

"Why not?"

"I've been paying my own expenses in cash. I'm financially independent."

She consults the file in front of her. "Did you make it clear that you do not wish to seek financial support from your husband?"

"Yes, Your Honor."

"Have you been employed during the course of your marriage?"

"That's correct," I say, holding her gaze. "I have."

Oscar scoffs, loud and derisive. "She's a liar! She never worked a day in her life."

Judge Perry's eyes snap to him. "Mr. Chambers, you will remain silent unless directed to speak. Counsel, control your client or the court will impose sanctions."

Oscar's attorney offers a weak nod. Oscar slouches back, face burning.

Judge Perry turns back to me.

"Mrs. Chambers, can you clarify your occupation for the record?"

"I'm a writer, Your Honor."

"And do you currently earn income from your writing?"

"Yes."

"Are you self-sustaining without assistance from Mr. Chambers?"

"I am."

There's a flicker of interest in her eyes. "Are you a published author?"

"Yes."

She leans forward slightly. "Would I know your work?"

"I write under a pseudonym. J.G. Bowler."

The courtroom shifts. A pause. Cameras click.

Judge Perry blinks. Then, “You’re J.G. Bowler?”

A murmur ripples through the room.

“Yes, Your Honor,” I say quietly.

Oscar snaps. “Liar!”

Judge Perry doesn’t even raise her voice this time. “Mr. Chambers, that is your final warning. One more outburst and you will be fined for contempt.”

Oscar sits back, seething.

And for the first time in weeks, I feel the weight begin to shift.

I glance at my dad and Jack; both of them wear smiles that seem to say, "You're going to win this." Arabella's smile beams brightly.

"What would you like to achieve from this trial, Mrs. Chambers?" she asks, her expression softening.

"I just want my freedom, your honor," I reply, my voice firm yet laced with years of suppressed longing for liberation.

Victoria and her team have gathered substantial evidence. Enough to shift the room’s center of gravity. A video plays. Maria’s face flickers on-screen, strained but steady. Her translator speaks with slow precision as she recounts the moment Oscar promised not to report her for illegal immigration, if she agreed to sleep with him.

She’d been desperate. Her mother lay in a hospital bed in Guatemala. Bills rising. Options vanishing. She said yes. Now, tension coils in the courtroom. Oscar sits motionless. But something in his eyes is fraying.

Weeks earlier, I'd sent Jack to find Maria. Not out of vengeance—just questions. I needed to hear her side. Why it happened. Why at my house. While she was still working there.

When Jack found her, she was half-shadow, worn down by fear and pregnancy and the weight of silence. But when she spoke, it unraveled something in me.

Her story wasn't sordid. It was survival. She hadn't seduced anyone. She'd been cornered. And just like that, my anger lost its target. My heart went to her, because I saw it clearly then: She was a victim too. Just like me.

Oscar hadn't just broken vows. He'd preyed on the vulnerable. Manipulated her with the same polished cruelty he once used on me. Only this time, it came with a cost no one should bear.

Jack found her near the southern border, dazed and pregnant, holding herself together with willpower alone. Jack called in a favor, an immigration lawyer with a reputation for impossible cases. Papers were filed. A case was opened.

It became clear soon after—Oscar had tipped off the authorities. A final attempt to silence her. Distance himself. Erase the evidence of what he'd done.

But he hadn't counted on Maria's resolve. Or mine.

I promised her that whatever it takes, I'll help. Her mother's care. Her safety. The child she's carrying. All of it. She'd cried then. Apologized for the chaos, for the pain. But she stood firm. Her testimony would be her reckoning, and Oscar's.

Now the truth is out.

And Oscar? He's still watching the screen. His facade holds. Not flawless. The smugness softens, yes, but doesn't vanish. It reshapes into something colder. Harder. Not fear. Not shame. Just calculation.

The courtroom pulses with tension. Truth rises like floodwater, but Oscar doesn't flinch. Each new piece of evidence lands, yet he stays upright, his back straight, chin lifted. Like a man convinced the storm will pass if he simply refuses to blink.

The gallery gasps. Some lean in for the spectacle, others recoil. Even the media stutter in their rhythm, unsure if they're watching a fall or a stand. But Oscar doesn't give them the satisfaction of collapse.

He folds his hands. Ignores his attorney's whispers. His gaze moves deliberately, one juror to the next. One camera. One judge. As if reminding them: *I'm still here. Still in control.*

Then, the scrape of his chair. He stands. With purpose.

The noise echoes, sharp against the hush. He doesn't flail or plead. He scans the room, not for help, but for challenge. For weakness.

What he finds instead is silence. Eyes that have seen enough. Faces closed like courtroom doors.

But Oscar doesn't shrink. He squares his shoulders.

Because in his mind, he's not the villain. He's the misunderstood man holding the line. And if the world won't see it, that's...the world's mistake.

"Enough! This is madness!" He finally bursts out, his voice echoing sharply through the courtroom, breaking the heavy silence.

The judge raises her hand, signaling for the evidence presentation to pause. She looks at him, her gaze piercing yet not unkind.

"Mr. Chambers, you may speak," she says, leaning back in her chair.

Oscar looks like a man at the end of his rope, his polished veneer shattered, leaving a pitiable figure in its wake.

His voice trembles, cracking with each word. He glares at me, his fists clenched at his sides, knuckles white. "This...this is all lies," he says through gritted teeth, his blue eyes narrowing into slits of fury. He takes a shuddering breath, his face flushed with anger. "Why would you make up all this nonsense just to destroy me?"

Wow. After everything he's done, cheating, shooting at me, throwing me out of the car, plotting to have me committed, and threatening my life. He actually thinks I'm the one who's lying?

His words hang in the air like smoke—thin, toxic, trying to curl into my lungs. A last-ditch attempt to rewrite the story, to make me question what I already know. To pull guilt from me like a confession.

But the ink is dry.

The damage is done.

The trust, dead.

Buried so deep, even memory struggles to find it.

I meet his gaze. My lips part, then close again. *You brought this on yourself* sits heavy on my tongue, but I let silence speak instead. My eyes hold his—not in anger, but in grief. A quiet mourning for what we once had. For the version of him I once believed in.

He's turned our marriage into a slow, grinding tragedy. And there will be no shared bow at the end. No applause. Just the dull ache of what could have been, dimmed by the theater of betrayal.

Still, he stares. Eyes hard, unblinking.
Like he could burn me alive with just the force of his denial.

But I don't flinch. Because it's over. And I think he knows that. He just doesn't want to look at the ashes.

The judge clears her throat, slicing the air. "Let's proceed," she says, voice clipped, pulling everyone back from the edge.

Victoria resumes the evidence presentation, her tone cool and deliberate. The final act is in motion.

I make one quiet call. I tell Victoria not to release the evidence about Alexi. Not yet. Not about the child. Maria's testimony has already pierced deep. The rest would only scorch the earth, and my father doesn't deserve to bleed for Oscar's fire.

If things turn, we'll use it. But not today. Not unless we must.

I'll face Alexi myself when the moment comes.

By the time the final witness steps down, the courtroom feels heavier, as if the walls themselves have absorbed the weight of what was said.

Oscar leans forward. His lawyer slides a document in front of him. A settlement agreement, clean, clinical, and final.

He doesn't ask questions. Doesn't look at me.

He signs.

Not out of remorse. Not even out of acceptance. But because there's nothing left to defend.

The judge glances at the papers, then nods. "The court accepts the stipulation," she says. "Judgment of divorce will be entered accordingly."

It's not over. Not legally. But the ending has begun. And this time, there will be no curtain call. Just the silence that follows when the play is done, and no one is clapping.

Except, my mother shoots me a deadly gaze.

# 26

# Moving On

Oscar's ratings nosedived in the weeks following the trial, crashing through the floor with each news cycle. His reputation, once polished and untouchable, lies in shreds. Political analysts speak of him in past tense.

His name is now shorthand for scandal. A punchline.

But he won't step down.

He clings to the campaign like it's the only thing keeping him upright. He still shows up—rallies, interviews, pressers—delivering speeches with hollow conviction, as if sheer willpower could resurrect trust from the grave. As if voters might forget.

They don't.

The polls keep sinking. His endorsements vanish. Even former allies stop returning his calls. The media smells blood. And Coumelly, sharp and opportunistic, exploits every opening, drawing a stark contrast between them at every turn.

Oscar keeps pushing forward. But forward only leads deeper into the wreckage.

Meanwhile, the trial's aftermath bleeds into my

private life in quieter, more personal ways.

My mother and ex-mother-in-law seize the moment. The courtroom didn't just expose Oscar—it gave them permission. Permission to unravel their disapproval like a parade banner. The texts start first—cold, clipped, weaponized.

"You've ruined everything," my mother writes. No greeting. No hesitation.

Then the voicemails. Long. Condemning. My ex-mother-in-law's voice, sharp as broken glass: "After all my son's done for you..."

There's always more. Always.

At first, I try to let it slide off, grit my teeth, toss the phone aside, tell myself they'll burn out. But they don't. They get louder. Meaner. The weight of their words seeps into everything, my work, my sleep, and my breath.

And in the middle of one ordinary afternoon, I reach my limit.

No preamble. No dramatic declaration.

I change everything. My number. My email. My voicemail password. I disappear from their reach. Not for revenge. Not even for peace. Just for air. I ask Marie and Dad not to give my new number to either of them, not even to Alexi.

Because some fires you don't put out, you just walk away from the smoke.

***

Marie's been counting down the days to her wedding ever since she started planning it months ago. She's been glued to wedding magazines and spent hours looking for the perfect venue online. As summer turns to fall and the weather gets cooler, she's determined to ensure her big day happens before the year's out.

When we walk into the wedding shop, I shoot a hesitant look at Marie, my older sister, and ask, "Is Mom gonna be in the wedding?"

Marie's hazel eyes harden. "You know I didn't want to invite Mom, right? She never liked Alden. She wanted me to marry her friend's son, a total narcissist. How do we end up with people like that in our lives?" She adds, lips tight.

We pause for a second, and I say softly, "Well, we can't really control who's around us. We can only control how we react to 'em."

Marie briefly studies me, then gives my cheek a playful pinch. "How'd you get so wise, little sis?"

I beam at her, proud of the compliment. Dad's always saying the same thing when he ruffles my hair.

But I don't let it rest and still ask, "So, is Mom coming?"

She stops browsing and looks at me, saying, "Well, I didn't want to invite her. But she kept bugging me about the plan, and when I told her she wasn't invited, she freaked out. So, I ended up saying yes. But, of course, I gave her one condition," she points her finger up, "If Mom causes a scene, Alden's friends are ready to escort her outside," she says with a smirk.

"Do you think she and Dad will...you know...make a scene?" I ask.

"Not Dad. But definitely Mom," Marie confirms.

"It's gonna be awkward." I say.

Now, I've got my Mom to deal with at the wedding. Just thinking about it gives me a ton of anxiety. I'm pretty much planning on avoiding her at all costs.

Marie's gaze lands on me again, and she says lightly, "But who's your plus one?"

I stammer, "No one," which is met with Marie's hearty laugh.

"Yeah, right," she chuckles. "Alden and I are still inviting Jack if you don't." With that joke hanging in the air, Marie returns to hunting for her perfect wedding dress.

After shopping for a wedding dress, Marie doesn't find anything she likes, so I suggest a coffee break. I need her full attention to discuss something important. Marie doesn't know about Alexi, Oscar, and their child, so when we sit down at the café, I decide to tell her everything.

We step out of the store, and I glance at Marie. She looks tired after spending so much time searching for the right dress, but I know she's determined to find it.

"Do you want to take a break? Maybe grab a cup of coffee?" I offer.

Marie nods slowly, "Yeah, that sounds nice."

We head to the nearest cafe and find a table in the corner. The smell of freshly brewed coffee fills my nostrils as we settle down and wait for our drinks to arrive.

Once the waiter sets down our drinks and steps away, I finally speak.

"Marie..." I hesitate. "You need to know about Alexi. And Oscar."

She stills, fingers wrapped loosely around her glass. Her hazel eyes widen, blinking once, then narrowing—not in suspicion, but dawning realization.

"You don't mean..." Her voice is barely a whisper. "They had an affair?"

I nod. Slow. Wordless. The truth sits between us like a fracture.

"And," I say, swallowing the sharp edge of memory, "Alexi was pregnant when I married Oscar."

Marie blinks again, then exhales. "That's...that's crazy. And nuts." She reaches across the table, wraps her hand around mine. Her touch is firm, grounding. Something inside me unclenches.

I wipe my eyes quickly and begin.

"I didn't piece it together on my own," I admit. "Jack found her. Found the messages. The timelines. He showed me everything."

Marie leans in, her brows pulling together.

"It started before the wedding," I continue, my voice low. "Alexi and Oscar...they were already involved. And it didn't end after I married him. It just got quieter. Deeper underground."

Marie doesn't speak, just listens—wide-eyed, stunned.

"The worst part?" I say. "I had no idea. Not really. No suspicions, no gut feeling, nothing concrete. I trusted them both."

I pause, swallowing against the shame I shouldn't feel but do anyway.

"The truth didn't arrive like a moment of clarity," I murmur. "It came in files. In dates. In digital receipts. Every detail Jack uncovered cut a little deeper."

Marie reaches for my hand, gently this time. No words. Just presence.

I glance down at the table.

"I didn't see it because I didn't want to," I add quietly. "That's what hurts the most. Not that they betrayed me. But that I let myself believe they never would."

Marie, with her heart-shaped face and gentle demeanor, sits across from me at the small café table, her eyes wide and questioning. I can tell she's still processing the news I've just shared with her.

"I can't still get over the fact that there's a child involved," she confesses, her voice barely above a whisper. "So, where's the child now? Is it a girl? A boy?"

"She's been placed with new foster parents," I say at last, my voice catching. "The last three didn't go well. The first couple who adopted her ended up in jail for drug trafficking. Child Services had to pull her from the last home, too."

Marie's eyes well up with tears at the thought of

a scared and hungry child. "We have to do something," she says firmly, wiping away her tears. "She needs to be with family who will love and take care of her."

I nod in agreement, grateful for Marie's empathy and compassion. "That's what I'm hoping the lawyer can help us with," I explain. "But it may take some time, and legal processes are involved."

"I understand," Marie says, nodding her head. "But we must try our best to bring her back to our family."

Marie's emotions are running high as she paces back and forth, trying to process the news of her long-lost niece. "Can we go and see her?" she asks suddenly.

"I don't think that would be wise," I reply cautiously. "The child is currently in the care of a foster family. It would be better for us to wait until the legal issues are sorted out before we try to meet her."

***

The past few weeks have been a blur of motion. Paperwork. Phone calls. Sleepless nights. My father, Marie, and I have thrown everything into the effort of bringing her home. Not out of obligation—but something deeper. A pull we couldn't ignore.

We've been in constant contact with Child Services, attorneys, and the foster family. Every update, every delay, every signature felt like it carried the weight of something sacred. Bella wasn't just a child in a system—she was ours. Already.

The process tested us. Background checks. Home visits. Legal barriers that seemed designed to wear us down. But we kept going, driven by something more powerful than frustration—love. Not the easy kind, but the quiet, relentless kind that doesn't need permission.

Then today, the call came.

Everything's approved. We can meet her.

The officer's voice was calm. Mine wasn't. My heart stumbled over itself as I thanked her, barely processing the words.

Now we're in the car, headed to the foster home. Marie grips the steering wheel tight. My father sits silently beside me, eyes fixed forward. The road blurs past. None of us speaks, we're too full.

Of hope. Of nerves. Of everything we've carried for weeks.

Bella is waiting.

And so are we.

As Marie and I step through the door, a wave of emotion catches me off guard. Part joy, part fear. My fingers tremble slightly at my sides. Behind us, Dad moves quietly, his presence steady as ever.

Marie's already crying. Not loudly. Just the quiet kind, tears slipping down her cheeks as she takes it all in.

Judy and Damian, the foster parents, greet us with

warm smiles. The case officer is there too, just watching as we reunite. There's something warm about the couple—something that puts you at ease without trying too hard. They know what this moment is. They feel the weight of it too. Still, they manage to make space for us, offering gentle words and the kind of comfort that doesn't ask for anything in return.

Then Judy says, "She's ready."

And Bella appears.

She's five, but so small it makes me catch my breath. She clings to Judy's skirt, peeking out from behind the fabric with wide, uncertain eyes. Her hair is soft and messy, a wisp of a child in a too-big world.

For a moment, no one moves. Then I kneel, lowering myself to her level. Not reaching. Not crowding. Just being there.

"Hi, Bella," I say softly. "We've been waiting to meet you."

She doesn't answer. Just looks at me. Curious, cautious. The kind of look that holds stories too big for words.

And that's okay.

Love, I've learned, doesn't always rush in loud. Sometimes it arrives like this. Quiet, trembling, and completely true.

Judy kneels beside Bella and smiles. "She likes to go by Bella," she tells us softly. "It suits her, don't you think?"

It does. Her name fits her like a favorite blanket—sweet, soft, and already loved.

"Hi, Bella!" Marie says, her voice bright but trembling. "I'm Marie, and this is Lila. We're going to be your aunties."

Bella blinks up at us. A spark flickers in her wide, searching eyes—not quite trust, not yet, but something close. Recognition, maybe. A sense that we are not strangers to fear.

Then her gaze shifts to Judy. "Do I have to leave again?" she asks, voice so small it barely carries.

The room goes still.

Judy crouches, eye to eye with her. "Yes, sweetie," she says gently, brushing Bella's hair behind her ear. "But this time you're going home—with them. They're going to be your forever family."

Bella's eyes lift toward me again, as if trying to measure the truth in that word. *Forever.*

I study her face. There's no mistaking it, Alexi in her soft curls, Oscar in those curious, watchful eyes. My heart tightens, not in rejection, but in awe. She's her own person. And she's already endured too much.

My father steps forward. He's been quiet all morning, standing a little apart. But when Bella looks up at him and asks, "Who is he?" he doesn't falter.

"I'm your grandpa," he says, steady but proud. His eyes give away more than his voice ever will.

Bella tilts her head, trying the word out. "Grand pa...?" It sounds like magic on her lips.

Marie's tears spill over again. She leans in and gently brushes her hand against Bella's cheek. "You're going to be so loved," she whispers.

Judy and Damian take time walking us through everything, Bella's bedtime routine, her favorite snacks, the stuffed giraffe she won't sleep without. Their love for her is woven into every word, every small detail. We thank them over and over. It still doesn't feel like enough.

As we leave, the air feels lighter. Not less serious, but full of something new.

On the drive home, my father is extra careful, hands steady at ten and two. Marie rides in the back with Bella, fussing with the seatbelt, showing her how the window works, making her laugh.

We had bought the car seat days ago. Because hope, real hope—plans ahead.

And now, she's here.

Ours.

Finally home.

# 27
# MIA

The early morning light spills over the horizon, casting a soft gold across the cottage windows. It's the kind of peace that makes you forget the world is still turning.

Then the phone rings, sharp, jarring.

I jolt awake, fumbling blindly on the nightstand. "Hello?" I answer, voice thick with sleep.

"Where is he? What did you do with him?" Alexi's voice crashes through the receiver—panicked, sharp, breathless.

I sit up, instantly alert. "What are you talking about?"

"Oscar," she snaps. "He's missing. And everyone knows you're the only one who ever held a grudge against him."

"That's quite an accusation," I say, trying to steady my voice. "I haven't seen him since...what, the divorce trial?"

She exhales heavily. "But where is he? Today's the big day. He'd never sabotage himself. Would he?"

I don't answer. I'm not sure I could.

"When was the last time you saw him?" I ask

instead.

"Last night. At the fundraiser," she says. "He told people he had to be home by midnight."

Typical Oscar. Always keeping control of the narrative, even if it's just an exit line.

"Who was with him when he left?"

There's a pause. "No one that I saw. He just... vanished."

My mind races. As much as Oscar made my life hell, I don't want him harmed. I wanted freedom from him, not this. Not mystery. Not fear.

"Mom said she needed to talk to him about today's event," Alexi adds suddenly.

My stomach tightens. "Have you talked to her?"

"She's not answering." Her voice cracks, just slightly. "No one can reach her either."

I grip the phone tighter. "Have you told anyone else?"

"His campaign team. They're the ones who told me. He never showed for briefing. Phones off. No tracking. They think it's either a stunt or...something else."

My chest tightens. "You think something happened to him?"

"I don't know," she whispers. "But you were married to him. He must've had a place, somewhere he went when things got bad."

I search my memory, but nothing rises. "I don't know, Alexi."

I pause, then add, "Maybe he just went out for

coffee. Or to clear his head."

But even as I say it, I don't believe it.

There's more silence, then commotion on her end—shouting, hurried footsteps.

"I have to go," she says abruptly.

Then the line clicks.

Typical Alexi. No goodbye. Just an exit.

I set the phone down and stare out the window. The light has shifted. The stillness of morning is gone.

Oscar's missing. And somewhere in all this, a thread has come loose. I can feel it.

I go to the kitchen to start the coffee, my mind still reeling from the news of Oscar's disappearance. But as soon as I walk in, Dad's already there.

"Morning, Dad," I greet, trying to act casual despite my inner turmoil.

"So, Oscar's missing?" he asks, getting straight to the point.

"Yeah...Alexi told you?" I ask hesitantly.

He nods grimly. "She called and then sent me a text. Have you heard anything else?"

"Nothing yet," I reply.

We both fall into a heavy silence, each lost in our own thoughts for Oscar.

It isn't until the coffee is done brewing that we start talking again. My dad sits at the kitchen table while I pour a cup on each of us and join him.

"Do you think something happened to him?" he asks quietly.

"I don't know," I admit truthfully. "But Alexi says

they're considering all possibilities."

My father let out a deep sigh and took a sip of his coffee, the warmth and bitterness bringing him comfort. "The timing couldn't be worse," he says with disappointment weighing heavy in his voice. "But if he wants to ruin his own campaign, that's on him." His words hold a sense of resignation, as if there's nothing more he can do.

Just then, we hear Marie's voice calling from the front door, breaking the tense silence. "Hello? Anyone home?" she greets as she enters. "We're here."

She texted us yesterday saying they would be over early in the morning because she had errands to run all day. Marie and I take turns looking after Bella. As soon as Bella sees me, she comes running with her favorite doll in hand and gives me a big hug. Her innocence and pure love never fail to bring a smile to my face. She then goes over to my dad and snuggles into his lap, wrapping her small arms around him as he holds her close.

The sun is just peeking over the horizon, casting a warm glow through the kitchen window as Marie pours herself a cup of coffee. She then sits beside Dad at the table, her brown hair in a bun.

"Have you heard about the news?" I ask, taking a sip of my hot drink.

"Oh yeah, Alexi called and informed me this morning," Marie replies, settling into the chair across from my father.

"Alexi called me too. She was asking about Oscar's whereabouts and seemed to think I had something to do with him going missing," I said with a sigh.

Marie let out a laugh, accidentally spilling some coffee on the table. "Oh, come on, like you would want to see him after everything he put you through."

I shrug, trying not to dwell on past hurts. "Well, it's water under the bridge now. I'm just glad the divorce is finally over."

As my dad finishes his coffee, he stands up with a sparkle in his eye and declares, "Well, my favorite girl and I are going fishing today. Care to join us, Marie?"

The warm sun shines down outside, the smell of freshly brewed coffee lingering in the air. Bella's face lights up with unbridled happiness at the mention of fishing.

"Oh yes, I love fishing!" she exclaims with the enthusiasm of a five-year-old.

Marie smiles and shakes her head. "Oh no, I'll pass. I have a busy day ahead of me."

I look at my dad with excitement bubbling inside me. "That sounds like so much fun!" I comment eagerly.

"Can you come with us, Auntie Lila?" Bella asks, looking up at me with her big blue eyes.

Feeling a tug at my heartstrings, I kneel to her level and smile. "Of course, sweetheart. I'll join you and Grandpa once I finish talking with Aunt Marie."

Dad chuckles and ruffles Bella's hair. "Okay, darling girl, let's go."

"You always say that, Grandpa. I'm just a girl. I

don't even know what *darling* means," she pouts, skipping beside him toward the garage.

He laughs, the sound deep and easy. "You're not just any girl, Bella. You're my darling granddaughter."

Her smile blooms—bright and shy. She slips her hand into his, his rough fingers closing gently around hers, and they vanish for their morning ritual: fishing, the old rods, the quiet dock.

Marie watches them go, her coffee cradled in both hands. Dark hair tumbles over her shoulder. When she looks at me, her eyes hold something weightier than concern.

"When do you think we should tell Alexi?"

The question lands heavily, cutting through the stillness.

I inhale, slow and measured. It's been days since we saw her.

"Bella's still...young. Too young to know all this." I reply.

Marie nods but doesn't look away. "I know. But we can't keep this secret forever. Alexi may not deserve the truth. But Bella does. She didn't ask for any of this."

A silence stretches between us, full of half-formed thoughts and invisible lines drawn.

"Maybe when she's older," I say. "Or maybe at your wedding. If Alexi shows up, Bella might start asking questions anyway. The resemblance is..." I stop short. We both know.

Marie reaches across the table, her fingers brushing mine.

"That could work," she says softly. "But we need to be ready. Whatever we decide...I don't want Bella to end up blaming us."

A heavy silence settles between us. The kind that doesn't rush to be filled. We sit with it, letting the weight of everything—Bella, Alexi, the lie we live with, press in on us.

Then Marie speaks, her voice low, almost hesitant. "What about Oscar?"

I look up. "What *about* him?"

"He's missing."

The words hang in the air like smoke.

I blink, caught off guard. "It's probably nothing."

But she doesn't look convinced. Neither am I.

By afternoon, it's no longer a private worry. The streets hum with it—rumors, half-truths, panic disguised as concern. His face is everywhere, beaming in photographs beside headlines that grow bolder by the hour. Candidate for Governor Disappears Hours Before Polls Open.

Oscar is officially missing.

The calls from Alexi start before noon. The first one is calm. The second, clipped. By the fourth, she's frantic.

"Where is he?" she asks, her voice like splintered glass.

"I don't know," I say each time. It's not a lie. But it's not the truth, either.

I say it again, and again, until the words feel hollow. Until I start to wonder if I ever really knew where Oscar was—at all.

I tuck Bella in, brushing a strand of hair from her face. She's already drifting, the kind of sleep only children know, untouched by the weight of adult disappearances.

"They couldn't find Mom either," I say, my voice barely above a breath.

Dad stands in the doorway, shadowed. He doesn't respond. His jaw tightens, a flick of muscle betraying whatever storm brews beneath. He says nothing. Just watches us for a moment too long, then nods and walks away.

Whenever I mention her, he retreats—like her name is a door he refuses to open.

Alone now, I sit beside Bella and let the quiet wrap around me, heavy and unrelenting.

Should I call Jack?

It's been weeks. Last time we spoke, he said something vague about a work trip, outside the country, urgent, no timeframe.

"Top secret?" I'd teased, trying to coax even the faintest smile. But he only looked at me. Too long, too serious.

He didn't answer. Just hugged me tight, the kind of hug that felt like an apology.

I wanted to ask more. I didn't. Because I already knew. With Jack, silence is safety. The less I know, the less anyone can take from me.

Still, some nights I wonder, was it just work, or

was he saying goodbye?

My relationship with Jack has always been a kind of fog—soft around the edges, hard to grasp. But if I'm honest with myself, I like him. Probably more than I should.

He's been there. Quiet. Consistent. Since the beginning of the fallout with Oscar. No grand gestures, just presence. And yet, he's also the kind of man who can disappear without notice, as if he's following shadows I'm not allowed to see.

Sometimes he shows up at just the right moment, like someone listening to a frequency I don't know I'm broadcasting. Other times, he's just...gone.

My heart doesn't know what to do with him. It lives in a constant state of contradiction: drawn in, then left waiting. Love, if this is what it is, feels more like vertigo than certainty.

Hours slip by. Oscar still hasn't turned up. What started as speculation has morphed into something colder, heavier.

I watch the news unfold in pieces. Quick flashes of his campaign headquarters, helicopters hovering low, panicked volunteers clutching clipboards. Then his campaign manager appears for a statement, face drawn tight, voice brittle.

"There's reason to believe foul play is involved," he says, before aides cut him off and hustle him away. No follow-up. No explanation.

The city holds its breath.

Whispers spiral into theories. Was it political sabotage? A staged disappearance? Something darker?

Even as the polls begin to close, uncertainty thickens. His name is still on the ballot, but without Oscar, the campaign buckles. Reporters circle like vultures. Voters are restless. And still, no word. No ransom. No trail.

Just absence.

And in that silence, I can't help but wonder: Was his vanishing the final card he played... or was he running from something only Jack knows?

# 28
# Plus, One

Marie's wedding day arrives, and she's glowing. Not the cliché kind of glow, something quieter, steadier. Like she's anchored, finally, in something good.

"We never heard back from your plus one," she says, adjusting her earrings in the mirror. There's a teasing lilt in her voice, but her eyes don't miss much.

I try to shrug it off, keep my voice light. But the moment Jack's name is spoken, something inside me stirs, sharp and sudden. I pretend not to notice. Pretend I'm fine. But it's impossible not to picture him. Not to miss him. No matter how hard I try, my heart doesn't know how to play it cool.

"Plus one, huh? Let's not pretend today's about anything but *you*. Honestly, you're the most stunning bride I've ever seen."

She rolls her eyes, laughing. "Flattery, flattery. You'll float off like a balloon if you keep that up."

But the smile lingers. She's radiant. Effortlessly so.

Then she shifts, gentler now. "Any news from Alexi?"

The name catches me off guard. I let out a dry

laugh. “Last I checked, she skipped my wedding too.”

Her smile fades, eyes searching mine. I regret the words the moment they leave my mouth.

“I’m sorry,” I say quickly. “I shouldn’t have...this day is yours.”

Marie shakes her head with a somber expression. "No... no... it's alright to bring it up. I remember that time vividly. But, she was pining for the wrong person." Her voice trails off as she remembers my wedding day. "But I wasn't a good sister to you either. I was so into pleasing our mother that I seemed just to follow," she recalls.

She takes a deep breath before continuing, her tone dropping to a hushed whisper. "Anyhow, if she does happen to show up, please don't mention Bella just yet. I fear it may stir up emotions we're not ready to face."

Nodding in understanding, I feel a twinge of guilt for bringing up the sensitive topic on her wedding day. Being honest with each other is more than I could ask for.

A small smile tugs at Marie's lips as she adds, "But just in case Alexi decides to make an appearance, I've ensured my wedding coordinator knows not to let her wear white. And if she somehow manages to slip through, Mylene has strict instructions to handle it."

The warm sunlight surrounds us as we gather at the outdoor venue for the wedding ceremony. It's early June, and the weather is perfect for such a special day. The air is filled with anticipation, joy, the sweet aroma of flowers, and the smell that comes with weddings.

As we prepare to walk down the aisle, my sister Alexi appears in a cream-colored gown that seems to steal attention from the bride. My heart sinks at the sight of her, knowing she has disregarded Marie's request for no white attire.

Marie's brows tighten. She doesn't speak, but her body gives her away—rigid, alert, eyes fixed on Alexi like a warning light. Dad holds her close, murmurs, "I'll talk to her," but it's already in motion.

Mylene steps in. Graceful. Unshaken. She greets Alexi with a practiced smile, then leans in—voice calm, but edged with steel.

Alexi pushes back. Says there's no time. Says the dress looks good on her. Of course it does.

But Mylene doesn't move. Doesn't blink. Just waits.

Eventually, Alexi turns. Her heels snap against the stone as she walks toward the bridal suite.

No apology. No glance back.

Just silence, thick and knowing.

As my father stands next to Marie, I can feel old feelings of frustration resurface. I thought I had buried them all when she cheated on me with my ex-husband.

The ceremony unfolds like a dream. Soft light filters through the trees, the air still and watchful, as if the world itself has paused to witness this moment.

Bella skips down the aisle, scattering petals with

careful joy, her dress swaying like something out of a storybook. She doesn't know the weight we carry. That's a mercy.

Marie and Alden exchange vows beneath the gazebo, voices low, steady. Every word lands like it belongs there. The match is real. You can feel it in the stillness.

For a while, I let the happiness wash over me. I want this for her. Peace. A clean slate.

But the unease never leaves.

Inside, at the reception, it returns—stronger now. Alexi's presence hovers like a sharp scent you can't scrub out.

She was supposed to be one of Marie's bridesmaids. But she missed the dress fitting. The shower. The rehearsal. Said she was chasing leads on Oscar.

Eight months.

Eight months since he vanished. No note. No footage. No demands. Just absence. Like he stepped off the map. Like Mom did.

Two disappearances.

No connection anyone can prove. No closure anyone can hold. Just questions that grow heavier the longer they stay unanswered.

And Alexi—she never stopped digging. Always convinced she's close. Always just one clue away.

But part of me wonders if the search is the point. If looking for Oscar keeps her from having to look at herself.

As the party climaxes, with the ceremonial cake

cut and the energetic dancing that ensues, Bella holds on to my father's arm.

In Alexi's intoxicated state, she stumbles over and asks my dad, "Who's the kid?"

Dad smirks, eyes on Bella. "Who do you think it is? Notice any resemblance?"

His tone is playful, but there's something behind it—something Alexi hears, too. Her expression tightens. The air between them shifts, sharp and brittle.

Before it cracks, I step in.

"Alexi," I say, light but firm. "Let's not do this here."

She rolls her eyes. "What's your problem? I'm just having fun." Her words slur slightly. The drink in her hand tilts. "This might be the last wedding I ever go to."

She turns to leave, but then stops. Smirks. Twists the knife.

"Oh... look who finally showed." Her gaze cuts past me. "Your plus one decided to grace us with his presence."

She cackles—too loud, too long—and disappears into the crowd, drink in hand.

I don't have to turn around to know who's standing behind me.

But I do.

And there he is.

"Jack..." The word slips out before I can stop it.

He stands just inside the room, still, composed.

Time slows. Not in a cinematic way, just enough

to feel the shift. The sudden awareness of him.

He hasn't changed. Tall, calm, unreadable. The kind of presence that doesn't demand attention, but takes it anyway. The low light brushes against him, catching the edge of his jaw, the line of his shoulders.

I take a step forward, then stop. Part of me wants to close the distance. Part of me wants to turn and walk away.

Too much has been said in silence. Too much left to guess.

His eyes meet mine.

And for a moment, the noise of the reception fades.

The tux fits like it was made for him. Clean lines. Quiet danger. His hair slicked back with sharp precision, like everything about him has been calculated, controlled. But it's the eyes that stop me—silver-grey, unreadable, watching me like I'm the only fixed point in the room.

When our eyes meet, the rest blurs. Just static and light.

My breath catches. I press a hand to my chest, feel the wild thrum beneath my skin. The fabric of my dress clings, heat pooling in places I can't name.

He smiles. Just a flicker. Just enough.

"I assume I'm your plus one?" he says, voice low and smooth, like it knows its effect.

I manage a laugh—small, unsteady.

He closes the space between us. "I'm sorry I'm late. I didn't see the invitation until this afternoon.

Renting a tux wasn't exactly at the top of my list, coming straight from the city."

He pauses. Holds my gaze.

"Would you care to dance?"

And somehow, the floor beneath me feels less certain than his hand held out, waiting.

When someone asks me to dance, I usually say no. I don't dance  and I'd shrug. Safe. Distant. Clean. But now, his hand outstretched, those silver eyes fixed on me—refusing feels impossible. Or maybe dishonest.

I take his hand.

There's a jolt. Not fireworks—just a current. Immediate. Unmistakable.

His grip is steady. Not tight. Not hesitant. He leads me onto the floor with the ease of someone who already knows I'll follow.

The music is soft, lilting. Strings. A piano. The kind of song that doesn't demand attention, only presence.

We sway.

Marie's voice drifts through the air like wind over water. "Take a deep breath..."

Alden's voice follows, lower, warmer. "Good to have you here, man."

And then they're gone. Their words fade, swallowed by laughter, glasses clinking, the distant hum of celebration.

Jack and I remain, moving in time, wrapped in something quieter than the music.

"So," he says, not looking away, "what does it take for you to say hi?"

His question lands soft. But it lands.

I open my mouth. Then close it again.

I take a breath, slow and steady.

"Hi," I say, and it feels like more than a greeting.

He smiles. It's quiet at first—then it breaks wide and easy, like sunlight slipping through clouds. I feel the warmth before I even understand why.

We move together, barely swaying. Not dancing, really—just existing, closely. The music hums in the background, blurred now, like everything else.

His hand rests at my back. Light. Anchoring. His laughter spills out in pieces, unpolished and real.

We talk about things. About nothing. And just dance.

And still, the question rises, uninvited.

"So," I say, eyes on the collar of his shirt, not his face, "what have you been up to?"

I feel him pause. Just slightly. Just enough.

The moment stretches, silent, taut—like a held breath before the drop.

A shadow crosses his face. Not dramatic—just enough to dim the light in his eyes.

They'd been bright a moment ago. Now they look distant. Weathered.

"I was out of the country," he says, like it costs him something. "Working."

His shrug is small, almost automatic. But his shoulders sag under it. The lines on his face are new—or maybe I just never noticed them before.

There's more he isn't saying. I feel it settle between us like dust.

"But this isn't the time or place," he adds, forcing a smile that doesn't quite hold. "I heard you bought a ranch?"

I laugh—nervous, a little proud. "Yeah. I know. Kind of surreal. I never pictured myself as a landowner."

He nods, and for a moment, I see something soften in him.

Maybe admiration. Maybe envy.

Maybe both.

A grin spreads across Jack's face as he teases, "Let me guess, half a dozen children and a wrap-around porch on your new house?"

I laugh, surprised by the ease of it. It slips out before I can filter it. For a second, I let the picture live: the swing, the sound of children, the sky going soft with sunset over the hills.

It's a good dream.

A quiet one.

The kind you don't say out loud too often. Not when you're alone. Not when the porch is still empty.

"Buying the ranch was the first step," I say, more to myself than him.

He raises an eyebrow, eyes dancing. "You do know those half-dozen kids won't show up without a man, right?"

My smile holds, but my chest tightens.

Then he adds, softer this time, "Do you have someone in mind?"

His gaze meets mine. Steady. Open.

The music keeps playing. The room keeps spinning.

But in this small space between us, something stills.

The music fades, dissolving into a hush. Still, I don't look away.

The dim light casts long shadows over Jack's face, sharpening the line of his jaw, the quiet seriousness in his eyes. A flicker of gold catches the edge of his gaze, like something burning just beneath the surface.

For a moment, it's just us. The crowd, the clinking glasses, the laughter—they all fall away.

I hesitate before answering, my cheeks warming with embarrassment.

"I might have one," I admit, my voice barely above a whisper. "But the problem is...I'm not sure if he likes me back, especially after I threw up on his shoes."

A beat, then his laughter breaks loose. Rich. Full. It shakes the air around us. Somehow, it makes everything feel lighter. And heavier at the same time.

I turn away, not wanting to see the teasing twinkle in his eyes or hear his response. A fear creeps over me, gnawing at my insides, that he will see through my carefully constructed facade and uncover the depth of my feelings for him.

I don't realize he's followed me until I hear the soft tread of his shoes behind me. The hallway lights are dim, shadows crawling along the walls like secrets.

Then, his hands. At my waist. Steady. Sure.

He pulls me in.

My breath stutters. My legs falter. I reach for him without thinking.

He holds me there, close. His forehead almost brushing mine. His eyes, silver in the dimness, fix on me with something that feels too much like hunger.

"I'll be damned if you found some rancher while I was away," he says. His voice low, edged with something sharp and unspoken.

Possessiveness. Fear. Want.

My heart flutters at his words, and I can't help but respond, "I think...I'll stick with the one whose eyes are like silver, and when he looks at me, he sees straight into my soul."

A smile tugs at the corner of his mouth, knowing.

His voice husky, and just above a whisper. "Then let me seal it with a kiss."

He leans in.

And just like that, the space between us disappears.

He captures my lips in unrushed passion.

There's no urgency. No theatrics. Just the quiet certainty of someone who's meant to be there.

The kiss is slow. Intentional. Sweet. A blend of warmth and something deeper, something that's waited too long to speak.

And it burns.

There's no chaos, no noise. Just the rhythm of

our breath, the pressure of his hands at my waist, the steady thrum building in my chest.

Everything else falls away.

This, this feels like claiming. And surrender. At once.

When we finally part, and breathless, his forehead rests lightly against mine. Neither of us speaks. We don't need to. The air between us is already full of everything we never said.

# 29
# Aftermath

The newlyweds bid their final goodbyes to the guests as they embark on their honeymoon journey to the Caribbean.

Panicked, I search for Alexi, but she is nowhere to be found. I turn to my father and ask, "Has she left?"

"I saw her and Rema heading out just before Alden and Marie left." My dad says, a hint of amusement in his voice. "They're probably keeping the celebration alive somewhere else." He shrugs, a small smile tugging at his lips, as if used to Alexi's spontaneous decisions. He seems to have come to terms with Alexi's strong-willed personality; after all, she is an independent thirty-year-old woman.

Tiny and serene, Bella lies cradled in my father's embrace, her breathing rhythmic and calm. As we reach the front entrance, Dad's car pulls up from a valet. He gently transitions her into the car seat, securing her without a stir from her deep slumber.

"See you tomorrow, Dad," I say. Planning to head out toward the bridal suite to collect some of Marie's forgotten things. Jack appears at my side, glancing at my father. "I'll drive her back to the hotel," he offers.

My dad nods, and they share a quiet, tense look before Jack turns to me with a reassuring smile.

As my father's car disappears into the dark, I catch Jack half-turned, laughing with a guest. Everything feels normal—for one more second.

Then a sleek black car tears into the driveway, tires shrieking against the gravel, stones spitting like sparks. The tinted window slides down with a mechanical hiss.

And there she is.

My mother.

Pale. Expressionless. A statue chiseled from ice.

Her arm lifts, slow and deliberate, until the barrel of a gun points through the open window. Steady. Unshaking.

And aimed straight at me.

I don't have time to scream. Or run. The car peels away, tires screaming. And then, a shot. A crack of thunder in my chest. The world snaps. I stumble. The ground lunges toward me.

"Lila..." Jack's voice cuts through the ringing, raw and close. His arms catch me before I hit the ground. Tight. Anchored. Holding me as everything tilts and spins.

My legs don't work. My body hums with a strange, hollow heat. No pain. Just silence under my skin.

"I think my mom shot me," I whisper to Jack.

It sounds ridiculous. Distant.

Then the darkness comes—quiet, absolute.

And I let it take me.

Light strikes first, sharp, uninvited.

I blink against it, lids heavy, vision smeared at the edges. Shapes move. Voices blur. Everything feels too loud, too fast.

I'm on a stretcher. The ceiling slides above me in jerks. Green scrubs surround me, pushing, guiding. The scent of antiseptic clings to the air.

Jack is there.

His face is tight, jaw clenched, walking beside a doctor I don't recognize.

A hospital. That much I know.

"Jack...?" I croak, attempting to sit up.

"Lila, it's going to be alright," he reassures me, his grip firm on my hand. "Your injury isn't critical."

The doctor's voice rises—firm, absolute.

"Stay here," he tells Jack, just before the doors swing open and swallow me whole.

I cry out for him, but the sound doesn't carry. It's swallowed by motion. By noise.

Fluorescent lights stutter above me, blinking in rhythm with my pulse. Everything tilts.

Voices blur together, urgent. Metal clinks. Wheels rattle. Someone calls for vitals.

I squeeze my eyes shut. Try to breathe. Try to stay.

A sharp sting in my arm.

And then, darkness wins.

***

A slow, rhythmic beep pulls me back. One note. And another.

My eyes open but just barely. The world is smeared and quiet, colors running together like watercolors left in the rain.

I blink. Shapes sharpen. I see him.

Jack, just beyond the foot of the bed. Seated. Leaning in close to my father. Their voices are low, too quiet to catch, but the tension is thick between them.

Neither of them knows I'm awake.

"Dad?" I rasp. My voice is paper-dry, barely a thread.

Jack turns first. His face shifts—relief, worry, something tighter underneath.

"How are you feeling?" he asks, inching closer.

"I've been through worse," I manage, the words dragging across my throat.

He gives a low chuckle, the kind that doesn't quite reach his eyes. "Have you been shot before?"

"Not really," I say, staring at the ceiling. "But it wasn't as bad as the last time I ended up here."

The words hang between us, too casual for what they mean.

His smile fades. My thoughts start spinning.

This is the second time my mother has done this. Not an accident. Not misfired rage.

Something else.

I shift my gaze toward Jack, searching his face.

"Did you tell my dad who shot me?"

The question lands heavy. I already know the

answer.

But I need to hear him say it.

Jack nods, his expression serious.

"I'm sorry it's come to this. This is all my fault." Dad's voice cracks at the edge, barely holding. He doesn't meet my eyes. Just stares past the bed, brow drawn, mouth a tight line.

A breath catches in his chest. He lets it go slow, but it doesn't steady him. His eyes are distant, fixed on something behind the moment, something old.

"I don't know if this is the right time," he says, almost to himself. His voice drops, quiet and brittle. "But I think... you need to know the truth."

The room stills. Even the machines seem to quiet. Outside, life goes on. In here, something's about to break.

Despite the sharp ache in my chest, I give him a firm nod. His eyes flicker with worry, darting between Jack, who stands close by, and me.

Dad glances at Jack. His hesitation is plain—shoulders slightly hunched, hands fidgeting against his legs.

"Would you mind giving us a moment?" he asks, voice low, uncertain.

Jack starts to respond, but I speak first.

"It's fine, Dad."

My voice is thin, raw. I shift, trying to sit up, but the pain flares sharp and immediate. Jack is already there, moving without a word. He slides a pillow behind me, careful, practiced. I flinch, jaw tightening, but force a smile.

"He can hear whatever's so secret," I say, breath hitching. "Do you mind?"

Dad looks at me, then at Jack.

"Not at all," he says quietly.

He takes my hands in his, gives them a gentle squeeze. His smile is small. Sad. Like he's about to unwrap something that's been locked away far too long.

"Edwina isn't your biological mother."

My father says it quietly, but it hits like a thousand whip on my back.

For a moment, I forget the pain in my side. And, I can't tell which wound runs deeper—the bullet, or this. My throat tightens. Words gather but won't come. My fingers move to my neck, scratching lightly. Reflex, habit, and panic.

I manage one question, barely above a whisper, "What do you mean?"

The room feels smaller. The walls closer. My voice is thick with something between grief and disbelief.

Because if she's not my mother... then who am I?

And why now?

"When Marie and Alexi were young, Edwina was rarely home. She spent most of her time traveling the world with her friends, mostly in Europe. We had to hire a nanny named Jasmine to care for the children. My relationship with Edwina had already changed by then. We weren't close anymore. And I..." He swallows hard, the sound loud in the stillness. "I fell for Jasmine."

The silence that follows is like an icy wind, stretching across the room, chilling everything in its path. "She got pregnant, with you." My breath catches in my throat, a sharp intake that echoes in the heavy air.

His eyes, now shimmering with unshed tears, meet mine. His voice cracks, burdened by the weight of long-held secrets. "She died giving birth. A heart condition. No one knew. Not even her."

"When Edwina came back and found out about the affair," my dad continues, "she was furious." He exhales, like the memory still burns at the edges. "I was ready to leave her. To start over. With you, with the girls. But she wouldn't have it."

He pauses, eyes flicking to the window, the past pulling at him. "She said a divorce would ruin her social standing. All her friends were still married. It was like... they had a silent pact. Appearances were everything."

He looks at me now. Softer. "She made me promise. That she'd stand as your mother, as long as I stayed. No divorce. No disruption. Just... the version of the truth we could all live with." His voice lowers. "She said you needed a mother figure. That it was for the best."

"Mother figure?" I say, the words bitter in my throat. "She's hardly a mother to me, Dad..."

The room tilts slightly. Not physically—just the weight of everything shifting. Anger flares, sharp and hot. Then confusion. Then something colder—betrayal settling in.

“How could you keep this from me for so long?”

He exhales. Slow. Shaking. “I know,” he says. “I know it was wrong.” His voice is thin, like paper rubbed too many times.

“But at the time...I did it to protect everyone. Especially you. You’d just lost your real mom. You were a baby. You needed a mother, and I...” He stops. Blinks hard. “I couldn’t do it alone.”

His words land with the best of intentions. But intentions don’t erase the years.

"But why didn't you tell me the truth when I was older?" I ask, trying to make sense of everything.

"Edwina made me promise not to tell anyone, or else it would ruin our family," my Dad explains. "She didn't want you to know or any of your sisters." I shake my head in disbelief.

I don't know how to process all of this information. My whole life has been built on a lie, a half-truth.

My father's eyes fill with tears as he speaks to me in a hushed tone. "I am deeply sorry, kiddo. It's all my fault. When Jack informed me that she had shot you, I couldn't believe it." His voice trembles and his posture slumps under guilt and regret.

"Do you know where she is?" I ask.

"She was caught while trying to return to Colombia," Jack answers.

My mind is confused as I try to process what I just heard. "Colombia?" I ask, looking at Jack for an explanation.

"Jack will give you all the details," my Dad says, his voice heavy with regret. "But right now, I need to go back to Bella. She's with Boyd." His words weigh heavily in the air as he leaves. I sit there, feeling overwhelmed by all the information that had been kept from me.

When my dad left, it finally hit me.

How could they have kept this from me for so long?

The truth unspooled in my mind, tangled and sharp. Emotions surged—grief, anger, disbelief—all at once.

For now, I'm just trying to make sense of it.

This secret.

This lie that's lived beside me for years; quiet, constant, and utterly unbelievable.

"I think you need to take a break before we dive into more details," Jack says.

"I'm okay, Jack," I reassure him. "So, has my mom been in Colombia all this time?" I ask, seeking clarity.

"Antonilla's dad, Don Quixito, is a big-time drug lord. He secretly helped finance Oscar's run for office because his daughter asked him to. But things changed when Antonilla found out on TV that Oscar was married. Her dad pulled his support. That's when Edwina stepped in, making a secret deal to help Oscar win the election." Jack relays.

"Despite all this," he continues. "Oscar started losing popularity—and even his prominent supporters, like the Senator, began backing away. That's when the CIA got involved. They traced the shady connections to Oscar's campaign and asked me—a retired operative—for help with the case," Jack relays.

"You're working with the CIA?" I couldn't hide my surprise.

"Temporarily until the case is closed," he replies, with a mysterious edge to his voice.

"Was it connected to me hiring you to investigate?" I ask out of curiosity.

He nods. "Yes, they found out I've been tracking Oscar and asked me to work temporarily with them."

But my confusion grows as I ask, "Where is Oscar now?"

"Well, Antonilla has taken him," Jack replies.

"What? Is he...is he still alive?" My voice trembles.

Jack's response is immediate and confident, "Of course. Antonilla made sure of that."

He gives a slight shrug, "She was furious when she found out Oscar had proposed to her while still being married to another woman. Well, that's you."

I told him to keep our divorce quiet, away from the media. But he wanted headlines, wanted the spotlight. Now it's caught up to him.

As I process all these things and swirl in my mind, a deep fatigue seeps into my bones. My eyelids grow heavy with exhaustion, and Jack seems to notice. He places a gentle hand on my shoulder.

"You need to rest," he murmurs, his voice soft with concern, then presses a tender kiss to my forehead.

“I’ll be right here.” His words are a comforting balm to my weary soul, and I let my eyes close, surrendering to the pull of sleep.

Yet, even as I drift off, one question burns brightly in my mind: why did my mother shoot me?

# 30
# The Reckoning

In life, those closest to us often inflict the most pain. Yet, ironically, they are also the ones we struggle to let go of. Despite the wounds they leave on our hearts, we cling to the fragile hope that somewhere within them lies a glimmer of goodness worth holding onto. We forgive, not because we are weak, but because of the bond that connects us. It is a thread through our lives, a golden strand of memories and experiences linking our past and future. It brings both vulnerability and strength, an unbreakable bond that unites us in our shared journey.

The heavy door creaks open. Footsteps, soft, and slow grow louder against the tile. The door clicks shut behind her, the sound sharp in the stillness. She stands there, in the frame. Watching.

My mother, or Edwina stands in the doorway, her eyes scanning the room. Then land on me. Something in her shifts. The tension arrives before she speaks, tight in her shoulders, cold in her expression. The orange prison uniform hangs awkwardly on her thin frame. Her posture is sunken. Smaller than I remember.

She walks over and sits across from me. Doesn't even meet my eyes.

"What do you want?" she asks.

Not cruel. Just empty.

I look at her. Really look. I search for the woman who raised me. Or maybe just for a name. The mother I tried to earn love from. Someone I thought I knew. But she's not there. She never was. Now that I know she isn't my mother, truly, biologically—what's left? Do I still want her attention? Or just the apology she'll never say?

I inhale sharply and muster the courage to confront her.

"Why?" I demand, my voice trembling with emotion.

She glares at me. "You ruined everything," she spits out bitterly. "If you had just stuck with Oscar, everything would have worked out. He'd be governor by now."

My blood boils at her words, but I try to remain calm as I retort, "Get over it. It will never happen."

Her expression turns cold as ice as she responds, "Well, maybe if you hadn't been so selfish and followed our plan, things would have turned out differently."

"Selfish?...*Our* plan?" I repeat, laughing under my breath. "Right. I'm the selfish one." I shake my head, lips twitching. "Because not wanting to be tossed into a psych ward without so much as a heads-up? Yeah—how totally selfish of me." I look at her, eyes sharp. "And funny...I must've missed the group text about *our* plan. Must've gone straight to junk."

I glance at her. She doesn't say a word, but something in her twitches.

"And how can you still stand by him?" I ask, my voice rising. "He cheated. Over and over. And you just, what? Looked the other way?" My hands are trembling now. "He's a liar. A serial cheater."

She rolls her eyes and responds, "Everyone cheats. It's just a part of life."

"Oh God, help me!" I mutter to myself, pressing my hand to my forehead. But my anger peaks as I demand an answer, "So you knew about his affairs all along, too? And you still supported him?"

She lets out a resigned sigh and replies, "Of course, I knew about Oscar's affairs. I warned him that women would be his downfall, but he never listened." She shakes her head sadly. "Look what's happened to him now."

My heart drops as yet another revelation hits me. I can't believe this is the mother I've known my entire life, and that throughout my childhood, I craved her approval. Now, I find myself questioning her morality, or does she even know the meaning of the word?

"And what about Alexi? Did you know about her, too?" I ask.

My mother meets my gaze. "What's surprising about that?"

Her words are like a blow I didn't see coming. "Do you know how sick that sounds?" I am appalled that I am in the middle of it and part of this family. "And how sick of a mother you are?" I add.

She is avoiding my gaze this time. I should not be surprised of how hateful and evil she is. But I am. How could she have chosen her selfish desires over the well-being of her own daughter?

"Then, on top of that, you shot me?" I ask incredulously.

Her hands tremble as she speaks, the guilt and fear evident in her voice. "I didn't mean to shoot you," she says, trying to explain herself. "It was only meant to scare you, but the driver accelerated, and before I knew it, I accidentally pulled the trigger." The loud bang still echoes in my ears, and I can't shake off the feeling of dread that fills me.

I scoff at her words. "Scare me? What kind of game were you playing? You pulled out a gun and shot me because you were angry, hurtless, and you want me dead...." Words flow out in me like venom, fueled by betrayal and pain.

Her face twists, shame, maybe. Regret. But after everything, I don't know if she's even capable of feeling either.

"You used to just accept things as they were," she snaps, like it's my fault the script changed. "What changed?"

I blink. My voice barely makes it out. "What changed?"

My jaw tightens. The heat rises in my chest, and I don't fight it this time.

"I *woke up*," I say, sharp. "I finally realized I don't

deserve to be lied to and cheated on by Oscar. And more than that, I don't need to keep pretending you're some kind of mother to me."

She looks like she wants to interrupt. I don't let her.

"Or maybe this has always been the issue," I add, voice low but steady. "Maybe you resented me from the start because I'm not really your daughter. Is that it?"

The words cut deep. They burn on the way out. Tears rise, but I blink them back. I'm not giving her that. Not now.

This isn't just a breakdown. It's the moment I stop pretending the lies ever held this family together.

The silence stretches, thick and sharp-edged. I wait.

Her eyes lock onto mine, burning. "No one was supposed to know that," she hisses, teeth clenched.

But I don't flinch. I stay rooted. Solid.

"You wanted me gone," I say, voice level. "Because you couldn't stand that Dad had a child with someone else. You blamed him for your life. And I was just the proof you couldn't erase."

Her breath catches. Nostrils flaring. I catch the sharp scent of her breath and bitterness as she exhales.

She stands suddenly, her chair screeching backward across the floor.

"How *dare* you accuse me of that?" she snaps, voice rising, cracking.

Her face twists. Fury, pain, maybe something

close to guilt. But I don't look away.

Because now, finally, she's unmasked.

All eyes are on us. The guard warns us to keep it down.

In a lower voice, I say, "It's not an accusation. It's the truth," I stand my ground, unflinching. "Deep down, you resented Jasmine for being Daddy's favorite."

"I never—" she starts to deny, but her body stiffens, and she looks away.

I lean forward, my voice cutting through the tense atmosphere of the room. "Why did you try to kill me?" I ask, staring directly into her eyes.

She slumps back into her chair, defeated and vulnerable. Her hands twist nervously in her lap as she avoids my gaze.

"Yes, I was jealous of Jasmine," she admits, her voice barely audible. She takes a shaky breath before continuing, "And even after she died...I couldn't escape that jealousy.

The weight of her words hits me. I had always suspected there was more to her actions than just pure hatred towards me.

"But why?" I ask, trying to understand her motives. "Is this why you treated me so horribly?"

She exhales, long and slow.

"Your father loved your mother more than he ever loved me," she says, her voice low.

Her face tightens. Grief, bitterness, or something in between.

"I couldn't compete with that. No matter what I did. I gave up everything—my friends, my life overseas, just to be near him. But he never really saw me. Not the way he saw her."

Something in me sinks. Not in sympathy, but in understanding. A dark, aching piece of the puzzle slides into place.

All these years. Her coldness. Her control.

It wasn't just me.

It was *her*.

"Do you have any idea how unfair that is?" My voice cracks, but I keep going. "You blamed me for something I didn't choose. I was a child. I didn't ask to be born into your mess."

Tears rise. I let them.

"I don't agree with what Dad did. But that was between you and him. Not me. Blaming me...treating me like I deserved your hate, it's cruel."

She doesn't flinch. But something shifts behind her eyes.

"I don't know," she says quietly. "Maybe because you were an easy target."

A beat passes.

"Maybe because you reminded me too much of your mother."

The air thickens with every word.

Memories rush in, years of silence, cold shoulders, being treated like I didn't matter. Like I wasn't there. Not worth seeing.

"I think you drove Dad away," I say quietly. "You

were never really there for him. Always chasing something, your image, your freedom. Never us."

I pause, steadying my breath.

"You left Marie and Alexi to figure things out on their own. And me... you just pretended I didn't exist." I pause, meeting her eyes. "You talk about me being selfish? Look in the mirror. You're the one who's cold. Self-centered. Always were."

The silence after is sharp. It rings. Her face is unreadable.

But I don't need a reaction anymore.

Something inside me settles.

This is what closure feels like. Not loud, not final. Just done.

I rise from the chair. No more words. No need.

I'm not carrying this anymore.

I stand up from the table and walk away, leaving her alone with her thoughts. She sits there, emotionless and silent, but I can only hope that deep down, she feels the weight of regret and guilt for her actions.

As I leave the facility, a sense of calm settles over me. It feels like I've let go of the ill feelings that once plagued me. Though forgiveness may take time, I've found closure in standing up for myself.

Confronting Edwina lifts a heavy burden off my shoulders. Still, a knot of anxiety in my stomach formed. Knowing that I have to face Alexi and confront her the truth.

***

The taxi ride takes an hour and a half, but it feels longer. I spend most of it staring out the window, rehearsing what I might say and discarding every version.

By the time I reach Alexi's building, my chest is tight. The weight of her betrayal, the silence, and the years of pretending feels heavier than the air around me.

I walk the hallway slowly, each step louder than it should be. At her door, I pause. Breathe in. And knock.

The sound echoes in the stillness.

When the door opens, she blinks in surprise. Her mouth parts slightly. She wasn't expecting me. Maybe she never thought I'd show up at all.

"Lila," she says, her voice cautious. "What are you doing here?"

"Can I come in?" I ask. I'm surprised how steady I sound.

She nods and steps aside.

Her apartment is sleek. Modern. All neutral tones and quiet perfection. We sit on her oversized cream couch. The silence between us settles, thick and uneasy.

"We need to talk," I say.

"Is it about Mom and Dad?" she asks, eyes narrowing with worry.

"It's about Oscar."

The color drains from her face.

"I know," I say simply. "I know about you and him. You don't have to pretend anymore. Neither do I."

It hurts to say it out loud. But the silence has hurt worse.

Alexi blinks, eyes glassy. She doesn't let the tears fall.

I take a breath. "Why, Alexi?"

Her voice is small when it finally comes. "I didn't stop loving him. I couldn't help it."

I flinch.

"Then why push him toward me?" I ask. "Why lie and say you were just friends?"

Memories crash back—how I avoided him, out of respect. How I believed her.

She swallows. "He said he'd leave me if I didn't make you like him."

My stomach turns.

I stare at her. "And that was okay with you? Letting him play us both?"

She can't meet my eyes.

"Don't you see how messed up that is?"

"He had me wrapped around his finger, Lila," she says, barely above a whisper. "I hated it...but I went along with it."

Tears slide down her face. She doesn't wipe them away.

"I'm sorry."

I stare at her, shaking my head slowly. "You're twisted," I say. "You dragged me into your mess."

A breath catches in my throat.

"If I had known you loved him...I would've stepped back. I could've let you have him."

My voice tightens. Not with anger this time, but with the sting of knowing I was never given that choice.

"Five years, Alexi. Five years I lived inside a lie."

I pause, letting the silence stretch.

"I let so much slide—because we're sisters. I gave you grace where you gave me nothing."

"But this? This was never a mistake. It was betrayal."

I pause, breath catching.

"This was betrayal from the start."

The room goes quiet except for the shallow, uneven sound of her breathing. Her usual edge is gone. What's left is just guilt—and maybe, finally, some truth.

She bows her head. "I couldn't refuse him, Lila. He meant everything to me."

"My God, Alexi," I say, my voice sharp. "Do you even hear yourself? That's not love. It's manipulation. It's toxic."

She looks up, eyes rimmed red, defiant and broken all at once. "Don't you think I know that?"

Her voice shakes. "You don't understand. He made me feel seen. Like I mattered. I love him. I still do."

She wipes her face with a trembling hand.

"I get it," I say flatly. "He had you under his thumb. And you let him hurt everyone around you because of it."

She says nothing.

I press forward.

"And don't even try to deny the child."

Her head snaps up, stunned. "How do you know about that?"

"Did you ever stop to wonder what happened to her?" I ask. "The child you never talked about?"

Her face collapses into something hollow. She turns away, the silence between us stretching—thick, punishing.

"Your actions were unforgivable, Alexi. But what's worse—you never even tried to ask for forgiveness. You didn't come clean. Not once."

I stand, blinking back tears. "Her name is Bella. She loves fishing. She says her grandpa is her favorite person on earth."

Alexi's voice cracks. "You mean...the child Dad was carrying at Marie's wedding...?"

I nod. "Yes, Alexi. That's your daughter."

She doesn't respond. Just stares past me, breath shallow, like she's still waiting for it to not be real.

I walk to the door.

"Lila, wait—" Her voice is soft, full of hurt and something that sounds like fear.

I stop, hand on the knob, but I don't turn around.

She doesn't say anything else.

Through the frosted glass, I catch her silhouette—small and shaken. Despite everything, part of me still aches for her. She's my sister, after all. But that doesn't mean I have to stay in the wreckage with her. I escaped Oscar. She's still clinging to the hope that he'll come back and finally see her for who she is. I found my freedom. She's still entangled in a fate that never loved her back.

I take a deep breath. Then I turn.

"Alexi," I say quietly. "You need to wake up."

She looks at me, eyes wide.

"Oscar's a manipulator. A narcissist. He'll never love anyone the way you keep hoping he will. Not you. Not me. He only loves himself."

She stares at me, but the words don't sink in. Well, not yet.

"I hope one day you see it," I finish. "Before he ruins what's left of you."

And then I leave.

# 31

# Here We Are

As I step out of Alexi's building, dusk folds around the city like a bruised curtain. The air is sharp, cool against my skin. Traffic murmurs in pulses, red lights blinking like signals from some distant conscience I ignored too long.

It's done. I said what needed saying. I didn't shout. I didn't cry. I just told the truth. That she and Oscar had been lying to me for years. That I knew. There's no relief in it. Just a kind of hollow clarity.

For so long, I let silence pass as peace. I told myself I was keeping the family together. But I wasn't. I was letting rot set in. I knew something was wrong. Always did, but pretending was easier. Cleaner. Until it wasn't.

You think you're safe by avoiding pain. But all you're really doing is letting the blade sink deeper.

I keep walking. The sidewalk slick with old rain. A man hurries past me, shoulders hunched, earbuds in. The world doesn't stop for heartbreak.

Was I right to confront her?

Maybe.

Maybe not.

But the lie was a sickness, and I couldn't carry it anymore. My marriage died under the weight of it. I nearly did, too.

Now there's Bella. Innocent, wrapped in all this mess. And Alexi—proud, reckless, broken in ways she won't admit. Oscar's shadow stretches across us both. Across all of us.

There's no clean break. But I'm not looking for clean. I'm looking for real. So I'm done hiding. Done pretending I'm okay with betrayal because it came dressed as family. I'll live with the mess. I'll find my way forward, one honest step at a time.

And maybe that's enough. For now.

God, I hope so.

As for my mother? Only time will tell.

As I walk, something loosens in me. The ache doesn't vanish, but it thins. The street buzzes, headlights smearing across pavement, and for once, I let myself breathe.

Then the ringtone slices through the quiet. Too loud. Too sharp.

I answer. "Hey."

Jack's voice slides in, low and steady. "What are you up to?"

"Just walking," I say. "Saw Mom this morning. Stopped by Alexi's. Now I'm out by her place."

A pause.

"You want to talk about it?"

I exhale, not realizing I'd been holding anything in. "No...it went better than I expected."

"Dinner?" he asks, quick.

I blink. "Now?"

"If you're up for it. I'll come get you."

"You know where I am?"

"You said Alexi's. I remember the street." A quiet laugh.

I slow. "Are you nearby?"

"You could say that." There's a rustle on his end. "Stay there. Ten minutes."

I lower the phone. My heart, traitor that it is, lifts. Just slightly.

I end the call and drift toward a bench. The wood is cold. I don't mind.

The city moves around me. Horns, heels, and a child's wail fading into silence. A violin cries somewhere nearby, melody drifts, slow and splintered, like it's remembering something painful. I'm not really listening. Just letting it all pass through.

People-watching becomes something else. Not just distraction. A craft. You can't build characters from thin air. You have to notice them, how they walk, stall, fidget, ache.

A woman in a red coat passes, eyes on nothing. A man speaks into his phone, voice low, almost pleading. Everyone's carrying something. I'm not alone in the unraveling.

Alexi lingers in my mind. What was said. What wasn't. The way truth never comes clean, only bleeding at the edges.

Jack pulls up, horn sharp but not impatient. His

car glides to a stop. He steps out, spots me, raises a hand.

He walks over like he belongs in the scene. No hesitation. Just presence.

He reaches for my hand. I let him.

When he kisses me, it's both. Fireworks and gravity. A steadying kind of warmth that sparks at the edges. The kind that makes your ribs ache because you didn't realize how tightly you'd been holding everything in, until something safe let you breathe again.

"Hi there," he says, his voice low, familiar. It sends a quiet shiver up my spine.

I manage a breathy "Hey."

"So... where are we going?" I ask, trying to steady my voice.

"I know just the place," Jack says, squeezing my hand.

He opens the car door for me with a half-smile. "In you go, madam."

I laugh at his playful attempts to impress me. But truth be told, I'm already smitten.

He slips behind the wheel, buckles in. "There's this restaurant with the best chef who could fatten you up!"

He throws me a wink. I pretend to roll my eyes, but I'm grinning.

"I can't wait," I say, excitement slipping through.

"You hungry?"

"I'm starving."

The car hums to life. As we merge into traffic, something in me quiets. There's a comfort in motion, in his presence beside me. I remember the first time I met him, and chuckle.

He glances over. "What's so funny?"

"Nothing." I shrug, but I can't keep the smirk off my face.

"Thinking?"

"Yeah." I shoot him a sideways glance. "About you."

He lifts a brow. "Dangerous."

I grin. "Just remembering how I threw up on your shoes when we first met."

He lets out a laugh. "Yeah, that was unforgettable."

"And disgusting."

"And effective," he says. "I haven't looked at Italian leather the same way since. But for you? I'd risk it again."

I shake my head, laughing. "Flattery will get you somewhere, Mr. Stone."

He nods solemnly. "I'm counting on it."

We both laugh.

We arrive half an hour later. The place is tucked between shuttered shops, glowing faintly under a flickering sign.

As we step out of the car, a broad-shouldered man with weathered hands and a thick Spanish accent hurries toward us. His face splits into a grin the moment he sees Jack.

"*Hola*, Jack! So kind of you to come," he says,

clasping Jack's hand with both of his. "Only for one hour, I promise. *Only for one hour!*" he repeats, breathless with urgency.

"There's a guest—special guest, from Spain—with his friends. They want the burger. *The* burger." He taps his chest. "And only you can make it right."

His English is broken, but his eyes shine with trust.

Jack nods without missing a beat. "No problem, hermano. That's why I'm here."

And suddenly, I'm not sure if I came here for dinner...or to watch a side of Jack I've never seen.

Then he turns to me, places his hands lightly on my shoulders, and grins. "I make a mean burger," he says, deadpan but proud.

Jack chuckles. "Let's feed my girlfriend first, *Hermano*. She's starving."

Hermano lights up, shaking my hand with both of his. "*Anything* for the girlfriend! Welcome, welcome!"

Jack leads me through a narrow hallway into the kitchen. The air is thick with the scent of garlic, grilled meat, something caramelizing. It smells like warmth.

"You cook here?" I ask, scanning the cluttered countertops, the hanging pans, the small wooden table pushed into a corner.

"Once in a while," he says, grabbing an apron. "When Hermano begs."

I raise an eyebrow. "So you're the mystery chef trying to fatten me up?"

Jack grins. "Let's just say I know how to make a burger you won't be able to resist." And with that, he captures my lips.

It's soft. Brief. A promise wrapped in smoke and spice.

Then he points me to the table. "Sit. Relax. I've got this."

He disappears into the kitchen, and I can't help but smile, already curious, already hungry.

The last time I had a burger, I didn't just eat it. I inhaled it.

I settle in, elbows on the scarred wood, chin in my hands. And I wait. Content to watch a story unfold. One bite at a time.

Fifteen minutes later, Jack steps out of the kitchen wearing a crisp white chef's coat. It fits him like it was made for this moment. In his hands, a single plate—burger stacked high, steam curling upward like a promise—and a glass of water catching the light. The smell hits me first. Charred meat, melted cheese, something smoky and familiar.

My stomach growls, embarrassingly loud.

"Wow," I breathe, grinning. "I could get used to this."

Jack chuckles, sets the plate down in front of me with practiced care. He leans in, his lips brushing mine in a soft, unrushed kiss.

Then, just above a whisper: "Five hungry guests await. Eat. I'll be back soon."

And just like that, he's gone again, leaving behind

the scent of grilled perfection and the echo of something deeper than dinner.

As Jack disappears back into the kitchen, the scent of sizzling meat and toasted buns wraps around me. It's warm, almost dizzying. My mouth waters, and I don't even try to hide it.

The first bite is heaven—juicy, sharp with mustard, softened by perfectly melted cheese. I eat slowly at first, then forget to pace myself. By the last bite, I'm full in the best way. Full and content.

I glance toward the kitchen but don't call out. I know better than to interrupt the rhythm of a cook in motion.

Instead, I reach for my phone and open my writing app. That's the beauty of my work, I can do it anywhere. And right now, surrounded by clatter, flame, and the low hum of kitchen life, I feel the stirrings of something worth writing.

Stories hide in places like this. Between bites. Beneath the noise. And suddenly, I'm ready to find one.

Lost in a flurry of words, I don't notice when Jack calls my name. His voice cuts through the haze and brings me back to reality.

"Is that how you do it?" he asks, curiosity shining in his eyes.

I scramble to refocus on him, asking, "What?"

"I've been trying to catch your attention, but you seemed spaced out," he explains with a small smile.

"I'm sorry, Jack...I..." I trail off, not sure what excuse to give for my distraction. Finally, I blurt out, "How did it go?"

His smile widens at my question, and he replies, "It went well, I hope. Are you ready to go?"

With a nod, I let him lead me out, away from the tangle of words and into the quiet of night. He reaches for my hand, and we slip through the backdoor, unnoticed. Hermano would've stopped him if he could.

"Let's go somewhere for dessert," Jack says, his fingers brushing mine as we head toward the lot.

The car glides through the narrow lanes of Mulberry Street, past warm-lit cafés and worn storefronts that lean into the sidewalk like they've seen everything.

We pull up to a place Jack mentioned earlier, famous for something sweet, though I can't remember what. Inside, the scent of sugar and butter wraps around us. Pastries cooling behind glass. Vanilla in the air. A slow kind of comfort.

We're led to a small table by the window. I sit, already half in love with the way it all feels—simple, warm, like something I didn't know I needed.

"What would you like for dessert?" Jack asks, eyes still scanning the menu.

I hesitate. "Maybe tiramisu? Or something else...I don't know. Desserts all kind of blur together. Sugar in different shapes." I flash a teasing smile.

He doesn't miss a beat. "Leave it to me." He stands. "I'll be right back with something you won't say no to."

A few minutes pass. Then he returns, balancing a silver tray with practiced care. On it: a delicate dessert, artfully arranged, and beside it... a small box.

He sets the tray down, then sits across from me. His hand lingers on the box, fingertips light, reverent.

"This is for you," he says quietly, a smile tugging at one corner of his mouth.

I stare at the box. Something about it stills the air around me.

"You know," he murmurs, "it won't open just by looking at it."

I swallow and reach out, hands unsteady.

The box is warm from his touch. I glance up, his gaze meets mine, steady and soft, silver in the dim light.

I open the lid.

And whatever I expected...it wasn't this.

My breath catches. Tears begin to well up in my eyes.

"Oh, Jack..." I whisper, as something behind my ribs quietly unravels.

A slow smile spreads across his face, reaching his eyes. Those small creases at the corners deepening, softening him.

"Well," he says, voice low, almost teasing, "you can't really raise six kids alone. Or write about them without a co-author." His gaze holds mine, steady. "So...will you do me the honor of being my wife?"

The question hangs there. Not flashy. Not rehearsed. Just him. Bare, sincere, and full of love.

He gently takes the box from my hand, and lifts out the ring.

Without a word, he slides it onto my finger. It fits perfectly.

I stare at it, at him. My chest aches in the best way. The kind of ache that comes with holding joy too big for your body.

"So?" he asks, his voice a whisper now. "Is that a yes?"

Tears blur my vision as I nod, the word catching in my throat. Then, finally, "Yes," I breathe. "Yes. A million times, yes."

And just like that, the whole world feels quiet. Like it's listening.

In one fluid motion, he draws me in. His arms wrapping around me like they were made for it. Strong. Certain. Safe. His lips find mine in a kiss that burns and steadies all at once, like striking a match in the dark and watching it hold.

For a moment, nothing exists outside of that heat. Just his mouth, the pull of his hands, the way my whole body answers without thinking.

When we break apart, I meet his eyes, those silver-grey depths that have unsettled me since day one.

"Thank you... Jack," I whisper, voice caught somewhere between tears and wonder.

He studies me. Quiet, curious.

"What?" I ask, trying for lightness.

"That look again," he says, a smirk playing at his lips. "Same one you gave me at the restaurant. Like you could see straight through me."

I laugh softly, remembering. "I was just admiring your eyes. They have this...like some magnetic pull on me, and the longer I stare into them, the more it feels like they hold some sort of magic."

"Magic, huh?" he teases. "Is that before or after you threw up on my shoes?"

"You're never letting that go, are you?"

"Never."

He kisses me again. Slower this time, less fire, more gravity.

Between breaths, I manage, "I love you...you ridiculous man."

His eyes soften. He doesn't say anything, but he doesn't have to. The way he looks at me says it all.

We've found something. Steady, improbable, and ours.

And whatever comes next, I know this: I won't face it alone.

# About the author

**Jane Fitcher** is a pen name born at the crossroads of reality and fiction. She often finds herself at odds with the characters in her head, most of whom ignore her edits and do whatever they please. When she's not wrestling with the sudden turns in her ever-growing maze of storylines, she's darting through the house like a character herself, one step behind her kids and two behind her own thoughts.

In real life, she's usually inventing new excuses to avoid chores. Time management isn't exactly her strong suit—especially when she's chasing children, reheating the same cup of coffee, and shouting reminders to play, do their chores, draw, read, eat, and everything in between. Meanwhile, her endlessly patient husband quietly pretends not to notice that she's once again using a plot twist to get out of folding the laundry.

She lives where the sun shines bright, hurricanes announce themselves loudly, and alligators swim in the lakes like they own it.

Her debut novel, *Lies I Can't Unsee*, pulls readers into a world of tangled secrets, jaw-dropping reveals, and characters who flat-out refuse to behave. Jane's writing is known for its vivid imagery, emotional gut-punches, and just enough suspense to make you cancel your plans and mutter *"just one more chapter"*—right up until 2 a.m.

**Check her out:**

janefitcher.com

# Thank You

**To all who read this book:** I am deeply grateful for your time. May these pages give you something more valuable than lost hours—a spark, a smile, a tear, or even a heartbeat you thought was no longer there. Or maybe... just the perfect excuse for a second cup of coffee, a quiet moment with tea, or a reason to pour a glass of red or white wine.

www.ingramcontent.com/pod-product-compliance
Lightning Source LLC
LaVergne TN
LVHW050918080826
845145LV00001B/128

* 9 7 8 1 9 6 3 4 0 4 0 0 5 *